"I came here wanting to kill you."

Though his shoulders were wide enough to bear a small vehicle on them, his expression was confused, as though he was unsure of what he'd gotten himself into. "But I can't imagine harming you, and it kills me to see what I've done to you already."

Ravin lunged across the bed and smacked Nikolaus across the forehead. Expecting to again be pinned by the vampire, she knelt there defiantly, fist raised.

Never had she been so close to a vampire and not had him either attack or flee.

He lashed his tongue to wipe away a trickle of blood that stained his lip.

Oh, of all that could go wrong. The odor of rosemary and ash that she had used in the love spell clung to her hair. Ravin remembered clearly now. The entire contents of the vial had spilled over her and, thanks to her magic, had absorbed instantly through her pores to course through her bloodstream.

"You don't love me," she muttered. "You're under a love spell."

⎯⎯⎯⎯⎯⎯ ✕✕✕ ⎯⎯⎯⎯⎯⎯

Please check out the
BEWITCH THE DARK
glossary of terms following the book.

MICHELE HAUF

has been writing for over a decade and has published historical, fantasy and paranormal romances. A good strong heroine, action and adventure, and a touch of romance make for her favorite kind of story. She lives with her family in Minnesota, and loves the four seasons, even if one of them lasts six months and can be colder than a deep freeze. You can find out more about her at www.michelehauf.com.

MICHELE HAUF

xxx

KISS ME DEADLY

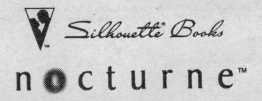

Silhouette Books

nocturne™

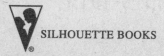 SILHOUETTE BOOKS

ISBN-13: 978-0-373-61771-5
ISBN-10:   0-373-61771-2

KISS ME DEADLY

Copyright © 2007 by Michele Hauf

www.silhouettenocturne.com

Printed in U.S.A.

Dear Reader,

Kiss Me Deadly is the second book in my BEWITCH THE DARK series, which features sexy vampires and mysterious witches. I was struck by the idea of doing a sort of "reverse romance." What if you had no choice but to fall madly in love at very first sight? Would that be a good thing? Would you learn to love for real, beyond the spell that had made you love for fake? And what if the person you fell in love with was the one person on this earth you hated so much you wished them dead?

The result is bewitchingly dark, dangerous and sexy.

Michele

To read more about Michele's books, find her online at www.michelehauf.com. Or if you prefer to write, drop her a line at Michele Hauf, P.O. Box 23, Anoka, MN 55303. E-mail is also good! Write to Michele at toastfaery@gmail.com. And for more info on all the Nocturne authors, go to www.nocturneauthors.com.

This one is for my fellow Vampire Vixens, and all the readers who stop by our Web site to support and cheer on the vampire romance genre. Get bitten!

Chapter 1

Two months ago, a slayer killed Nikolaus Drake.

Not any slayer, but a vigilante witch with death in her eyes. As if acid, her blood ate into his flesh. Felled in an instant, Nikolaus had gasped for breath, and could not find it. His heart had stopped beating.

A vampire isn't supposed to survive the death cocktail—that's what vampires call witch's blood—but, after being hit, Nikolaus had collapsed onto the body of one of his dying cohorts. Crazed by the active decimation of his body, he'd drunk from his friend, racing to take the blood before death's release of the mortal soul made it useless.

The blood had served to restart Nikolaus's heart. He wasn't sure how he'd made it home, or how he'd been able to stop the caustic effects of the death cocktail.

And it didn't matter anymore. Nikolaus had survived. He was now a vampire phoenix, risen from ash and blood. But his injuries had forced him into seclusion, for a witch wound proved a stubborn heal. He still bore scars and could yet feel his left lung wheeze when he exerted himself.

Before being transformed into a vampire, Nikolaus had been a surgeon, a man who had witnessed many people survive incredible odds to recuperate and heal. But yes, sometimes they also died.

Experiencing recovery for himself had changed him. It had fixed a lust for vengeance into the scarred sinews of Nikolaus Drake's soul. He, a man who had always strived for peace, now desired a bloody revenge.

Foremost, Nikolaus could not stand back and do nothing when he knew the witch yet stalked the shadows in search of one more vampire to make ash.

Summer solstice arrived in two weeks. That night, Nikolaus planned to return to tribe Kila.

Yet he could not do that until the anger that had brewed within him for two months was settled. Before the attack, Nikolaus had led tribe Kila and served them well for twenty years. The tribe was wary, but none were safe from the death cocktail—save Nikolaus. He possessed immunity now—the witch could not again harm him—so he would fight for his tribe and destroy the enemy.

One thing could tip the scales and return his mind to the peaceful resolve needed to lead properly.

Tonight, he would kill the witch.

The witch's name was Ravin Crosse, and she rode a big black street chopper with the word *venom* curved across the gas tank, and wore more black leather than Nikolaus did. Small, but imposing in her costume, which also included visible weaponry that could annihilate a vampire in less than a minute, the witch walked as if she owned the earth.

She was the only slayer in the Twin Cities area that Nikolaus was aware of.

Not for long.

Nikolaus had located the witch's hideout. She lived at the edge of Minneapolis, but three miles west of him, at the top of a warehouse recently rehabbed for luxury flats. Nice, but not half so spendy as his digs in the Mill district.

He did not give a fig for a witch, her life, or her nasty soul. Let her burn. And he would proudly present her ashes to his men.

He had been observing, at a distance, her comings and goings for the past ten days, the first days since his pseudo-death that he'd felt able to leave his home.

The vampire killer went out three nights a week on the hunt—Tuesday, Thursday and Saturday. Nikolaus had not witnessed her execute a kill.

His own tribe numbered eleven, and had claimed Minneapolis's inner city as territory against two rival tribes.

There were a few independent vampires, not aligned to any tribe, but they were stealthy and kept to the shadows, and very often, the suburbs and smaller towns in the state.

Minnesota was not a vampire hot spot. This surprised Nikolaus. The state offered a healthy six months of winter, which meant little sunlight and plenty of dark basements in which to hibernate. And a vampire could regulate his body temperature so the below-freezing weather affected him little. A bloodsucker's haven, if you asked him.

Tribe Kila was small, but not stupid. Nikolaus had purposefully kept their location away from New York, Miami or New Orleans, major vampire breeding grounds. The average metropolitan area hosted perhaps a hundred vampires, or less. By no means were they in the majority, let alone a countable minority.

He had prided himself on leading the most civilized tribe in the States. While others, such as Nava, Zmaj and Veles stalked the night, wreaking havoc and creating blood children indiscriminately, Kila strove to keep their bloodlines pure and peaceful. No accidental transformations, no witnesses, no mistakes. That had become Nikolaus's personal mantra.

There were a few incidents to be overlooked, though.

Hell, they were vampires, not tamed lions. The blood hunger was a powerful thing, and not to be ignored or put aside as if it were a habit one could easily break.

They, all vampires, were called *the dark*. But none in Kila murdered for the sake of taking blood to sustain life.

Over the weeks since the witch's attack, Nikolaus had slowly healed. Initially, Gabriel Rossum, his closest ally, had brought him donors daily. The infusion of warm, mortal blood to his system had been supplemented with a weekly draw from Gabriel.

Vampire blood proved more powerful in the healing process as opposed to mere mortal blood. Flesh had grown over Nikolaus's exposed ribs within three weeks, and slowly the charred skin on his arms and torso began to heal.

Now only the skin on his left arm, up along his neck and down his left side to his hip was puckered with pink scarred flesh. It looked abysmal, but Nikolaus wasn't concerned with appearance. He'd once wandered the streets bald, exposing a scalp full of tattoos, and a defiant growl to anyone who would cringe.

That was when he'd thought his life was over.

It *had* been over. Dr. Nikolaus Drake no longer existed. Hell, to imagine performing brain surgery around all that blood now?

At the sound of the front door sealing shut, Nikolaus set down the fifty-pound hand weight and strode out to the living room where subdued evening light snuck through the one window Gabriel had commandeered for an assortment of huge, leafy plants.

After the witch's attack, Gabriel had returned to the tribe

with word their leader was still alive—a phoenix—and that he required time to heal.

A month ago, Gabriel had moved in with Nikolaus after losing his apartment to a pissed-off girlfriend. It had been easier for the non-confrontational vampire to walk away than to divide up belongings and listen to her angry wails. He was on the lookout for new digs. Though now Nikolaus didn't require twenty-four care, he appreciated the company and was in no hurry to rush Gabriel out the door.

"Tonight the night?" Gabriel asked as he tossed the day's paper onto the coffee table and flicked the sunshades open. The electrochromic blackout glass seamlessly changed to clear, providing an evening view of the Mississippi River and the industrial barges moored on the opposite bank. "It's still too soon for you to be going out on the hunt. You sure about this?"

"Never been more sure of a thing in my life," Nikolaus growled. He punched a fist into his opposite palm.

Maintaining the anger was part of the plan. Not that it was difficult. But fair-haired and dimple-faced Gabriel always played angel-on-the-shoulder to Nikolaus's feral need to get things done, be it by force and fury or by talking through a vexing issue.

A man learned patience in the medical profession, and Nikolaus had spent a good number of years doing so. But along with his mortality, his patience and empathy had been sluiced away with the blood that fateful night of his transformation.

"It'll close a chapter in your life."

"It'll feel damn good." Rubbing a palm up his torso, Nikolaus strode across the room. The scar tissue on his side always drew his attention. It sent out the message "not whole, incapable" to any who might see it.

As he strolled into the kitchen, he punctuated his mood with a slam of his fist to the gray marble counter.

He needed the witch's limp body sprawled before him. That was the only ointment that would completely heal his wounds, both physical and emotional.

In the fridge, he eyed the bottles of wine Gabriel kept for his evening sacrament. He sniffed. The corks gave up the rich aroma of eighteenth-century soil steeped with raspberries and limestone and the poignant cry of tiny black grapes plumped to bursting from the sun. "You pick up the fish oil?"

"In the bag on the counter."

Much as blood served his only means for regeneration, Nikolaus believed some natural remedies certainly couldn't hurt. Wouldn't the AMA get a chuckle over that? A former neurosurgeon using natural remedies. Of course, he'd always held the belief that the brain could not heal itself if a person insisted on bombarding his or her body and blood with chemicals.

Flexing his left arm, he eased his palm over the rippled flesh.

"You know," Gabriel commented, "you've got an opportunity to steal some of the witch's magic if you don't do the deed too quickly."

Right. Nikolaus was immune to her poisonous blood now. Or should be. A risk he was straining at the leash to take.

And should a vampire manage to drink witch's blood without harm, the witch's magic would flow into him. "Bewitched" is what they called the ancient vampires who were once able to enslave a witch and consume her blood in order to increase their own strength.

Nikolaus had never met any of the ancients, though tales told of half a dozen that yet lived.

"Any blood magic I gain will be a bonus," he said as he slipped on his dark sunglasses.

He was a phoenix. And though he'd yet to test his strength, he wondered about the legend that a phoenix was indestructible. He didn't *feel* it, but he was still recovering.

He glanced to Gabriel. "The kill is what I'm after, and nothing but."

"Do you know how odd it is to hear such a declaration from you?"

Nikolaus shrugged. "Yes." For he preached avoidance of the deadliest drink.

"You know this is necessary, Gabriel. I do this for the entire tribe. One less witch in this world is one less nuisance for the vampire nation. I'm out of here."

"Have a nice evening!" Gabriel called.

Nikolaus smirked as he strode for the front door.

Nice? He hadn't known so sublime an emotion since before he was turned. Since before, when he'd been the newest neurosurgeon to grace the Mayo clinic, the smart young resident with dreams of changing the world in hand and a self-righteous God complex to put the most arrogant men to shame.

The world was not nice. The world…demanded presence. And tonight Nikolaus Drake intended to return with a vengeance.

Chapter 2

Making a deal with the devil Himself is always a bad idea.

Three obligations had been set to her, in exchange for the valued skill of the Sight.

When offered the deal months earlier, it had been a no-brainer. To gain the ability to actually see her enemies—and rule out the possible mistake of killing a mortal—Ravin had jumped at the offer.

Jump wasn't exactly the word. A guarded "sure" had sealed the deal. For her soul was no longer her own. She hadn't so much sold it to the devil as loaned it.

Marked across the chest with a palpable tally, she had then set to obligation number one. So easy, she almost had to wonder why she'd lost sleep about making the deal. To merely locate a sin eater and shut down his protection wards, seemed to have pleased Himself immensely, so Ravin wasn't about to question whether or not she had gotten off easy. When the devil was happy there could be no doubt as to who was the winner of that round.

There remained two obligations to repay her debt—and to see her soul returned. Right now, she focused on the second— another deceptively simple request.

Bent before the cupboard between her refrigerator and the stainless-steel sink, Ravin looked at a six-inch glass vial, her tongue sticking out of the corner of her mouth.

All week she had gathered ingredients for a love spell— a child's innocence and a cat's seventh life being the most difficult to come by. After careful measuring and summoning, she'd brought the whole batch to a boil, and then let it cool for an hour.

Now she hefted the copper brewing pot over the vial and poured. Spiced-pear air freshener scented the room, overwhelming the stench of the pot's contents. She was careful to ensure not a single drop was wasted.

Unless the entire contents were consumed, spells could prove less than effective. In this case, six ounces of liquid could either be drunk or spread over the skin like a moisturizer; it wasn't particular, as long as the ingredients were absorbed into the bloodstream. Magic would render the absorption rate instantaneous.

"A freakin' love spell," she muttered.

Setting the pot back on the cool burner with a clang, she straightened and searched the counter for the little square of plastic wrap she'd cut out earlier. Overhead, a jungle of hanging spider plants tendriled down, some tickling her head. Plants gave her vital energy and kept the apartment's balance.

She sighed wistfully and shook her head. "This is so not what I should be doing right now."

On the other hand, the occasional dabbling in actual spell craft and mixing kept her skills from fading. And it helped to tilt the balance back in her favor—or so she hoped.

Ravin was a witch, had been for more than two centuries. Though she had mastered earth and water magic, air still eluded her—and she had no intention of touching fire.

She didn't spend much of her time sitting about, brewing up spells or chanting. In fact, it was rare she indulged in her own magic for any purpose other than to ward her home against intruders. Which is why her life was dangerously misbalanced right now. A witch wasn't a real witch without consistent practice of spell craft.

So where had her focus gone over the years? Ravin strived to make a mark on the world. As a slayer, Ravin's job required she destroy vampires. The only good vampire was a pile of ash.

Out in the living room on the rosewood coffee table, a row of empty shotgun cartridges waited to be injected with her own blood before she went on patrol this evening. The Kila tribe had been stalking the suburbs, stirring up the wolves. Ravin had nothing against werewolves, so their enemies were hers.

Not that she needed a shove to go after a blood-sucking longtooth.

But by slaying, as opposed to using her craft, she pushed her life balance far to the dark side.

"And I am the light," she murmured, though the declaration was absent of all the belief her ancestors had instilled in her since an early age.

Witches were *the light*. Vampires were *the dark*. And while they were just terms used by the witches for centuries, it was the rare witch who abandoned the light of the craft to surrender her soul to darkness. And those who did?

In the eighteenth century, after she had mastered earth magic, Ravin had watched a fellow witch take revenge against a farmer for raping her by blighting his crops. That revenge was not so singular as it should have been. The farmer's entire family starved to death that winter. And the witch, drawn to the dark by her act of vengeance, continued to wreak havoc against any slight. She became a hag with a grotesque aura all creatures could see, and all chose to avoid. Eventually she was consumed by darkness.

Since witnessing that fall to darkness, Ravin had vowed that she would strive for balance. While slaying was necessary, it also marked her soul darkly. So she would always use her magic for good to keep the balance.

Of course, if she didn't practice magic, her balance angled out of whack. And, having dealt with the devil, she was now quite desperate to begin bringing light back to her out-on-loan soul.

Which is why she'd bargained for the Sight in the first place. Sacrifices had been made, but ultimately, it would be for the greater good.

Referring with a glance to the instructions from the dusty old grimoire she'd dug out of grandmama's trunk, the potion now had to sit high and loosely covered overnight. A courier would arrive at daybreak for pickup.

What happened after the potion left her hands should concern her. Ravin suspected Himself wished a certain mark to fall in love with another certain mark of opposing forces for reasons that would summon a demented thrill in Himself. The playing of enemies against one another? Right up the devil's sinister alley.

Ravin looked the other way. It did not serve to poke one's nose into this type of business.

Standing on tiptoes—though some would label her short, Ravin liked to think of herself as average for a seventeenth-century woman—she carefully placed the vial on top of the refrigerator. The plastic wrap fluttered over the circular opening, but she didn't press it to seal over the glass lip.

"See you in the morning—"

Arms still raised high, Ravin averted her attention from the vial and focused her senses in all directions of her periphery.

A nonmortal being was close. She always felt such a presence as an intuitive clamp tightening her scalp. Who or what…?

A discernible wave shuddered through her apartment, as if it were a frisson moving the air. She could actually see the air molecules and walls and furniture be displaced in a wavery movielike shiver.

Her heart dropped two inches. Her mouth grew dry.

Couldn't be.

"My wards are breeched?"

Impossible. The entire block was warded to warn her of impending danger. The apartment building was cloaked and set to alarm should an enemy cross the threshold to the first-floor foyer. And if anyone, creature or being, got past all that, the repulse ward she'd set up to span twenty feet about her property should have alerted her like a punch to the gut.

"Something must have glitched."

Again, impossible. But Ravin felt the intrusion like a blade to her side.

Wood creaked. Heavy metal bolts tore from hinges.

Weapons. She needed to protect herself.

A loud slam echoed from around the corner of the kitchen. The crash of the front door to the floor made Ravin jump.

Chaotic commotion vibrated throughout the apartment.

Ravin spun around, but her elbow hit hard against the refrigerator door handle. Splattered with an officious rain of potion, she scrambled to right the vial, but swallowed and gasped at the dripping mess.

"Screw it!" She didn't have time to deal with the nonessentials.

Someone—or something—had invaded her home. And her closest weapon was in the artillery closet across the living room.

Ravin took two steps and slammed into a force so substantial it set her back and thumped her shoulders against the fridge.

A man stood in her kitchen. Big and imposing. Dark, so dark. Coal-black hair flowed about his head and broad shoulders like a wicked flag warning against cutthroats. Black leather creaked as he fisted his fingers. And he snorted like a bull for the red cape.

Droplets of the spell dribbled down her forehead. Ravin spat at the liquid.

She saw the intruder for his truth—a vampire. Their kind wore an aura like glittering rubies shadowed with ash. Indeed, the Sight was valuable. She'd never regret making a deal with the devil.

But that this creature had permeated her wards and stood in her home staring her down as if she were his next meal, infuriated her. How had he entered without verbal permission? A vampire could not cross a private threshold uninvited.

Whatever the glitch that had allowed him entrance, Ravin wasn't about to bemoan her privacy, or her safety. She didn't need weapons. This one she could battle with her hands tied behind her back.

Ravin bit the inside of her cheek, tasting the blood and sucking it into her saliva. The longtooth would be ash in no time.

Chapter 3

Stupid, brave little witch. Standing there with fists raised and defiance shining about her like diamonds dipped in oil. He'd waited a long time for this moment. The road back from ash and bone had been difficult, if not impossible at times. And it was all because of Ravin Crosse, vigilante vampire hunter.

Nikolaus crossed the kitchen floor in three strides. Fitting his hand up under her chin, he slammed her against the refrigerator. The room reeked of herbs and smoke and a spiced sweetness. Witch smells. No doubt she'd been brewing a wicked spell.

He lifted her petite frame with ease, crushing his fingers about her windpipe. And yet, she struggled. She was feisty. Her bare feet hit every part of his thighs and even glanced across his groin.

He felt nothing, so long as he kept his eyes burned onto hers. Brown, they were, like mud. She slashed at his chest and arms with fingernails that would have drawn blood had he been wearing anything but leather.

And then she spat on him, hitting him directly on the cheek.

She stopped struggling then. Nikolaus supported her fey weight completely. Wide, enraged eyes took in his reaction.

Or rather, his nonreaction.

"That's right, witch." With his free hand, he swiped away the spittle and showed his fingers to her. The blood sat upon his flesh as if nothing more than mud kicked up in a fight. "Your blood is like water to me now."

The risk had been worth it. He'd not doubted for a moment her blood could have harmed him further than it already had.

"Impossible," she croaked. "You're a vamp! Who—who are you?"

Moving his hand from her throat and slamming his other palm against her shoulder, he held her pinned. As he lunged into her, her foul witch smell laced with herbs and a piquant citrus scurried up his nostrils and into his sinuses. The essence of witch disgusted him. He should be done with her right now.

But he'd waited for this moment too long. Not once had he rushed anything important. He would make his suffering mean something for the entire tribe.

"My name," he said, "is Nikolaus Drake. I am lord of tribe Kila."

"Oh, yeah? Last I checked, Truvin Stone was leading those infidels," she said.

"Stone merely fills in while I have been away."

"Yeah? Nikolaus Drake is dead."

The nerve of her. And he stood right before her!

She clutched his forearms with both hands, but he did not relent his grip. "I killed Drake, I know it. A stinking vamp!" Again she spat, landing on his chin. "You smell like one. You look like one. But—"

"But your damned poisonous blood has no power over me now."

Twice now she'd spat upon him. Any other vampire would have been a sizzling pile of ash right now. Nikolaus knew the feeling. Too well.

"You don't remember me, witch?"

He slammed her hard to get her to stop struggling. Dark liquid spattered her forehead, nose and cheeks. Blood leaked from the corner of her mouth. The sight tempted him. Gabriel's reminder that he should take some of her magic distracted him momentarily.

"Two months ago you attacked tribe Kila. Why? Without provocation? That night, I became another notch on your gun. Well, erase that notch. I didn't die."

"I don't understand."

"I am a phoenix." To recite the word filled him with pride. Any vampire who survived the death cocktail was termed a phoenix, for the vampire literally did rise from char and ash to struggle back to life.

"Bloody hell," she marveled. "No, it's impossible to—You're a phoenix? But that means you would have had to—"

"Kill me once," he growled. "Never again."

Wheezing as he drew in a breath, he ignored the ache in his lung and dug his fingers into her shoulders. The blue T-shirt she wore stretched under the pressure. Slamming his hips against her torso, Nikolaus pinned her effectively.

A mist of something rained down from above the fridge, splattering the witch's angry red face.

"Now it's my turn, witch. I've waited two months for this day. You don't know how I struggled to come back from a half-burned walking hunk of flesh. A vampire can never completely heal from your death cocktail—"

"Cry me another one," she said. "Let me go, asshole, and we'll handle this with blades and stakes."

"And another of your blood bullets? Go ahead," he hissed against her cheek. "Drown me in your crimson poison. I will bathe in your taint, and wear it proudly as a warrior displays his victories to the world."

He glared into her eyes, so dark, almost black. "I intend to drain you dry, witch. It'll be the sweetest drink I've ever tasted."

As he slammed against her, her head fell back against the stainless-steel door, exposing the pulsing carotid—breakfast, lunch and dinner.

Opening his jaw wide, Nikolaus clamped on to the witch's neck. He fought to wrangle her slashing legs with his own. Holding her with his jaw, he gripped her wrists with each hand and spread them out from her body.

He would not put her into reverie by using his innate per-suasion—he wanted her to feel every moment of terror.

Canines pierced flesh and artery. As he'd predicted, the first gush of blood tasted awful. Witch blood. Reeking of rosemary and salt and something inexplicable he couldn't name but felt as a sour tingle at the back of his throat. It brought back memories best left to the grave. A grave he'd once walked across, but had no intention of lying in.

"No!"

Her protest spurred him on. Wrenching her head down and to the side, Nikolaus drew out his sharp teeth from her neck and drank the warm blood that spilled to the surface. It grew much tastier as he swallowed. Hot, rich and spiced with the forbidden. Also, laced with adrenaline, an addictive drug to all vampires.

"This can't…" she murmured, "…not right. The…the spell…"

No remorse surfaced as he drank. The witch's death would

fulfill a craving no amount of blood could ever match—that of revenge.

It was a crime Nikolaus had to commit to ensure the safety of his men.

As her muscles slackened and her protests ceased, he supported her upper body across his left arm. Want had been served. Yet he could drink all day and never fill up his need.

The swoon fell upon him with a startling attack. Tossing back his head, Nikolaus gasped out a cry of pleasure. The high of blood extraction dizzied his brain and swirled his thoughts. He must have dropped the witch to the floor, because his hands moved before him, grasping and searching.

He turned, lifting his feet from the heap that held him weighted to the ground. The room wavered in black and white, darkening, and then brightening so that he winced. Yet he did not reel in pain.

Breathing deeply, he felt each inhale and exhale as a sensual attack that heated the very molecules of his body. The air caressed his pores and shimmied brightly down his throat in the wake of the life-giving elixir. He grew hard with desire—a usual reaction to drinking blood but entirely unexpected in this situation.

This swoon—it was different. It had come on too suddenly. It lasted too long. And he hadn't even begun to drain her.

The witch must die. Pick her up. Finish the task.

Something wasn't right. And yet, it was all very right. The crazy heat gush of orgasm filled his veins and thickened his erection. Similar to sex, and yet more intense, for it traveled his entire system. Poisonous witch's blood tracked his extremities and staked claim to his soul.

She filled him. She sweetened him. She possessed him. She…claimed him.

"R-Ravin?" Nikolaus gasped in searching wonder. "Where? Ravin?"

Landing on his knees, he crept across the tiled floor. Blood spotted the white and black kitchen tiles. Fine, fragile glass shards *clicked* beneath his knees, protected by his leather jeans. His fingers dove into the thick black pool of her hair.

Salvation. Here is where you belong.

This is wrong. Why did you…? How could you?

She lay in a heap, her head tilted to the right to expose the deep wounds he had inflicted. Blood streamed down her neck and across her chest, staining the blue T-shirt stretched tight across her breasts.

No anger. No fight. Utterly silenced, his gorgeous witch. Hurt? Had he…?

Nikolaus scooped Ravin into his arms. He pressed his lips to her forehead. She didn't feel inordinately cold. A steady pulse beat against his palm where he slapped it over her neck.

"What have I done to you, my love?"

Chapter 4

Two months earlier

Jamming the syringe into the gel-tipped shotgun cartridge, Ravin filled the last of a dozen bullets with five milliliters of her blood. She did this every Sunday night. It was a ritual. She needed rituals. After two centuries of living, rituals kept her life on track and her focus sharp.

She'd been stalking the Kila tribe for weeks. They laid low and never made a mistake. She attributed that to their leader, Nikolaus Drake, who was known to keep a very tight rein on the tribe members. No unnecessary kills—that was their law.

A dead vampire was never an unnecessary kill, as far as Ravin was concerned.

A count over the weeks had determined two dozen in the tribe. The number of enemies didn't faze Ravin. She was a witch. So long as she kept her back to a wall, and her gun loaded, no longtooth was going to mess with her. The vampire's choice was to either run, or take a blood bullet and explode into ash.

She preferred the exploding part as opposed to running. But they could run forever; she'd never give up her quest to annihilate every bloody longtooth on this earth. It was a promise she'd made to her parents on the eve of their deaths.

Ravin checked the sawed-off shotgun for a full load and fitted it into the leather holder strapped across her back. Another belt strapped at her thigh secured a silver dagger, the edged metal soaked in her blood. She wore leather chaps over tight-fitted black suede pants and a black T-shirt beneath her leather vest. A big silver cross swung around her neck.

Reaching back, she secured her shoulder-length dark hair out of the way with a rubber binder. Her gloves slid on and snapped, and she donned clear safety glasses to protect her eyes from vampire debris.

The only thing that could take her down tonight was reluctance or fire.

Neither would bother her. For beyond the innate determination lived an indelible image of her parents' dying faces. No matter the notches Ravin marked on her gun, or the plunge toward darkness that occurred when slaying tipped her balance, that image would never be erased.

Not once did she question her relentless quest. For if she did, the truth might be harder to face than a tribe of blood-thirsty vampires.

The wolves had sent a messenger stating that there would be no communication-gathering this night. The nerve of Severo, the leader of the northern pack. He insulted Nikolaus with his blatant disregard for the vampire/wolf relations.

The vampires had always considered the city their territory. The wolves kept to the suburbs and countryside. And while he preached peace to his tribe, Nikolaus would not stand back and watch the wolves creep onto his grounds and begin to terrify Kila's source of nourishment.

"We'll snuff him out of his lair," Truvin Stone, second in command to Nikolaus, suggested. "I'll gather the troops?"

"No. They have shown us their fear. It is enough." For Nikolaus would not march his men into needless battle. The werewolf pack had retreated, offering a bloodless victory this day.

He could sense Truvin's tension, the need to react and charge into danger, as it stiffened his cohort next to him. Never would Truvin completely accept the peaceable ways of Kila, but Nikolaus was reassured in knowing that he did try to embrace them. The man had not killed for survival in the three years he'd been with Kila.

With a whistle, Nikolaus called the nine vampires who had accompanied him and Truvin into a circle in the middle of the dark alley. They would regroup and disperse.

Too late, he realized the bad tactical move. He'd drawn them into a tight target.

The first cry of "Witch!" froze Nikolaus's blood.

Two of his cohorts went down in a flash of sizzling flesh and blood. Their cries were unreal, choking screams as their bodies were destroyed by the surprise attack. It could only be a vigilante witch, armed with blood bullets—the death cocktail.

"Bitch," Nikolaus swore, and sought the direction of the attack, while calling out to the others. "Retreat!"

Another comrade—a friend for fifteen years—exploded before Nikolaus. He caught bits of flesh and blood against his palms.

So quickly they were taken down. Not right. How to stop it?

Truvin caught his gaze and nodded. He was on his way out—every vampire for himself, and woe to the fool who did not flee.

Nikolaus turned and spied a glint of silver in the narrow alley between two brick buildings but fifty strides away. The witch. She stalked the shadows, sure and relentless.

There were two vampires left standing besides himself. Panicked, they raced toward the approaching menace.

Nikolaus caught Cory in his arms. The man had been hit, but he would not be reduced to ash like the others, for he was a mortal supplicant to the tribe, one who sought immortality, but first must prove his dedication to *the dark*. He dragged his dying body behind a rusted Dumpster.

A bullet shrilled past Nikolaus's head and hit the brick wall right above his shoulder. A glass-tipped bullet that contained witch's blood.

A scout had once obtained one of the bullets for the tribe's study. But a drop of witch's blood, infused into a vampire's bloodstream, took a manic trip through his body and ate him from the inside out. It proved a quick yet excruciating death.

Something stung his shoulder. Fiery bites ate along his neck and cheek. Nikolaus dropped Cory onto the tarmac and slapped at the incredible pain. It sizzled down his torso and up, under and along his left arm, eating into his leather clothing and gnawing at flesh.

"No." He'd been splattered from the bullet that had hit the wall.

Staggering against the unreal pain, Nikolaus dropped to his knees, landing beside Cory's body. The death cocktail sizzled into his torso. His heart pumped furiously, as if trying to outrun the inevitable. He slapped at the burning flesh, rolled over it to make it stop, but did not cry out. He was dead to the witch.

And in a moment of clarity, he knew what had to be done. He needed blood. Lots of it.

Even as his flesh fell away from his bones, Nikolaus ripped into Cory's throat, drinking his blood and slapping his hands over the mortal's gaping chest wound to coat them in blood. He bathed himself in Cory's fleeting life, but it didn't seem as if he could ever stop the burn.

Listening, keen for the intruder, he realized his own pulse beats ceased. His heart—

He gripped his chest but felt his insides. Blood. Ribs. Organs. His vision blurred. Breath stopped.

Drink!

Or die at the hands of a witch.

Chapter 5

The Present

He laid the witch on the end of a king-size bed that mastered the whitewashed floorboards in the bedroom. A thick white comforter cradled her as if she were an angel resting on a cloud. A bloody angel that he'd...not killed.

Nikolaus straightened abruptly. He smoothed a palm over his face and drew it down his chin. *You almost killed her.*

But he hadn't.

Why didn't you kill her?

Ravin Crosse, this...witch? Vampires and witches were enemies.

What the hell?

Fists formed. Nikolaus hissed through his teeth. Rage emerged and flooded his system. Stalking the floor from door to wall, he resisted the urge to growl, to howl out his frustration.

She lay there, inert, her hair splayed, black curls across white. Silent. Unable to lash out, to fight, to challenge him.

This was the witch who had once injured him so badly he had touched death. His heart had stopped. He'd had to feed on a friend to survive.

Heat flushed Nikolaus's neck and shoulders, and filled him from skull to fingertips to heels. A storm of vengeance raged for release, but—

This felt different. Unusual.

For where the rage should have felt substantial and insistent and uncontrollable, it merely settled, and became an emotional reaction Nikolaus had not touched for what seemed like ages.

Heartbeats quieted. Fisted fingers snapped open. Anxiety fled, softening the thick tension holding his neck stiff.

He bent over the body sprawled across the bed, his palms sinking deep into the plush down quilt.

This witch, this gorgeous woman, deserved—

He swept his head lower, over her face, but stopped short of touching her mouth with his. Blood coated her neck. It smelled different. Not like mortal blood. There lingered an odd herbal aroma to it. Before, the scent of rosemary had come to him, but it had changed. This scent was organic. Cherry? Or musk and then…cloves? Nikolaus couldn't place it.

Curiosity held him over the bed, the tips of his dark hair sweeping across her bloodied neck and chest. Swiping a forefinger through the blood, he observed the crimson glisten near a lamp that glowed at the head of the bed.

So deadly this small drop of life should be. It had once eaten through him, literally, to his heart. It had rendered dead six of the tribe Kila in less than five minutes.

Death cocktail, this. Dangerous. To be avoided at all costs. *It brings so much pain!*

Yet now…he wanted more.

He did?

"Not right," he muttered, then licked his finger clean.

The taste of her shimmered through him, warming his belly, and revisiting the earlier sexual desire. With the blood hunger always came the need for carnal satisfaction.

"Not right," he murmured again, "but not…wrong."

He glanced over the havoc marring the witch's neck. He'd not taken much from her; she should be coming to soon.

A tangle of wavy black hair scattered across the snow-clean quilt. A heart-shaped face finished at the sharp chin, and above that, a generous red mouth, partially open, hushed out soft breaths. A viscous brown liquid trailed down her forehead and across her cheeks and jaw.

Dark brows arched a wicked slash above each closed eye. A sprinkle of pale freckles danced upon each cheek. Yet, there, at the corner of her mouth, a scar curled down toward her jaw.

A tiny scar. *Unlike mine*, Nikolaus thought, with a stroke along his neck where the convoluted flesh ever reminded him of his survival.

Even unconscious the witch looked imposing, ready to strike. Must be the black jeans jealously hugging her narrow hips, and the T-shirt stained with blood. No bra beneath, for the pebbled texture of her erect nipples formed clearly in the thin cotton shirt.

Nikolaus licked his lips. The sight of her breasts, full and high, stirred a need that the taste of her blood had pushed to the surface. He hovered a palm over the points of her nipples. But not to touch.

She is poison!

No, he possessed immunity to her blood; in proof, he'd survived the extraction that now saw her unconscious.

Tracing his lower lip with his tongue, Nikolaus scanned the

room, lit by the white shadow beaming from a small halogen lamp. It had been just after midnight when he'd arrived. Less than an hour had passed. Safe yet, for the sun wouldn't peek over the horizon until five-thirty. He'd walked here, but he may need to call his driver for a fast dash into a dark vehicle and a secure ride home.

The room was large and stark. But the bed and a few pieces of clothing were scattered across the whitewashed hardwood floor. A huge plant with leaves the size of elephant's ears sat near what must be the bathroom door.

One entire wall was fashioned of bookshelves—also white-washed—stuffed from ceiling to floor with volumes that varied from ancient, gilt-embossed spines, to glossy, colorful paperbacks.

The north wall was lined with windows, the shades pulled against streetlights.

No matter what trials Nikolaus had overcome and survived, give him but a minute or two in direct sunlight and his flesh would begin to sizzle. Though, even as a phoenix, he'd not yet summoned the sanguine carelessness to test his still-healing flesh against the sun.

Compelled to stare upon the witch, Nikolaus rubbed his jaw. Should he leave her here alone to wake wondering what had happened to her? Would she know?

He'd not used persuasion to erase the memory of his bite, yet he had licked the wound. The vampire's saliva was necessary to heal the bite and to prevent the vampire taint from transforming his victims to vampires themselves.

He couldn't abandon her. He…he cared about her.

Impossible! She is a witch.

Difficult to argue with his rational inner voice. And yet, Nikolaus knew, heart-deep, that he did feel genuine concern. Ravin Crosse was…why, she was *his*.

Yes, to claim her felt right. He rubbed a hand across his chest and stopped over the pounding beat within. This woman belonged to him for he felt her in his heart. It was as though she occupied him. Her mysterious scent lived in his nostrils and her taste filled his mouth and body. Instinctually, he wanted her.

And yet, did she return the sentiment?

He wasn't sure about her feelings toward him. It was as if she'd just appeared in his life, and yet he'd known her even before he'd been born. A stupid notion. Nikolaus did not believe in reincarnation or soul mates. Man had but one life to live, though certainly that life could be drastically altered and lure him to encounter a strange new world of creatures he'd not once imagined to be true.

Like werewolves and vampires and witches.

"Do I know you, Ravin Crosse?" He traced the fringed darkness of her hair. "Of course I do. How can a man *not* know someone they care about?"

Where was it? The confidence of soul he had always felt when leading his men, or the utterly intoxicating power when he'd once held a surgical blade in hand. This new, strange feeling encompassing his being, so opposite—it was the absence of control—rendered him helpless. Unsure.

Nikolaus had always clung to love, grasped for it, and embraced it whenever it had come to him. It had been...so long. He'd not loved a woman since before he'd been transformed.

Dare he believe love was once again his?

The world had changed and that was never a good thing. Everything felt...horizontal. And it smelled different. Not a repulsive smell, but an untamed scent that should set up her hackles.

Danger. Predator.

Ravin realized the low, murmuring sound she heard was actually herself. She moaned. She ached. Her neck hurt.

A pair of deep blue eyes hovered above her. Getting closer. As if…he was going to kiss her.

Instincts kicked in, and Ravin smashed her fist into the creep's jaw.

He reeled upright, smoothing a palm along his face. But instead of the expected anger, he leaned back over her and grinned a rogue's saucy smirk. "I love it when you play rough, sweetness."

The second punch cracked his nose. Ravin scrambled to sit upon the thick comforter.

Shaking his head and sliding her another roguish grin, the big brute of a vampire swiped blood from his upper lip and chuckled. "The left side next time, okay? Wouldn't want you to knock a tooth loose. Might need it for breakfast later."

So she wound up for punch number three—on the same side.

The vampire clamped a hand about her fist and wrangled her other wrist into a tight clasp. "That's enough." He slammed her backward and pinned her to the bed. Tension salted the air with a strong urgency. "Or you'll get me thinking you're as madly in love with me as I am with you."

He crushed a kiss to her mouth. Brutal and forceful. He wasn't going to let her beat him. It was all Ravin could do to twist her head aside. She felt him grin against her jaw.

Tall, Dark and Ruthless had developed a weird method of dispatching his vengeance. She slapped away his hand before the vampire could stroke her face.

Stroke her? As in *gently?* A vampire?

To his favor, the vampire didn't react to her defensive move with another body slam or kiss, though he knelt on the bed, leaning over her body, hands above her shoulders, and that dark, pitiful expression but inches from her face. Yeah, it was more pitiful than predatory. Kind of a puppy dog stare, if she had to label it.

A vampire was in her home. On her bed. Close enough to— "What the hell? Aren't you going to kill me?"

"Changed my mind," he offered. Her attempts to knee him off her fortified his efforts to remain on top of her. "Obviously, when I first arrived here, my thoughts were clouded by our past encounter. Got a little carried away."

"A little…? You came here to kill me. You're supposed to get carried away! What the hell are you doing now—don't you dare kiss me!"

"I… If it's what you wish?" The imminent kiss aborted, he raked a hand over his mane of dark hair and sighed, looking as confused as Ravin felt. "Don't know what got into me. I don't normally attack those I care about."

Enough of this.

Ravin kicked against the vampire's chest with one foot. Yes, a freakin' vampire! Care about her? What fruit salad of drugs had he sucked out of his last victim?

"Get away from me, you bloodsucking longtooth!"

As she scrambled backward across the bed, her head hit the wood headboard, stopping her cold.

Ravin cursed her need for sanctuary, a quiet room filled with things that calmed her, such as books and scented oils and luscious, nine-hundred-count sheets. No weapons in the room. Not even a lousy cross at hand!

The vampire sat on her bed—on her own quilt that she'd saved from granny's belongings—as if they were chums or pals…

"Back off, vampire!" She lifted her wrist to her mouth, prepared to bite, but then the disaster that had just happened flashed in her thoughts.

The spilled love potion. (No wonder she smelled nasty.)

The front door. Yeah, it lay on the floor, her home open to the world, or anyone who should walk down the hallway.

But the most vivid recollection was of the hulking vampire pinning her to the fridge—and biting her.

Ravin slapped a hand to her neck. "Ouch!"

He shrugged. "I rubbed my saliva into it, though it does seem to be healing rather slowly. Your blood doesn't clot as quickly as a mortal—"

"You bit me?" she spat. "Who do you think you are? What are you doing? You're— We're—"

The world had tilted completely off its axis. Normally a vamp should be fleeing her for fear of a droplet of her blood splattering any portion of its flesh. But this one had *drunk* from her. A lot, to judge from the open wound on her neck and the still-woozy feeling that dizzied her brain.

"Feels as if I've been punctured by a nail gun. Get off my bed!"

"Don't be so mouthy, woman. Can't you see I—I just…" A heavy sigh. Two worry lines appeared on his forehead as he lifted his brows and delivered another sigh. "Love you, is all."

From where had this vampire escaped? The Count's Home for Wayward and Manic Vampires? When last she'd checked, all the insane ones had high-tailed it for New Orleans. He must have tallied numerous kills to his chart, for the *danse macabre* had driven him insane.

"You don't love me."

"I do. Damn me, but I do." He delivered her a wink and a rogue's grin that was beginning to irritate her more and more.

Ravin did not do flirtation. Most especially with a—

"I'm a witch. You're a vampire. Do you get that? Don't you remember you came here to kill me?" She recalled his impassioned speech just before he dug his teeth into her neck. "I…killed you?"

"Tried." That smile kept sliding back onto his mouth. A triumphant, roguish grin that exuded sensuality and put Ravin on high alert.

He settled onto the bed, a big loafing greyhound who would not be put back no matter how many times he was kicked. A few of the metal grommets on his leather jacket glinted with blood. *Her blood.* "I survived your attack."

"Apparently."

"Barely." He tugged at the collar of his black shirt. Ravin saw scars on the side of his neck, nasty scars that looked pink and brand new.

"I know I came here wanting to kill you," he said.

Running his hands through his hair, he searched the walls, as if to avoid her gaze. Though his shoulders were wide enough to bear a small vehicle on them, his expression was confused, as if he was unsure what he'd gotten himself into.

"I'm not sure what happened between "I hate you, witch" and "I'm sorry, Ravin," but I can't imagine harming you, and it kills me to see what I've done to you already. Can you forgive me?"

Ravin lunged across the bed and smacked the idiot across the forehead.

Expecting to again be pinned by the vampire, she knelt there defiantly, fist raised.

He bowed his head.

Ravin was simply floored. Stunned. Not in her history had she ever been so close to a vampire and not had him either attack or flee.

"What the hell did you say your name was?"

"Nikolaus Drake." He lashed out his tongue to wipe away a trickle of blood that stained his lip.

"Tooth loose?"

"Not the important ones."

"Then let me have another go."

"Chill, sweetness. You're all about showing your affection with little love taps, aren't you?"

Love taps? Of all the…!

Disgusted, Ravin slid off the bed, staggered, but when she sensed the vampire jump up to grasp for her, she swayed forward and caught her balance. "Hands off!"

He retreated with hands raised to show compliance.

Why did the idiot think he was in love with her?

Oh, damn, of all that can go wrong. The odor of rosemary and ash that she had used in the love spell clung to her hair. Ravin remembered clearly now. The entire contents of the vial had spilled over her, and thanks to her magic, had absorbed instantly through her pores to course through her bloodstream.

"You don't love me," she muttered. "You're under a love spell."

Chapter 6

She stalked away from him, into the bathroom. Fluorescent lights blinked on, highlighting the bloodstains splattered down the left shoulder of her T-shirt.

Nikolaus sat silently on the bed and observed.

Tilting her head to the side, the witch noted the havoc in the bathroom mirror, then let loose a string of curse words. Nikolaus bowed his head and shook it, yet he smiled. The woman could paint a blue streak.

"Look what you did!"

Stepping into the doorway between the bathroom and bedroom, she pointed out his handiwork with an angry thrust of her thumb.

Sore, swollen flesh surrounded two prominent bite marks just below the sharp line of her jaw.

"It'll heal," he said calmly. "I should lick it again, to make sure of it?"

"Back off! Stupid love spell. I sure hope it's—"

Focused on more than the witch's temper tantrum, Nikolaus pricked his ears toward the living room. "There's someone at your door," he said.

"Tell them to go away. Wait. What time is it?" Ravin rushed back into the bedroom and grabbed the gray sweatshirt jacket mounded in a heap near the foot of the bed.

"It's almost morning." He glanced toward the windows, shades pulled, each and every one of them. No sunlight yet, but soon. "You slept all night. I didn't want to wake you. You looked so serene."

"Why don't you leave? Get out of here!"

He fitted his thumbs into his front pockets and drew up to stand tall. He didn't take kindly to such treatment, especially from someone he loved. It stirred up too many memories of broken hearts and shouted curses.

On the other hand, she seemed genuinely peeved he was here.

I know I've only just come to her home. There can't be things between us already. Can there?

But of course, there was one very obvious *thing*. The way he felt about her.

"I'm not leaving until I'm sure you're going to be okay," he said. "Even then…I don't want to leave, Ravin. It can't be this way between the two of us."

"This way? There is no *way* between us."

Now Ravin heard the rap at the door. Couldn't be the door, because that lay on the floor of her living room.

"You are going to hate yourself when the spell is broken," she snapped.

She zipped up the sweatshirt jacket, but it didn't cover the wound, so she tugged up the hood and tied it tight, which gave her a South Park-esque look. "You don't love me. Get that idiot nonsense out of your tiny little brain."

"The human brain is the largest in all the animal kingdom, save the whale. Three pounds. Though I've put my hands to a four-pounder once. It wasn't healthy; had swelling in the cerebral cortex due to infection."

Ravin lifted a brow. That comment had thrown her. It was good to surprise them; kept them on their toes.

"I've a delivery pickup," she said on a snarl that Nikolaus was starting to assume was her standard expression. "I'll be right back to explain."

"Explain what?"

"That you're under a spell," she hissed, and trotted out to the living room.

A spell was making him love the witch?

It's the only way something so heinous could ever happen.

Nothing, but nothing, could make him consider kindness toward a witch.

A skeleton of a man waited in the space of Ravin's front entryway. Flesh clutched his bones, cheeks sucked to his tonsils, and a manic look in his gray eyes glittered. He tilted his fist to rap the door frame again.

"Pickup?" Ravin asked. "Hang on. Give me two minutes. Do not move from that spot, got it?"

He nodded, meek enough to lower his head and look up shyly. Not a mortal, she knew that from his sallow coloring and red eyes; possibly an imp. Himself employed them copiously. Probably didn't own his soul.

Ravin knew the feeling of not owning your soul—and wanted it to go away. But more so? She wanted the vampire to go away.

She detoured into the kitchen, where the evidence of last night's fiasco made her want to retch. Brute smell of vampire aggression clung to the air, mixing with the spilled herbs and smoke of the spell.

"He thinks he loves me," she muttered. "I guess the spell was successful. Now how to reverse it?"

It was not reversible, she knew. At least not by her. The only one who could reverse a spell was that person who had ordered it. She always designed her spells that way. Otherwise, she risked being called in to render null so many nasty spells.

And the one who'd ordered the spell?

"Crap. My soul isn't getting any closer to being returned."

The glass vial lay on its side on top of the fridge, held in place by the suctiony white plastic buffers between the two doors.

Ravin retrieved it carefully. About an ounce remained inside.

"Not enough to do any damage. But I'm not about to tell Himself I didn't finish the job. I did finish it. And I tested it, like it or not."

Plucking out a small, finger-size vial from the junk drawer, she filled it with the remaining potion and stuffed in a small red plastic stopper. Sealing that in a Ziploc bag made it look more official.

Dangling the pitiful thing before her, she blew out a heavy breath. "This'll never work."

But at the moment she had worse things to worry about. Worse than the devil's disappointment?

"Oh, yeah."

She had…tamed the untamable, it seemed. The man was a phoenix, a leader among his kind. Phoenixes were rare, and possessed amazing strength and—she hadn't heard of one in existence for centuries. Was he really what he said he was?

Phoenix or not, the vampire was here in her home, making moon eyes at her and whispering sweet nothings. Not good, not good at all.

Clutching the sweatshirt hood around her neck, Ravin hoped the courier wouldn't notice the bite marks.

"Here it is," she said with forced cheer as she rounded the corner and stepped onto the fallen door. "Be careful with it."

"This is it?"

She narrowed a glare at him. "Is that what you do? Ask questions? Because I don't think you have the authority to ask questions, am I right?" She crossed her arms and cocked her hip out.

Yeah, I'm tough. Just try me.

So long as it wasn't a six-foot-plus love-struck vampire standing her down.

"Right. Er…" The imp let his gaze roam over the door, then opened his mouth but didn't say a thing. No questions. Good boy. "Thanks."

The little man skittered away.

Ravin bent to lift the large, solid-oak door, and it moved much easier than she expected.

"Let me help."

Stunned she hadn't heard, felt or smelled the vampire come up behind her, Ravin slid away from him and paced across the floor. She shoved back the sweatshirt hood and increased her pace to a fitful stomp. Maintaining distance was all she wanted right now.

The vampire fitted the door into the frame and inspected the hinges. Biceps as large as coffee tins flexed beneath his soft black shirt. Long hair dusted across a wide back. She'd always been a back woman. Strong, wide and muscled is how she preferred—

Whoa! What was she thinking? Ravin unzipped the sweatshirt jacket and deposited it on the couch with a fling.

"That's the wrong way, vampire!" she called as he fitted the door into the hinges.

"This is right," he said.

"No, *you're* supposed to be on the other side."

"Ah. You have a sense of humor." He rolled that one

around in his thoughts. "That must be why I love you so much." He fitted the door into the splintered wood frame, and left it there. "It'll need new hinges, but for now it will serve. Who was that?"

"No questions." Arms akimbo—and thoughts scattered—Ravin paced between the kitchen and living room. "You're going to hate yourself with a bloody vengeance when you finally wake up from this spell, you know that, vampire?"

"My name is Nikolaus. It's considered rude to use the other term, unless by my own kind."

"Yeah, I know, *vampire*. I'm a witch, what do you want from me? And why is it you were able to drink my blood without exploding into a million bits?"

"I'm immune to it now I've survived your initial attack."

"Right. A phoenix," she muttered.

The one who got away. How impossible was it to survive a death cocktail? The vampire couldn't have taken more than a minimal hit, and even with that, he had to have wiped most of the blood away immediately.

"Took me two months to recover," he offered. "I'm still not completely whole."

That long to get over a few splatters of her blood? Well, she hoped he had suffered. Small recompense for not dying, in her opinion.

He approached her slowly, his arms arced out at his sides like a weight lifter's. Yeah, he had muscles, lots of them. And black leather everywhere, wrapping his legs and his thick thighs. The leather jacket strained over his shoulders.

But despite the costume and the imposing build, his expression was eerily compassionate. Darkest eyes sat on a long face with defined cheekbones and a square jaw. A broad forehead was swept clean of the long straight hair that spilled past his shoulders and to his elbows.

He was huge and powerful—and love struck.

That was some hell of a spell if he knew she'd tried to kill him, and yet continued to proclaim love toward her.

Nice work, Ravin. You could go into business. Too bad Himself will make you pay with flesh for this screwup.

That is, if the vampire didn't pock up her flesh with tooth marks before then.

"I've still scars all up the left side of my body," he explained. "You really did a number on me."

"Show me," Ravin demanded. If he were going to claim damage, then he should have proof, yes?

"Right now?"

"You say you love me? Don't you want to share your most intimate secrets with me? Oh, stop." She put out a hand as he slid off the leather jacket and tugged up his shirt to reveal rock-solid abs. "What am I saying? Put your jacket back on. This is all very wrong."

It was difficult to remain angry and look at him at the same time. Every part of the man was hard and taut and oozed a come-and-touch allure. Even the crimson-and-ash aura he wore looked sparkly and inviting.

Deadly? Oh, yeah. But also…evocative.

Ravin shook her head and steered her gaze anywhere but toward Nikolaus Drake.

"Now, listen and try to understand," she said. "You are a victim of a misdirected spell. You don't love me because you *want* to love me, you love me because of the spell shooting through my bloodstream at the time you bit me. This spell." She swiped a finger over her forehead and showed him the dark residue. "Got it?"

He quirked a brow, a dark check mark that highlighted the vivid blue eyes beneath.

"I remember that I came here to—"

"To kill me!" And don't look at his eyes, she coached silently. They do not resemble jewels.

"You've been smoking some witchy weed, sweetness. I would never stand still long enough to allow a witch to bespell me."

"The spell was already in my bloodstream, Einstein. It spilled over me when you made your crashing entrance into my home, death in your…eyes." She tore her gaze from what were sapphires fixed into a dark, deadly setting. "You drank the spell when you drank my blood."

He shrugged. "I'd never allow a witch to put a spell on me."

"Oh, yeah? Tell me how a man…make that vampire, falls in love with a woman…make that a witch…in less than the snap of a finger? Oh!"

Gripped by a sudden burning bite to her chest, Ravin clutched her ribs.

"Ravin? What's wrong with you?"

The pain was brief, but it did not fail to level her to her knees. Landing on the floor but inches from Nikolaus's scuffed leather biker boots, Ravin wobbled and tried to keep from collapsing into his waiting arms.

Chapter 7

She swayed before him, on her knees, her head tilted way back to reveal the havoc he'd done to her neck. Nikolaus held his arms out to catch her, but she shook her head and mumbled that she'd rather die than have a vampire touch her.

The statement sliced him like a surgical blade to the heart. He felt relegated to a realm of monsters and creatures. He'd struggled for years to overcome that kind of thinking after his transformation. Now he accepted that he was one of *the dark*.

But I will never become a monster.

And yet, a monster had harmed this woman.

Why he'd bitten her—so sloppily, as if he had intended harm—was beyond him.

No, it's not. You knew. The left side of your brain—that logical thinking part—knows you intented to murder the witch.

Yes. Because she had killed his men, and had attempted to kill him. This awful, selfish, petite…defiant, *gorgeous* woman.

What the hell? He didn't want to hurt Ravin. He wanted to hold her close and fall into her arms. Which was a strange thought in itself, because Nikolaus was the furthest thing from romantic. He didn't have relationships. He had sex with women to relieve a need that always accompanied the hunger. He didn't trust women. He didn't trust himself with mortal women. He…

…was in love with this witch.

If his tribe ever got wind of this they'd flail him alive. And he'd remain alive after the beating, because a little flailing wasn't going to kill any vampire, most especially a phoenix.

How could he return to Kila now? Would they smell the witch on him?

What of her blood? It coursed through his veins. Along with…a love spell?

"What's happening to you?" He knelt before Ravin. Her fingers clasped into his, but she withdrew as if touched by a flame.

Finally she settled into him, her stained forehead falling to rest on his shoulder. She smelled good. Like blood and sweat and some sweetness that could only be woman.

"Is it from me? Are you still weak from blood loss? I didn't take that much before I—" *Fell in love.*

Was that it? He'd fallen. Tumbling. Arms spread and completely unprepared for such a fall—into love.

Huh. This condition could prove a bitch when he finally shook it off.

Ravin pushed away from him and landed her back against the brown leather couch. A long-leafed plant shivered on the round table just behind her shoulder. Tugging up her T-shirt, the witch revealed three dark horizontal scars just below her breasts, each about eight inches long. Two of them had slashes through them. The second looked fresh.

She grinned and muttered, "Two strikes. Ha! One left, and the old soul is mine again. And it can't happen soon enough."

"What does that mean?" It confounded him that she was in pain and he hadn't a clue how to help her. And yet, she seemed quite pleased with whatever had just transpired. "Talk to me, sweetness."

"All right, vampire."

"Don't call me that," he muttered.

"You insist on calling me sweetness, I'm going to have to call you vampire."

"What's wrong with sweetness?"

"It's a term of endearment! You are not endearing to me, nor should I be to you."

Fist raised, he bent before her, but a strange whisper in his brain made him soften the fist to a splay of fingers, and then he gently stroked across her brow to swish aside her hair. "Sorry, sweetness, but I can't change the way I feel about you. I insist you call me Nikolaus."

"Not a possibility. Too personal."

"Then Drake, please?"

The struggle in her eyes fascinated him. Not muddy as he'd originally decided. The dark irises resembled burnt wine with glints of gold flaking.

"Sit down, Drake," she commanded, pulling her gaze abruptly away. She stood and, still rubbing her ribs, pointed to the couch.

"I prefer to stand."

"If you have such free will then— fine. I know you're not responsible for the part of your brain that makes you feel love right now."

"You know about the ventral tegmental area of the brain?"

"The what?"

"Located in the brain stem. It's the command center for emotions such as joy, sadness and love."

Huffing out a sigh, she again pointed to the couch. "Please. Just…do whatever you want."

Nikolaus decided sitting was acceptable. He settled onto the couch and rested his wrists upon his knees.

She stood over him, an angel with wavy black hair and a cherub face that had never seen a bow and arrow, and if she had, most certainly had never shot the weapon out of love.

Nikolaus's gaze followed the curves of her body. She wasn't long or lithe; in fact, her curves were healthy and luscious.

He liked a woman with meat on her. Both for biting and for holding while having sex.

Her T-shirt was still rucked up. Nikolaus had never before seen the like. Long slashes streaked across her flesh as if some taloned beast had dragged its claws over her. But she seemed not to be in pain.

"It's a debt I owe," she said, tugging the shirt down to cover the incredibly toned abs that screamed for Nikolaus's attention. "Three strikes and I'm out. I've only one more obligation to complete."

"Whom do you owe the debt to?" he wondered.

She had a manner of narrowing down her brows. It was a look that might make some take a step back. Especially if it was another vampire, and she held up a wrist dripping with her own blood. Yet, Nikolaus found her self-assurance fascinating, so commanding. There was nothing about the person standing before him he did not admire.

"It's more of a loan than a debt. I loaned out my soul for something only another witch would find valuable," she said. "You wouldn't understand, and I'm not going to explain."

"Your soul? Have you—?"

"That's all you're getting from me, Drake. Now, let's get you briefed and out of my hair, shall we?"

"Briefed on what?"

"On this ridiculous nightmare we've both been dragged into since your abrupt entrance into my home last night."

"There's nothing ridiculous about it."

He stood and Ravin stepped back, putting up her hands, first as fists, but quickly spreading out her fingers merely to placate.

"All right, don't get your dander up," he offered patiently. "I won't touch you," he added, but felt chastised for having to say it. "Not for a few minutes, anyway."

"Take your chances, vamp—er, Drake. I can defend myself until the end days."

"I've never thought it necessary to defend oneself from a kiss. You've an interesting set of values, sweetness."

"You kiss me again, I bite you back."

He whistled. "You do tempt me."

And if her fiery sense of defiance didn't do it, then the underlying scent of her being was there for backup. Nikolaus sniffed, a habit he'd developed with his vampirism, for his senses had become so heightened there were times he could smell a person before they stepped out from a car, or even days after they had been in his home.

Ravin Crosse's scent was a heady variety of strange and wondrous fragrances. Salt. Honey. Musk. Acrid anger. A trace of something fruity, probably from her shampoo or soap. The metallic, meaty aroma of dried blood. And the erotic vibrance of warm flesh.

But most prominent? The vampire in him demanded further sustenance, because he wasn't feeling at all sated after the first draw. His canine teeth descended, for normally they remained in line with the rest of his teeth until the blood hunger demanded.

"Oh! You," she started, completely unaware of the struggle going on inside his brain, and in his mouth. Squeezing her fist before him, she closed her eyes and let out a frustrated noise.

His teeth tingling in their sockets, Nikolaus hungrily observed her rub at the wound on her neck. The dried blood attracted him. He'd spent the past two months drinking from donors Gabriel had captured and brought to him as if he were a caged rat. Tonight he'd gone out into the world and had taken nourishment himself. And he was feeling it in his bones. Normally he'd be flat on his back now, exhausted merely from the intense healing his body was engaged in.

Now he felt invigorated. In fact, a deep breath did not draw a wheezy wind through his left lung. And yet, he needed more.

"Are you listening, vampire?"

"Huh?"

"Back off, bloodsucker. Get those teeth out of sight."

"Make me."

"I'll—" The fire in her held her fist high, but Nikolaus watched as the flames dimmed and she realized there was nothing she was capable of doing. "This is not you. Trust me."

"I don't require an artificial means to know I love you, Ravin."

"If you say you love me one more time, I'm going to get out the stakes. They're sharp and have break-away glass tips loaded with my blood—oh, hell." Running her hands back through her hair, she paced the floor away from him. "Like that's going to help."

"You are defenseless against me now. But I won't use that against you, I promise."

"Listen, I know my blood won't do it for you anymore, but I'm pretty damn sure a stake to the heart will take you out."

Doubtful. His heart had already been partially reduced to ash thanks to the witch's blood that had burned deep into his body. It had stopped beating. Then restarted. Nikolaus felt sure it was now tougher than ever. Should he test the stake to prove it?

Nikolaus shook his head. "What did I do to make you so angry with me?"

"That's it." She walked off, her arms pumping furiously. "Time for the stake!"

"Wait! I don't know what kind of lover's spat we're having, but—very well, maybe I *am* under a spell."

Nikolaus slid around behind the couch and blocked her path from the stakes, wherever she kept those.

Hands shoved to her hips and bare feet tapping, she always wore a sneer. Did the woman not have a smile to her arsenal?

"Did you put a spell on me to make me love you because we had an argument?"

"Please. I would never bespell a vampire to love me. I despise your kind. Always have, always will, got that? Always. Will."

"But—"

"I hunt your kind! I was hunting the night I thought I'd killed you."

This was all fact. He knew it as he knew he loved her. He knew the brain was processing the information, sorting and responding logically, and yet the right half of his brain was winning on the emotional front.

Was he deceiving himself? It was not out of the realm of possibility. And that was the troubling part. "But we've overcome our differences?"

"Aggh! No, we still hate each other." She lifted her shirt and drew her finger under the second horizontal line that had a slash through it. "I finished obligation number two. Now you're love struck. Not because you want to be, but because of a spell. A *spell*."

"Huh."

It made sense. Ridiculous sense. Maybe.

Why would he need a spell to love this woman? She was perfect and gorgeous, and he wanted to kiss her. To settle her ire and calm her.

Thinking was for dummies. Real men took action.

Gripping her shoulders, Nikolaus leaned in to kiss his sweet, angry witch. He was accustomed to the struggle. Often, he'd seduce his victims, have sex with them, then, when he flashed his fangs before the bite, they'd scream and shove and kick. But not for long. The vampire's bite was only initially painful to mortals. Soon enough, the swoon of orgasm would cease all struggle.

But he wasn't biting now. And little Miss Witch remained intent on making a simple kiss as difficult as possible. Damn, she tasted fiery and urgent and all those things that turned him on for reasons he'd never sort out.

A kick to his knee brought him down.

Ravin backed into the kitchen. "Keep your filthy mouth away from mine!"

She sorted through a drawer, drawing out a huge silver cross. Wielding it at the end of her outstretched arm, she defied him to act.

So Nikolaus stepped forward, arms spread, and pressed his chest to the cold silver object.

"Shit." She gave the cross a shake, as if to jolt it into vampire-killing mode.

"Sorry. My parents were scientists," Nikolaus offered. "They believed in the theory of evolution and space travel and the power of reasoning over faith. I'm not baptized."

Ravin drew back the cross, twisting it in her grip to hold as a dagger. Nikolaus noted the end was pointed, a worthy stake.

"Fine." He put up placating hands. "I keep my distance. No stakes. Agreed?"

She looked him up and down. That sneer of hers pushed him close to an edge. It was so sexy. If only he could taste it, master it, and ultimately wrangle it into a wanting, cooing sigh.

"Fine. For now," she agreed. An expert twirl of the cross showed her prowess with weapons. Setting it on the counter with a slam, she then crossed her arms over her chest. "Though why I'm even agreeing will surely see me in hell faster than any devil's bargain. I'll give you ten seconds to leave. If you're here during second number eleven, you're ash."

"I'd be happy to oblige, if that's what you really want, but…" He pointed to the windows, shaded by blinds. "Daylight."

"What, you forget your SPF100?"

"Did I mention your sense of humor is what I like most about you, sweetness?"

"Enough! So you can't leave. What new hell is this day, anyway?" She tapped the counter. "I'm going to see about a reversal incantation. With luck, I'll have you hating me in less than an hour, and you can be on your merry way. Of course then, you won't kill me when you hate me, because you *will* owe me one."

"I'd never kill you unless it's between the sheets," Nikolaus said as he approached her. When he was inches from stroking her cheek, he pulled back. A grin offered the acquiescence her sudden wielding of the cross dagger demanded. "Over and over until you can't cry out any longer and the pleasure reduces us both to molten reverie."

She cast him such a horrified look Nikolaus laughed. The last time he'd had to struggle to get a girl to accept his kiss had been, well, never. The challenge intrigued him.

"What? You can't imagine making love like that? Let's do it now, Ravin. I need you."

"Back off!"

It was obvious she wasn't going to be convinced of some early morning sex. Fine. He'd attacked her; she needed some time to get over it.

And he needed to put a finger on this weird abundance of emotion that kept him bouncing back for more and more punishment from someone he should be hating.

Nikolaus sat on a bar stool across the counter from where the witch stood. For the moment, she paged through a thick black leather book, ignoring him. But he could sense her regard. She was very aware of him.

This was madness.

Was that it? Somehow just intending to kill had visited the *danse macabre* upon him? For when a vampire killed he took the victim's nightmares into him, and would relive them as if his own later. The more kills led to madness.

No, you're not being logical. Use the parietal lobe, that's what it's for.

Yeah, she was tempting to look at. Nikolaus could appreciate women, instead of seeing them only as either food or sexual fulfillment. Or both. To know they required tenderness, no matter how hard a front the woman wore. Yes, a slow seduction, a journey of her body, soul and mind was required.

"What are you doing, Nikolaus?"

"Nothing." She'd used his name. She was softening already. And he hadn't accessed the parietal, but instead the visual, occipital lobe. What was up with that?

"You're doing nothing very loudly. Go and sit on the couch, away from me."

He propped his forearms on the counter and bent down to catch her elusive gaze. "No."

"I can't do this with you watching me."

"Maybe that means you should save it for later. Right now you need to relax. You're strung tighter than a bow. Your anger is so strong I can feel it. And you do need to take care of that wound."

"What am I supposed to do about it? Stitch it up?"

"Let me lick it again. My saliva will—"

"If you so much as lay a finger on me—let alone, a tongue— I will strike for your eyes and tear them from your face."

"You see? Such vicious anger. Where does it all come from? You need to chill."

She slammed the grimoire shut. Black lacquered finger-nails tapped the stone countertop.

"Are you a Goth?" he suddenly wondered.

"A—what? I am not!"

"You dress like one."

"I could argue you dress the same. You've more black leather than a damned cow."

"Cows are Goths?"

"Now you're just trying to piss me off."

Nikolaus met her furious gaze—and smiled. He loved her fire. He knew there was a reason behind the strange feeling.

"I stink," she finally said. "I smell like love spell and vampire. I need to wash you off me. I'm going to take a shower."

"I'll join you."

"I shower with a stake in hand."

"You're not serious."

She leaned forward, fluttering her lashes. "Try me."

"I'll wait out here."

"No, you will not. My need to shuck off your scent leaves a convenient moment for you, the enemy, to quietly slip away, never to be seen again."

"What about the spell? I thought you were going to reverse it?"

"If only. I can't reverse it. The creator of the spell can never do that. It requires the owner—the one I created it for—to recite the reversion chant."

"So who ordered the spell?"

She chewed her lower lip. *Let me*, Nikolaus thought.

"None of your business. So take a hike, will you? You must have a means for traversing in the daylight. A driver? Dark glasses and a hood? Go on. The spell doesn't bind you to my home."

"Spell or not, I am bound to you with this." He pressed a

hand over his heart. It had been a long time since he'd spoken words like this—and meant them.

"Oh, for freakin' sake!" She charged past him, peeling her T-shirt over her head as she did so. As she wore no bra underneath, Nikolaus stepped from the stool to go after her for further investigation. "Don't be here when I get out of the shower. I wasn't lying about having a stake in the bathroom, and I will use it."

Glancing toward the windows, he noted the slash of sunlight that beamed in around the edges where the vinyl shades had curved back from age. He did have a driver who was on twenty-four-hour call. Leaving wasn't the issue.

"You can't get rid of me that easily, witch," Nikolaus called to her retreating back.

Part of him knew the truth—they were enemies. He should not be here.

But a bigger part of him made Nikolaus walk over to the couch. Putting up his feet, he laid his head back and made himself at home.

Chapter 8

Was there anything worse than having a vampire in love with you?

Having a vampire sit on your couch and declare his love in sappy sweetness?

Yes, that was worse.

But he would rage when the spell was lifted. To be tricked into feeling love for his natural enemy? By the very witch who had once killed him?

Ravin closed her eyes and bowed her head. Water beat upon her shoulders and neck. The bite wound didn't hurt anymore. But it pulsed, reminding her of her stupidity.

She had been bitten by a vampire before last night—many times. And despite the movies and books that would have one believe a vampire bite a sensual experience, it hurt like hell.

But this was the first time the biter had lasted longer than thirty seconds after sinking his teeth into her vein. There was a reason vamps called witch's blood the *death cocktail.*

So how to kill a vamp immune to her blood? That was the only option—a mercy killing. It was a hell of a lot more humane than allowing him to suffer under a love spell.

Would Drake be immune to another witch's blood? Hmm…

Ravin had only lived in Minneapolis six months; she hadn't encountered another witch, though she hadn't gone looking for any, either. Like vampires, her kind were in the minority.

Certainly a stake should do the job nicely. Shove it in between a couple of ribs, twist and tear, and rip his heart open. If the vampire's heart could be torn beyond repair, he would die.

Though, she wasn't up on phoenix lore. He'd come back from ash? That was too incredible. Could the vampire take a stake and remain standing? And yet, he was obviously not at full strength for the glimpse of scar she'd seen on his neck.

The idiot was enamored, blubbering about love and dismayed over the harm he'd done her. How sneaky would it be to take him out as he declared his undying love for her? To maybe let him kiss her…while she held the stake ready behind her back?

Sneaky, but effective. He would never see it coming.

Who was she, if not a hunter who never allowed her prey rest?

Ravin soaped up her hair, kicking herself for leaving the vampire alone in her living room while she skipped off to get naked. In the same house? Was she stupid?

Obviously. Though, there was the dead bolt inside the bathroom door, and the Charlie bar, and the silver cross tipped with her blood. She took security very seriously. As well, a gun and an arsenal of blood bullets and stakes were fitted in the cabinet behind the towel rack.

She never welcomed anyone lightly into her home. Even her friends. In her line of work, it didn't pay to have a lot of friends. In two centuries she could count on the fingers of one hand the faithful friends she had garnered—friends she would trust with her life.

Even those she did trust were never left alone. There were things in her home they could touch, and ruin and, well, destroy. Weapons, spells, protection wards. She was a private person, and she liked it that way. She didn't do relationships, or—heaven forbid—*love* because she didn't have time, the inclination or the patience for it.

Love was for people who possessed the capacity to care.

She shook her head under the stream of water and turned to press her hands against the slick tile wall. The awful smell from the spell had rinsed away and now the coconut body scrub filled her senses. To stand here all day would be the ultimate luxury. To not think about a thing. To not worry or have to communicate with the world.

Time to get back into hunt mode. Today, Ravin would rack up another notch on her stake. A notch that should have been permanent two months earlier.

At least she'd received credit for the botched spell.

Tracing a finger over the new slash mark, she smiled. So maybe the devil *could* be tricked? Ha!

The shower curtain slid open. Ravin choked on a stream of water. Steam fogged the small white bathroom and blurred the hanging spider plants to verdant blobs, but the large dark image was unmistakable.

How had he...? She hadn't heard another door crash to the floor.

A naked vampire stepped into the bathtub.

"No." She lifted her leg to kick at him but lost her balance on the slick porcelain surface.

Nikolaus caught her wrist, stopping her from a graceless fall against the shower tiles. "I need you, Ravin. You need me, too. Let's do this."

* * *

She resisted his attempts to kiss her so desperately, Nikolaus almost gave up. He could find street whores gladly willing to service his needs. But he didn't need to be serviced. He wanted to dive into this woman and hope upon hope she'd allow him an inch.

He got an inch. Maybe it was because she had slipped under the hot rain of water. He didn't care. That slight alteration in her stance moved her lips against his, and when he grabbed the back of her head to support her, she ceased to protest. And she began to indulge in the kiss as much as he wished her to.

"I know nothing of your kind," he murmured against her ear, "but I intend to learn. All of you."

For this moment he wouldn't venture off to any other parts of her body. Only her lips. Inside, her mouth was as warm and wet as outside. Slicking his tongue across her teeth, he cautioned against nipping the plump lower lip. *No teeth. Keep it sane.*

One of them moaned. It was Ravin. A deep rumble in her throat that wasn't admonishing or angry, only wanting. She had begun to respond to him in ways that didn't hurt him.

Deep. Yes, she allowed him a long lazy kiss. Slide down inside her. Feed her moans with another, and another kiss. Control her with a few directing fingers along her spine, pressing the slick curves of her groin against his hips. *Make her yours.* And then softer, teasing kisses that led him from her mouth up to the tip of her slick nose.

Nikolaus shifted his entire body against hers, effectively holding her against the wet tile wall. Every pore on his body drank in her essence, the heat-steam misting from her like a wicked witch's potion.

Like the potion you drank from her blood? Watch it, Drake, you'll allow her the upper hand, no matter the conditions of the silly spell. You are not enslaved to her whims; she is yours to do with as you please.

He dropped her arms and slid his fingers over her breasts. Heavy and firm, they were too large for a handful. He liked that there was so much of her to hold. To possess. Rock-hard nipples skimmed beneath his palms. The feel of them tightened him, made him hard.

Nikolaus growled out his need. He wanted to take her right now. No sane man could hold back the burgeoning want. The hot water pinpricked the thick head of his cock. Every touch, sensation and slide tempted him closer. He had to be inside her.

But he must be patient, not push too hard, for only moments earlier she had been ordering him to leave and never return. A man never gained headway by charging the front. (If the occasional door had to be battered down, that was different. The bathroom door had come down with one kick after he'd knocked off the hinges.) Yet Nikolaus had never been one to grasp and snatch. Slow and sure had never led him wrong before.

He bent to bury his face against her hot velvet breasts. A dash of his tongue tasted the ruddy texture of a nipple.

The slap of her palm tingled across his cheek. She shoved him hard against the shoulder. "Get out!"

"Make me," he said, knowing this slip of a witch might be able to fire some bloody bullets at him, but she would never be able to physically move him. He towered over her by a foot, probably more. "You want this, too, Ravin. I can feel it in your kiss."

"You're going to feel something a lot more painful if you don't step back!"

Instead of beating on him, or attempting a few expert shin-kicks, she stepped out of the shower. Steel curtain rings *zinged* across the shower bar with her exit.

Nikolaus pressed a hand to the tile wall and jerked back his head to flick the water from his eyes and disperse the hair from his face. A grimace quickly became a wistful grin.

"Why does love have to be so difficult? What am I doing wrong?"

His erection, heavy and taut against his stomach, wasn't about to go flaccid anytime soon. Sex wasn't love, he knew that, but the key body parts involved weren't as up on the intellectual aspects of lovemaking.

With a glance over his shoulder he spied Ravin stomping out of the bathroom, dripping wet, her dark hair long eels slithering across her shoulders.

Nikolaus flicked off the water and stepped out. Barely avoiding clonking his head on a hanging plant holder, he dodged toward the vanity. Amid the fog of coconut steam, he could see there were no towels on the counter, so he went after Ravin, but she walked out of the bedroom and on into the living room.

"Where are you going?"

"Stake time," she said.

He followed her wet trail, enlarging her scattered drops to puddles as the water poured from him. If she wasn't going to play hostess, there wasn't much he could do about the mess.

Besides, who could think about the nonessentials when the steam misting off her body carried the scent of her blood to his nose? Again, not so much appealing, as intriguing. It was different, and that drew him for further exploration and discovery.

"I can understand you're not of the right mind, but I've lost all patience," she insisted in the tough-girl bark that gave Nikolaus a chuckle. "You touched me!"

"I liked it. You did, too!" He rushed to pass her and slammed his shoulder against the closet door where, he guessed, she must keep the stakes. "You think to tease me by stripping naked but a room away, and expect I'll just sit out on the couch twiddling my thumbs? I couldn't not touch you, Ravin."

"Get out of the way."

"Make me."

"Oh, my goddess." She turned and stomped the floor with an ineffectual slam of her bare foot. "Don't stand there like that."

"Like what? Naked?"

"Yes!"

Hands to hips, Nikolaus stood tall. And erect. "You don't like what you see?"

Avoiding eye contact, the witch snapped her gaze away from his torso, then back, then away. "You are so going to hate yourself for this later, I assure you."

Now she took off in a jog back into the bedroom.

When he entered the room, she sat on the bed and twisted to face him. Her hand pulled something out from under the mattress. A pistol with a wooden grip and platinum barrel.

Deadly eyes held him from behind the barrel.

Nikolaus crossed his arms and stood at the end of the bed. He didn't say a word. She'd find out soon enough. His erection bobbed against his stomach. Damn, but her audacity was making him all the more hungry.

"What the hell?" She jerked the gun toward his left side. "What is that? On the underside of your arm, and…your torso."

He lifted the scarred appendage to display the witch's handiwork. "Your work, Ravin."

"That's from the…*my* blood?" She walked across the bed on her knees, bringing the aimed gun on target with his heart. But her focus took in the havoc stretched along his side. "That's…a lot of scarring. Why didn't you die? You should have!"

Nikolaus took it all with calm resolution. Which surprised him, because he did not suffer anyone who held a weapon on him. A supernatural swiftness and agility allowed him to dodge bullets and sink in his fangs in but a blink.

But she needed to know him if she were ever to return the love he held for her.

Turning, he displayed the pink convoluted flesh marring the underside of his arm and all down his left side. It didn't hurt to touch it, though it did bring back flashes of that dreaded night. Burning embers in the shape of a friend. Ash raining over the tarmac. Cries of terror. And Cory, fallen, and dying in his arms.

"One of my fallen cohorts bled on me. I…took from him, and it helped to stave off further desiccation. With Cory's blood, I was able to fend off the immediate blaze of poison, keep it from spreading over my entire body, but it ate into my organs."

"I don't need names, vampire."

"Why not? Cory Grant. That was his name. I'd known him for six months. He was just a kid, mid-twenties. Worked nights as a mechanic to pay child support for a baby he wasn't sure was his, but loved all the same."

"Enough."

"Not enough." Nikolaus tilted up the barrel of the gun so it pointed directly at his eyes, and focused on the witch's flickering gaze. "My heart stopped that night—I was literally dead—but I remained conscious the entire time. Drinking. Feeding off a friend. Cory Grant was mortal. Your bullet killed some baby's father."

She cringed, and her sneer stretched wide. But her reply was almost too quiet to be heard. "That's why I needed the Sight."

"The what?"

Ignoring his question, she resumed her tough-girl stance. Naked and dripping, with but a towel wrapped about her torso. Her eyes did not stray, though Nikolaus willed her gaze to glance lower. To see his want, his need.

Her aim fell away.

It was the moment Nikolaus required.

He lunged onto the bed and tore the towel away from her hips. The pistol landed on the pillow. One push and she landed on her back. Before she had time to react, he grabbed her behind the knees and pressed himself upon her. "This is happening, Ravin. Don't make it a chore."

"You call sex a chore? Oh, now, that's romantic. Try adding rape to your list of seductions."

"No, I didn't mean…" He released her legs and rolled to his back to lie next to her. The textured ceiling sparkled with glints of sunshine that peeked through the tops of the shades. Not direct; he could not be burned. "I don't want to force you."

"Then take a hike." She sat up, going for the towel again. "And please, cover that thing up." She waved at his groin.

"Does it interest you?"

"No!"

"I think it does."

He gripped a hank of her wet hair and pulled her back. Twisting his leg over her hips, he pinned her shoulders into the thick bedding. Gliding his tongue from her shoulder down to her breasts, he managed a cry from her as he tugged at her nipple without using his teeth.

"You like that," he murmured. "That wasn't a moan of disgust."

"I…"

Guiding her hand lower, he placed it around his cock. She didn't let go, but didn't tighten her grip. Nikolaus felt himself thicken against her palm.

"You want what I can give you, sweetness."

"This is insane."

He walked his tongue up her neck and kissed her. Fingers compressed about him, tugging slightly.

"I would never force you, Ravin. I swear it to you." He clasped a hand about hers, and when he thought to direct her, she began to slowly slide her palm up and down him. Expelling a tight breath against her neck, he whispered, "You want this?"

Mutely, she nodded.

Chapter 9

It was happening, and it was so wrong. But Ravin couldn't summon a single protest. Because it didn't *feel* wrong. Not physically. Desire, long muffled and shoved aside, began to unfurl. A wanting need she'd once fed, but had learned to starve, gasped. Hell, this was not something she wanted to fight.

This man knew her body. There wasn't a touch, glide, lick or kiss that didn't hit the center of the target.

Should she distract herself by thinking of reality, of what was really happening?

There were just some things a woman—if she were smart—should not refuse. Like gorgeous roses. Expensive jewels. Or a roughly erotic session of petting and kissing.

Because she was already there. The orgasm snuck up without warning. It circled like a tiny hurricane right there at the pinnacle of her nerve endings, building, preparing, ready for release.

He had only touched her breasts. Kissed her, yes. There. And there, and oh, right there beneath the curve of her breast. And what he did now with his tongue, tracing it roughly over her nipple, and then barely flicking at it—oh.

And here she lay, arms sliding above her head and across the quilt, ready to rip away the protective barriers she had put up over the decades to fly free in a man's arms.

A struggle with her conscience could be set aside for later. Now was for feeling the sensations she had denied herself through intense and determined dedication to her work. Extreme pleasure could be hers. She'd not lost the ability to reach that indescribably intense release.

Ravin lost her breath.

She'd take his.

Drawing down his head, she kissed her lover as she'd never kissed before. With intent. With urgency. With knowing.

This is wrong.

Her balance was bottoming out, sinking into the dregs of the darkness.

She didn't care. All she wanted, right now, was to surrender.

Arching her back and raking her fingers through Nikolaus's glossy hair, she cried out as the vampire mastered her body.

Though the vinyl shades let in much sunlight around the curved and torn edges, none of the rays beamed lower than standing-head-level above the bed. It was like lying beneath a criss-cross of laser beams used to protect museums from burglars, Nikolaus mused.

He wasn't worried. He never slept more than a few hours a day and sometimes even left the electrochromic shades open in his home because he had never denied himself the sight of the sky during the day. Sun, his desire, his killer.

It didn't take long, just minutes before a vampire's flesh

would begin to burn in sunlight. He'd learned his lesson the first time he'd arrogantly thought to test it by striding outside on a hot July afternoon. But unless a sunbeam hit him directly, he was good to go.

So here he lay. Next to a witch.

Everything was wrong about this picture, and yet it didn't disturb him at all. There was something about this witch he loved, and obviously it was enough to make him look beyond the learned fear.

Ravin Crosse could not harm him, so he could not hate her. And why did he hate all the rest? Simply because they *could* harm him? That was akin to a man hating a certain race of people because one day, one of them may decide to harm him.

Interesting. He'd never been one to jump on a bandwagon, or to follow blindly, and yet he'd accepted the vampires' hatred for witches as part of the package.

Stretching out a leg and shifting onto his side, Nikolaus tilted his head into the soft nest of Ravin's hair littered across his shoulder. Smelled like coconuts, kind of beachy and fresh.

"God, I'd love to go to the beach again someday," he muttered. "Make sand castles. Swim in the ocean."

"Fry in the sun," she murmured. "You got a death wish, Drake?"

So she wasn't sleeping. He hadn't been sure, so silent she'd become, nestled beside him, her eyes closed and her breathing even slower than his.

"Not at the moment, though I'm sure you'll hook me up should the urge ever strike."

"You know it."

"Do you regret what we just did?"

"It's not what I want," she muttered. "I hate you."

"I wasn't getting the hate vibe when I was pumping inside of you, sweetness."

She tapped a finger against his torso. Nikolaus sucked in a breath. No one had touched his scars, save Gabriel, and that had been purely for restorative purposes.

"If I say yes, I do regret it," she said on a sigh, "I'm not sure if I'd be lying to myself. The sex was good, there's no denying that."

"I figured after about the third orgasm you were pretty pleased."

"Call it surprised that a man would even care to give a woman such attention."

She traced a fingertip from his ribs to just below his armpit. Nikolaus couldn't feel the entire journey, for some of the scars were simply too thick. "I did this."

Not a question. Was she admiring her handiwork?

"The first few weeks you could see organs," he said, leaning in to kiss her on the forehead.

"And you can lie here now, calmly kiss me on the head, and forget the pain?"

"You got it, sweetness. Can we do it again?"

He nudged a leg between hers to clue her into his growing arousal.

Following the heat scent of her blood, he licked a trail across her neck and gave her a hard—but toothless—bite on the thick carotid artery.

"Hey, vampire, be careful. No teeth."

"I won't bite. But if I did, there's nothing to worry about."

Her shove did little more than zing one of his nipples, for Nikolaus wasn't going to be pushed away. "Maybe not for you, but being bitten hurts, you know. My neck still aches."

"It's supposed to be pleasurable."

"Eventually, sure. You ever get bitten by a wolf?"

"Almost." He was faster than the loping weres that were more bark than bite.

"Well, it's the same. Teeth cutting through flesh and muscle, and oftentimes tearing. Very painful."

"Sorry." He rested his chin upon her diaphragm, tilting his head to nudge his cheek against her breast. "Forgive me?"

Her sighs made him wonder about her regrets. She had them, but maybe she just didn't know how to deal with them. He intended to waylay her concerns for as long as physically possible.

"A vampire is asking forgiveness for biting me?" she wondered.

"Couldn't have been any more painful than receiving these dreadful marks." He traced the lowest of the three tally lines that were nestled across the bottom of her rib cage. "I wish I could kiss away the pain."

"Yeah, and I wish I could kick you out of my bed. Here I am, lying naked, allowing a vampire to make love to me. Not even allowing, more like…"

"Participating?"

"Yeah, what you said."

"Denial is usually a cry for more experience, sweetness. If I have to make love to you another eight hours, I'll do so."

She giggled as the touch of his tongue sent a shiver of thrill through her system. "Oh, I can't believe I did that."

"Laugh?" He moved lower, drawing a glistening trail in his wake as his tongue marked out a path on her stomach. "I bet that's something you haven't done for years."

"Try decades, maybe longer. Never had much to laugh about."

"Your other lovers not make you laugh?"

"Oh, no, you're not getting details. Ooh…yes."

"Do that again—that moan," he said against her belly. "Let me hear how much you like what I'm doing to you."

"Drake, I—" Ravin surrendered to the giddy sparkle of sensation as Nikolaus moved lower.

Intent on a gentle stroking cruise of her inhibitions, he vanquished them quickly. He loved to feel her fingers rake through his hair, grip it tight, then tug as her body arched and surrendered to yet another no-holds-barred orgasm.

Spreading his hand across her stomach, he closed his eyes and propping his chin on her hip bone, followed the ride as her muscles tightened and released and the pleasure worked her body at its own volition.

This one really surrendered to the flight. She let out her voice and rode the wave, unembarrassed to give him a glimpse of the marvelous woman who really knew how to take pleasure and give it, too.

A few giggles slipped out in the wake of her climax, and Ravin finally managed to say breathlessly, "Have you used reverie on me?"

"Never." Sliding up alongside her, he stroked stray hairs from her eyelashes.

The reverie was a way to seduce and calm the vampire's victim by matching the pace of their heartbeats. Once matched, there was a certain persuasion the vampire could exercise upon his victim's thoughts. Most often Nikolaus used it to persuade his victims that nothing had happened, no more than a sore neck, and they would never recall the dark stranger's face, voice, or drinking bite.

"You want me to?"

"No," she said. "I don't need persuasion."

"Not even this kind?"

Pinching her nipple, he then sucked the hard peak.

"Drake, you're killing me."

"I owe you one."

She smirked. "You make it so difficult to concentrate, to want to…"

"Come again?"

"Hate you."

He sensed her determination. The fight would not leave the slayer. But she reacted to his touch—likely against her better judgment—and spread her legs. Nikolaus slid inside her.

The heat and the squeezing tightness of her coaxed him to a quick release. Nikolaus scooped up Ravin under the shoulders and brought her to his chest to hold close. Loose and relaxed, she let him embrace her longer than was necessary. He didn't want to lose hold of her, to stop this sweet moment. A victory he'd been wanting for months.

"Looks like there's a new slayer in town," he said.

He'd killed the witch. And he would kill her again, with orgasms, over and over until she cried for mercy.

She'd made love with a vampire. All freakin' day.

Ravin lay in bed—next to a vampire. And she didn't feel compelled to jump away and grab for the stake.

And yet…

"This is not how it should be," she murmured.

Despite her reluctance, Ravin moved her littlest finger, which traced the smooth muscle of Nikolaus's powerful thigh. Wandering higher, she drew along the edge of a scythed black curve that formed a sharp tip on the elaborate tribal tattoo positioned mid-back and stretching up from shoulder to shoulder, and wrapping the back of his neck, and—she could guess—across his scalp.

Must have always been a tough character, because he had to have got this tattoo *before* becoming a vamp. Vamps couldn't get inked because their incredible healing abilities would push out the design within hours of the painful process.

Who was the man beneath the vampire exterior? What had he been before his transformation? How long ago had it happened?

Oh! She did not care. She didn't!

"Of course." The sheets slithered as he moved in to whisper lazily against her ear, "I should be romancing you."

"No, I didn't mean it that way." The heat of his breath started that funny swirling feeling in her chest again. Her heart raced and she wanted to—

Suddenly the warmth of his presence moved away as Nikolaus sat up. Ravin slid her hand over the sheet, but then quickly tugged it back to wrap across her stomach.

Where are you going? was the question she wanted to ask, but she didn't want him to think it mattered.

"We've been making love all day. Damn, lazing around in your arms? That felt good," he said. "But it's night."

"Ah. That makes you a free man. Have you been counting the minutes until sunset?"

"No. I have a driver. I can leave whenever I wish."

"You mean last night when I wanted you to leave? When I was in the shower…?"

"Yes." He shot her the rogue's wink over his shoulder. "I'll go now. I have something to do."

His exit from the bed left a warm hollow against Ravin's back. Too quickly it cooled. She turned away and didn't watch as she listened to the man pull up his pants and button his shirt. Well-worn leather pants and a dark cotton shirt conformed to his every muscle and bulging bicep.

Mmm, Ravin snuggled her head into the pillow and closed her eyes. After sex always left her drowsy and sated. An entire day of sex left her depleted, but giddy. Like alchemy, he'd performed sex magic on her. Incredible sex. Really. She'd never before had the like.

The thought that she should be arming herself and blasting away at a vampire left as quickly as it had disturbed her.

He leaned in to plant a kiss on her eyelid, and she snuggled into a tight ball of smiling comfort. "Think you can make it until I return?"

"Return?"

"Nothing could keep me from your warm bed, sweetness. I'll give you a chance to catch some shut-eye, and then be back for round two. Or did we already do round two?"

"Don't come back."

"Easier said than done."

"Because of the spell."

"Because...I love you, Ravin. See you soon."

The front door closed. Ravin rolled to her back and spread her hand over the wrinkles on his side of the bed.

Why did something so wrong have to feel so right?

Chapter 10

The vampire had gone.

Ravin sat up in bed and stretched out her arms. Her legs ached and her wrists were sore from Nikolaus pinning her down as he'd slaked his lust. She hadn't minded being pinned down. In fact, it had turned her on more than she'd thought possible.

Most of her sexual encounters had been brief affairs with near strangers. Not the kind of men who knew how to satisfy a woman, much less *care* about her satisfaction.

After two centuries it now took a lot to impress her sexually. She'd once chosen her lovers for their handsome appearance and roguish manner, and then had graduated to wealth and a certain unavailability that came from a married man. Over the centuries, such vain, selfish requirements had ceased to matter, and, not sure anymore what she needed, she lately resorted to one-night stands. Quickies.

So why did she do it?

Contact. Validation. Every woman required connection, if only for a few moments of bliss.

Sure, she'd had some great lovers in her history. Daniel had been a printer who aspired to engrave monograms, but his eyesight wouldn't allow him to do the detail work. Hadn't kept him from learning her body with his lips, though.

Dominique San Juste, a faery changeling, never left her memory. Unfortunately, he'd been more in love with absinthe, and the memory of his dead wife, than Ravin. She hadn't told him about the pregnancy, a surprise to her at the time. There had been no need to tell him.

The miscarriage brought up an awful longing. Ravin had never considered herself maternal, but with a child in her belly, she'd quickly taken to the prospect of becoming a mother.

She still didn't know if it was because a faery and a witch should not procreate, or if it had simply been her womb, unable to carry to term.

Was it possible, after so long, that she may have finally found a man who could satisfy her in every way?

She felt sated. Beyond satisfied. A slip of skin lying on the sheets, empty and waiting to be filled again.

"Sex magic," she suddenly said. Ravin sat up abruptly and sat cross-legged on the sheets. "Blood sex magic."

Her heart started to pound. She pressed a hand over her chest. "I can't believe I didn't think of that."

It had always been mere legend to Ravin. Tales told and passed down over the ages, from one witch to another. The history of their kind. The reason why vampires and witches rubbed against one another like oil to water—and the result of what could happen should the two succeed in coming together.

Blood sex magic. When a vampire drank the blood, and/or had sex with a witch, he took into him some of her magic. It made him stronger, fortified his soul, and even gave him some of the same abilities the witch possessed, such as earth, air or water magic, but to a lesser degree.

It used to happen all the time, when the vampires had once enslaved the witches for just such a purpose. But then the witches got smart and cast the great Protection spell, which rendered their blood poisonous to vampires.

"He's stolen my magic," she gasped.

No, not stolen.

"I *gave* him my magic, willingly. Oh, damn, this is not good. Not only is the man a freaking phoenix who cannot be destroyed, now I've decided to go ahead and toss a little magic into the mix. What have I done?"

No matter. It wouldn't happen again.

Scrambling off the bed, she paused in the center of the room. What to do?

She had to set up wards to keep the vampire from again crossing her threshold. Until she could convince Himself to reverse the spell for her, she was responsible for— For what? For contributing to the destruction of a perfectly sane vampire.

Or was she enhancing him?

At the risk of her own enslavement. She would not become Nikolaus Drake's supplicant. That way lay danger.

"Oh hell, don't even go there. He is not for you, Ravin. Get that into your thick skull. So the two of you had awesome sex. That was it. No more. There will be hell to pay should he ever return—aggh!"

Sudden, vicious pain in her sternum streaked outward through her muscles and flailed her backward so she landed outstretched on the bed. Invisible claws ripped flesh from her body.

Slapping her hand to her chest, Ravin felt the burn of a very familiar touch. Moaning, she slid from the bed and landed on the floor in a sprawl, and then snapped abruptly upright.

Beneath her fingers, the slash mark had been erased. "No."

"Oh, yes. Can't be having a cheat in my ranks, now, can I?"

She didn't look. The brimstone was evident.

In fact, if Ravin could keep from looking she wouldn't be forced to gasp at his utter beauty. That was how it worked with the Old Lad Himself. He appeared to all others in the guise of their greatest temptation. To a man he could look like a gorgeous woman; to a woman, an attractive man.

In the few times she had seen him over the past decade, Himself appeared to her looking like Johnny Depp, pre-pirate days, with dark, shoulder-length mussed hair and a sexy aloofness that made her drool and want to break out the condoms.

Condoms? *Damn.* Not once had she considered using a condom with Nikolaus.

"You have been a naughty girl, Miss Crosse."

He even sounded like the actor. But Ravin suspected the actor did not wear the horrid perfume of sulfur on his person. The scent was strong, unmistakable.

The bed sagged next to her as she felt Himself sit across from her.

You're naked, girl.

Oh, hell. She tugged up a corner of the sheet but a gorgeous man—*just a* figment *of handsome, Ravin*—sat on it, so she was able to barely cover one breast.

Ravin wouldn't give the bastard the pleasure of showing shame, so she dropped the sheet and stretched back her shoulders.

"Did you think you could put that little trick past me?"

No fooling the devil.

"No." She winced once more at a streak of pain in her chest. "There was an accident. The potion spilled. I didn't have time to make more before the pickup imp arrived."

"Demon, not an imp."

"Looked like an imp to me."

"So you thought to send along a sip and hoped I'd not question it."

"Sometimes a sip will do the trick. Erm…" It wouldn't do to lie to one of the greatest deceivers ever. "Goddess of Mercy. So I screwed up. You have every right to be angry—"

He scoffed.

Ravin didn't dare turn around.

"I don't subscribe to frail mortal emotions," Himself announced.

"Anger isn't—"

"Of course it is! It is for the weak. The ridiculous. Anger is nothing more than jealousy and the inability to express sadness. I prefer the sublime human emotions such as grief, curiosity or envy. Of course, lack of anger does not disqualify the need for punishment. Your soul is still mine, witch."

Heat flayed across Ravin's torso, burning deep into the middle line that no longer bore the slash mark of a completed obligation.

Ravin clutched her chest and rolled to her side, coiling her body inward to fight the pain. There wasn't a thing she could do to stop it, and no argument would suffice. The hot poker pressed deep—it felt as though it seared her lungs. She gasped, choked and clawed at the sex-scented sheets.

"Sorry?" Himself asked.

She nodded.

"I didn't hear that," he sing-songed gaily.

She forced herself to react, to push beyond the pain, and springing to an upright crouch, shouted, "I'm sorry! Forgive me!"

And like that, the pain stopped.

Ravin collapsed onto her back. The room felt too large, too pale and no longer warm. *As it had been when she had been in Nikolaus's arms.*

It wasn't fair that she was to be shoved back to reality so quickly after an afternoon spent in fantasyland. But it was just. And she was all for standing up and accepting punishment when punishment was due.

Opening her eyes, she looked up at the face looming over her. "Oh, hell, why him?"

The actor's face cracked a brimstone smile. He looked to the left where a full-length mirror was attached to the back of the bathroom door. Himself didn't know how he appeared to others until he looked at his reflection.

"What is it with you and actors? Who was it last time?"

"It's always Johnny."

And keep it that way, she thought. At least it wasn't Nikolaus Drake leering over her now. That gave her immense hope that this afternoon truly had been just a tumble in the sack. A very wrong tumble—that had felt so right.

A glance to the side sighted a horned red reflection in the mirror. When viewed in the mirror by others, Himself's true diabolical form showed. Ravin looked away. The image was too horrific for any eyes not demonic.

Himself leaned forward and sniffed loudly over the sheets. "Who have you been banging? Ravin, my wicked little witch, it's been months." He took another sniff. "Strong. Tainted with salt, sweat...hmm, coconut. That's yours. But what is that? A hint of expensive men's cologne? Not your usual stud. You must have come over and over."

"Six times."

"Good for you, girlie."

"Yeah. Well. Why the hell not."

"'Bout time you found someone to satisfy you."

And she so did not need to be having a girlfriend-after-sex chat with the King of Hell.

"What was it this time?" he asked. "Let's see...you've

done a faery, a familiar and countless others. Was it a wizard? A dragon-shifter?"

"None of your business. I'll make you another batch," she offered.

"Of course you will. And I'll watch."

"Why not? I'm all about sharing the love. Let me get dressed first."

He gripped her arm as she edged toward the foot of the bed. The contact crawled over her flesh like corpse worms wriggling from the light. No, never Johnny.

"I prefer you this way. Love spells in the nude, it'll be. Now, get to work."

Sighing, Ravin consented with a nod. A shower to rinse the sex from her body was all she wanted. Remove all traces of the vampire from her pores. It was as though he'd entered her, and now he lingered in her soul.

On the other hand, she wasn't currently in possession of said soul, so there was that.

And perhaps keeping the vampire's scent on her for a while was the thing. A reminder of her mistake.

"Rough night?" Himself asked, stretching out across the bed, and again inhaling the sheets.

Ravin wandered to the mirror and shrugged her fingers through her tangle of hair. Cream rinse was required to smooth out this nest. "What makes you ask that?"

"You've a bite mark on your ass."

She swung her hips around to study her rear in the mirror. "That is so not funny."

"Did I laugh?"

"No, but you were think-laughing."

"I'd guess a vampire, but I know how you abhor them, witch. Perhaps it was a wolf?"

Thrusting about, hands on hips, Ravin had no intention of

giving the devil his due, at least not on the matters of who or what she'd been sleeping with.

The Don Juan DeMarco version of Johnny starred at her, his hair falling to chin length and a billowing white shirt open to reveal his taut, smooth chest. Too perfect. Too tempting.

But could he make her come with but a lick of his tongue and a smoldering wink? She didn't think so. And she wouldn't. No sense in giving Himself fodder.

"Do you have to look like him? I mean, it's distracting, especially when one is naked."

"Do you want me, Ravin?" He flicked out an inordinately long tongue and waggled it. "Come and get it."

Steeling herself, she forced herself to think of worse troubles than the devil's teasing sensual temptation. Like having sex with a vampire. It worked. She couldn't summon an ounce of desire for the man lying on her bed.

"I think I hear a grimoire calling my name."

He shuddered, wracked by nightmare—the *danse macabre*.

Nikolaus found Gabriel in the hallway, kicking and dragging his boot heels across the hardwood floor, and pulling at his hair as he struggled against the inner demons. His victims' nightmares.

The *danse* only came with the kill.

Nikolaus sucked in a breath as he realized his friend had killed. Had to have been recent, either today or no more than a few days ago.

Bending before Gabriel, he tapped his knee, offering silent support. This was wrong. Kind, gentle Gabriel had not killed since he was first created two years earlier. He knew better than to steal life. What could have made him do such a thing?

For twenty years Nikolaus had successfully led the tribe. He had mentored many a new vampire confused by his transformation and unsure of the new life given him. And he'd weaned just as many from the kill to watch them grow stronger and confident, a humane creature of the dark.

In less than two months, Truvin had succeeded in completely reversing Nikolaus's vision.

Truvin Stone was an old and heedless vampire who hailed from the eighteenth century. Just three years in Kila, he'd never needed the boundaries Nikolaus believed necessary to survive in the mortal world, and yet, he'd accepted the no-kill rule.

According to Gabriel's reports, the tribe was now embroiled in a turf war with the wolves, and he wasn't sure Kila would rise above it without great damage to its members.

As well, Truvin's penchant for the kill had, reportedly, returned. Stone had been leading the brotherhood down a treacherous path, instilling in them much mindless destruction.

Violence and death were not necessary for a vampire's survival—though certainly the blood was.

Nikolaus stroked away the sweat-drenched hair from Gabriel's forehead. The man had begun to settle, though he still clenched his jaw.

Truvin had to be stopped. Gabriel was too good. He couldn't handle the kill.

"Take your rest, Gabriel," Nikolaus said lowly. "They're not real. Just images from another life."

"So awful. An attack…brutal. With a knife. Christ! What mortals do to one another— I'm sorry, Nikolaus. The *danse*…it is as awful as you warned."

"We won't talk of it. It's done."

Nikolaus rested his head against the wall as he stood over Gabriel. To his right, he flicked the switch that turned off the window blinds. The sun had set. A string of glittering lights danced across the river, probably a party boat cruising slowly by.

"I've spoken to Truvin," Gabriel said after a while. "He wants to meet with you before the Solstice."

"Why?" He hadn't showered. Nikolaus suddenly wondered if Gabriel could smell the witch on him. "Does he intend to take me out before I can return to the tribe? That's not playing fair."

Nor was luring Gabriel to the kill. Bastard.

"He wants to talk," Gabriel said. "I trust him."

"You do?"

When had he lost control of Gabriel?

Nikolaus studied his friend's face as he nodded agreeably. It wasn't a part of Gabriel's nature to want to destroy or harm, which is why he'd distanced himself from the tribe since Nikolaus had been away. But obviously that distance had grown shorter.

"In proof," Gabriel said, "Truvin wants to meet you at Cue, Saturday night at ten."

A ritzy restaurant located in the Guthric Theater. A scuffle would not be tolerated there. Saturday? Three days away.

"I won't be hungry," Nikolaus said. He knew there had to be a trick, some reason Truvin couldn't simply wait for his return.

On the other hand, why not talk it out with Truvin first? If Nikolaus's suspicions were true—that Truvin would not give back the leadership easily—perhaps they could discuss and work out the reasons beforehand.

"Fine." Nikolaus walked away from Gabriel's pleading pout. "I'll go. I need a shower, then I'm going out again."

"Hot date?"

Slapping a hand against the door frame to the bathroom, Nikolaus paused and thought of his hot little witch sitting on the center of her bed, the sheets strewn and her hair tousled. A rosy blush of satisfaction had glistened on her cheeks.

"You could say that," he called back.

Chapter 11

An hour later, Nikolaus had showered, slapped on a little cologne and combed back his hair. It was getting too long, he figured as he secured it in a loose ponytail at the base of his neck with a leather strip. Forgoing the long-haired, hippie trends of the sixties, he'd once worn it short and styled.

Until life had hit him hard. After his surgery, he'd shaved his head bald, and had kept it that way for about a year. (Which was also when he'd gotten the skull tattoos.)

Smirking at his reflection, he shrugged and turned off the light.

The TV was on, but no one was about. Gabriel must have gone out. He always left the thing on, claiming he liked the background noise when he was reading. Switching it off, Nikolaus left his home, ensuring the double dead bolts were secure, and tapping the invisible ward. He wasn't able to craft a ward himself; that's what wizards were for. And any vampire who valued his heart—unstaked, thank you very much—invested in warding.

Instead of checking in with Jake, his driver who lived on the first floor, for a chauffeured ride, Nikolaus decided a walk in the warm summer night was the perfect thing.

He lived close to downtown in the Mill District, and walked along Washington Street, marveling at the late-night crowds. The never-ending stream of barflies seemed to change little decade to decade, save their appearance. The clothing grew skimpier, the age younger, and the men were more blatant in their sexual advances, as were the women.

They were all so busy searching for something to fulfill their empty mortal lives. Maybe if they'd spend some time at home, sober, and started to look inside themselves, they'd have that something.

Nikolaus smirked at his philosophizing. Who was he to claim that ineffable *something* so easily? He was still in search mode—and yet, he may have found just the thing.

The last time he'd spent such a languorous afternoon having sex with a woman had been back in his college days when he'd skip class and know he'd ace the tests because he'd had a photographic memory.

Surgery had changed that. Surgery had changed everything about Nikolaus Drake. It had put him in a position to be changed. And the devastating results of said surgery had pushed away the only woman he'd loved.

Julie Marks, first-year NIC-U intern to his first year as attending on the neurosurgery floor. Long frizzy red hair, tamed with one of those leather pieces and a stick, had been her signature. It had been the summer of '66. Free love abounded. But Julie had been cool about sex, claiming she wanted to wait until after they were married. Nikolaus had honored her wishes. He hadn't felt deprived at the time, and he still did not regret his choice.

Now he loved another. And despite her protests, he knew he'd never fear her rejecting his sexual advances. Perhaps a struggle, but that only sweetened his want.

It neared midnight. Though he'd fed just last night, he felt strangely empty. The blood hunger lingered. The witch's blood had not satisfied his need.

Odd, that. But besides the pangs of hunger, he actually felt vigorous. Much more so than he had for the past two months. Recovery was coming along nicely. Had sex with the witch done that?

He recalled Gabriel mentioning that taking the witch's magic could make him stronger. Had he seeped away some of her magic when drinking her blood? Through sex? And had it worked to make him feel so…alive?

"Too easy. Couldn't be."

He paused before a flower shop and studied the art nouveau design painted around the front window. It was called Pushing Up Daisies, and seemed to cater to the Goth crowd, judging from the skulls looped in and out of the gray ribbons dancing around the shop's logo. And it was still open this late at night.

"Perfect."

Nikolaus stalked inside among tight rows of blood-red roses and white lilies. Stone gargoyles and dragons clung to walls or peeked out from behind frilly ferns. Everything sparkled with a fine coating of glitter, as if a faery had been sliced open and shaken over all.

Faeries were not Nikolaus's favorite creatures. They were tricky and malicious, and the women, while sexual athletes, were too interested in their own pleasure to consider their male partners. Besides, their ichor tasted nasty—not his favorite bite.

A particular iron cross, situated between a vine of climbing silk lilies and some sparkly springy stuff made Nikolaus veer down the next aisle to avoid the holy. Not that holy icons disturbed him; it was sort of a learned behavior from Gabriel. The device, no matter it a cross, rosary or what-have-you, had to actually touch a vampire to do harm, and said vampire had to be baptized and to have once believed.

Nikolaus also avoided lingering over bunches of similar items. For some strange reason he'd figured out early on, vampires have a propensity to count. More than once he'd gotten lost beneath a tree on a warm summer evening, neck craned back, finger marking out the leaves as he simply counted, despite himself.

When he spied the black roses, he went immediately to them.

"Gorgeous, aren't they?" the female behind him noted. Must be the cashier. She wore a colorful head of dreads and three nose rings. Cinnamon drifted from her cleavage, a scent that lifted Nikolaus's hunger. Thin and fey, she smiled easily. "We can't keep them in stock. The Goth crowd, you know."

He didn't know that crowd, beyond that they liked to play at being vampires. *If they only knew*. Blood drinking wasn't all it was cracked up to be—because wouldn't a nice juicy steak fit the bill? And the ostracization from society? He'd take mortality, if offered.

Then again, screw mortality. Nikolaus had become accustomed to his vampiric nature; he'd now been a vampire longer than he'd been mortal. It fit, if a bit too snuggly at those times when he pined to stand in the sunlight.

"How many do you have?" he asked.

"Total?" She smiled a sexy crooked smile and rubbed the back of her head, which set the dreads to a colorful bounce. "At the moment, about six dozen."

"Give me all of them. And have you red?"

"Of course."

He envisioned the red silky petals, nestled among the black. Red like blood. *Her blood drooling down your lip.* Red silk slithering across her curves. *Trailing across your dark hair as she slides up to tease you with a peek.* Would Ravin Crosse wear a dress? *And dance for you, shaking her hips in a sexy come-on.*

"And the same amount of red."

The cashier nodded approvingly. "Shall I have them delivered?"

"No, I'll take them."

"Twelve dozen roses? Mister, you're big and all, but that's a lot of flowers to carry down the street."

"It's okay." He slid a Centurion card out from inside his jacket pocket—million dollar credit limit—and handed it to her. "I'm in love."

"Hold her arms, man. And slap a hand over her mouth to shut her up."

Nikolaus paused at the edge of a street corner a block down from the strip joint Déjà Vu. He easily picked up two male voices. Down the alley, to the right, he picked up the strong scent of aggression. Yet even stronger, fear. Female mumbles carried to him as well. A distressed female.

"Hurry, man, before someone comes."

Detouring around the corner, Nikolaus separated the huge bouquet he'd been holding and fisted it in two clumps. Arms pumping, he stomped onto the scene.

Two young men, looking like teenagers, but with the sallow, sunken cheeks of junkies, held a wide-eyed blond girl with a skirt high enough to advertise against the brick wall. She might be a prostitute, but this was one job she hadn't asked for.

"We don't need any!" one of the men yelled at Nikolaus. "Take your stupid flowers to the corner, dude. Just leave!"

Swinging up one bouquet, Nikolaus clocked the man holding the woman's arm pinned under the jaw. Black and red petals flew. The man let go of the girl and grabbed his bloody jaw.

The snap of a switchblade alerted Nikolaus. As did the acrid scent of defiance. The aggressor waved it before him.

"You—" Nikolaus pointed to the girl "—leave. And you two stay."

The girl slipped by and ran down the alley, spike heels clicking frantically.

The switchblade cut the air before Nikolaus's face.

Blood trickled down the chin of the one at the wall. "He cut me, man, with those stupid rose thorns!"

The scent of blood gave Nikolaus a thrill. The blood hunger would not relent, nor did he wish it to. He dropped the other bouquet and, lowering his gaze on the man with the knife, sent the persuasion into him. "Stand down," he said calmly.

The knife dropped, though the man still held it near his thigh, and his shoulders relaxed as he took on the reverie.

"What are you doing, man?" The one at the wall bounced nervously.

Nikolaus gripped the bleeding man by the throat and shoved him against the wall. "He's decided he likes to watch. You wanted to get lucky? Try me, asshole."

Pressing his palm over the man's mouth, Nikolaus bent to bite his neck. The adrenalized blood rushed through his system, threatening a high that he desired, yet didn't want to deal with later. So he only took a taste, then licked the wound and dropped the idiot in an unconscious heap.

Turning to the one still holding the knife, Nikolaus gestured with one finger that he approach. The man did so and conveniently tilted his head to the side.

"Thanks," Nikolaus said, and bent for another bite.

* * *

Thankfully, there were ingredients remaining from the previous batch for the love spell. Except the child's innocence, which Himself was able to produce upon his palm with a wicked grin.

"How young?" Ravin asked as she scraped the ashy substance from his fingers and into the spell pot. "No, don't tell me."

"Twelve," Himself said with a satisfied grin. "Orphaned just this morning before school. Sweet, eh?"

Slamming the copper cover over the pot, Ravin closed her eyes and wondered why she even cared. She'd gone beyond caring about mortals decades ago. Didn't matter to her what happened to them. They existed in a completely different realm than hers. Hers was all about vengeance and taking what she needed. Theirs was a pitiful quest for survival unfulfilled by the religious promise of everlasting life.

But she could relate to any child abandoned or endangered. *Or orphaned.* It wasn't right; it was never right.

"If I'm not mistaken," Himself—a la Johnny—said from the other side of the granite kitchen countertop, "that looks like a vampire bite to me."

She'd forgotten about her nakedness. Now would have been an excellent time to own an apron.

Ravin swiped a palm over her right ass cheek. The swelling had gone down some. Because of the vampire's healing saliva?

"Ha." She tried to make her voice sound glib. "Imagine that. A vampire biting a witch. Did you see any piles of ash when you arrived?"

"Don't be flippant with me, chit. That's a vamp bite. I know my havoc. And you're a witch, enemy numero uno to vampires. Explain."

"Don't you know everything?"

She swung around and rested her elbows on the counter—

she wasn't shy about her nudity, but it felt wrong exposing herself to her movie idol. Of course, the thrill of fandom had been shattered by the brimstone and attitude. Johnny was so history in her dream catalog.

"Can't you look into my eyes and tell me everything I've done for the past twenty-four hours?"

"I can tell you what you've done every hour of your life, every breath you've taken, every breath you've stolen—but you won't like it."

Ravin knew that was a warning against a sort of soul-read only Himself could perform with but a touch. Putting up a palm, she nodded. "Yeah, don't look. It was a vamp."

"But—"

"He's immune to my blood," she said, because it wouldn't make things any easier to beat around the bush.

"Delicious danger."

"Whatever."

"Someone must have spilled a love spell all over themselves last night," Himself sing-songed. He reached up and snapped a segment of leaf from the spider plant and shoved it in his mouth.

"Only because he breached my wards with supernatural ease. An angry vamp, with blood in his eyes for me, comes charging through my door. Doesn't even need permission, just walks right through my wards and slams down the front door."

Which reminded her…she needed to fix the front door and reinforce the wards. Were there any protection spells against a vampire who was immune to her?

"The same vampire I thought I'd killed months ago. He's a phoenix."

"Oh, this is rich." Himself chuckled grandly, nearly toppling from the stool. "Well, if he is a phoenix, that means he's suffered your blood and survived. Makes him immune to your particular blood, ever after. You two are bonded, which also negates the need for permission to enter your property."

"Peachy."

She stirred the officious brew as it began to boil. A snap of her fingers set it to a fine bubble. Water magic was easy. She'd learned to boil water when she was a kid, nothing more than a parlor trick.

"Let me guess," Himself added, twirling another bit of plant between two fingers. "He chawed at your neck and sucked down the love spell. Or was it your lovely bottom that drew him in for the drink? Interesting scenario, if one thinks on it."

The brimstone-coated enthusiasm leaking into the room was in direct proportion to Ravin's gut-curdling disgust.

"Right, but this vamp wants me dead. Repayment for me killing him, and all. At least, he *wanted* me dead, before he went all lovey-dovey moon-eyed on me. I think I would have preferred death to what he did instead."

Ravin turned and peeked in the pot. It needed to cool for an hour before she could package it up and send Himself on his merry path to hell. Joy.

"I need to reverse the spell."

"Impossible," Himself said.

"I know that, Einstein."

Himself looked startled. He patted his hair. "Have I changed to the scientist? Where's a mirror? I've got to see this!"

"No, creep, you're still…him."

One should probably laugh at Himself's attempts at humor, ingratiate oneself to the dark lord, and all, but Ravin had worse matters to attend.

"I ordered the spell," Himself said, "and thanks to the particulars of your spell crafting, that means only I can reverse it. Not that I will. What wicked joy to see you pursued by the very creature you most hate. Though it couldn't have been all too hateful in the sack. I don't see struggle marks."

"Can I please take a shower?"

"When will the potion be ready?"

"An hour. Half, if we rush it. It just needs to cool."

"Fine. Go wash away the evidence of your sins."

"Having sex is not a sin."

"Just so." He steepled his fingers before Johnny's face and flashed those gorgeous brown eyes at her. "But two different species going at it—"

"Enough!"

Johnny leaned forward and caught his chin in his palm, contemplative. "You know what? I like you, Crosse. I am going to reverse the spell for you."

Sounded too good to be true. Which meant it was. Ravin traced the second line on her chest, sans slash mark. "And what will I owe you in return?"

"Nothing. I've already gotten a good laugh out of the whole fiasco. Laughs are so rare in my line of work."

"So you'll do it while I'm in the shower? The world will be good and evil when I step out?"

He shrugged. "Probably not. I'll get around to it when I'm in the mood."

Of course. It couldn't be that easy. "I can't ask for anything more."

"You certainly can not."

Ravin went and showered, and when she had finished Himself was gone, along with the love spell.

"Great. Didn't need you, either, ugly plant-eating, brimstone-stinking…" She sighed, not feeling the energy to summon an angry diatribe.

Treading into the bedroom, she retrieved a soft black silk

two-piece pajama outfit and slid it over her skin, but she didn't feel the least bit tired.

It wasn't even midnight. Today was Monday…not her usual hunting night.

"So!" She slapped her palms together and the sound rang in her empty apartment. "Time to re-ward the threshold and look up a number to call a carpenter in the morning."

She was a witch, after all, not an expert in construction.

The doorbell rang, and the front door—still unhinged—fell down into the foyer.

Ravin peeked out the bedroom door, knowing to expect a vamp, but seeing only a pitiful clutch of red and black roses.

Chapter 12

"Did you rob a graveyard?"

Nikolaus stepped over the fallen door. "You want me to fix that for you? Can't be easy for the wards to keep out the undesirables."

"Yes, and obviously, it isn't working."

He ignored her sarcasm. She'd come around.

"The flowers are...broken."

Nikolaus shrugged. He handed her the lackluster bouquet, truly upset that it wasn't as he'd intended. Though he was thankful for the snack. Turning his face from her imploring gaze, he lifted the door and set it into place.

"Is there blood on that one?" she wondered aloud. "No don't answer that. You know, a single rose would have served. Not that I'm saying I like flowers..."

Again he ignored her lack of kindness, because he didn't

sense her usual venom. Besides, he knew how to reduce her to an agreeable silence.

Soon enough.

"Has no man ever given you flowers before?"

"Nope."

"Then it's about time. I'm starved for you, sweetness. You been thinking of me?"

Sexy little number she wore tonight. Short silky bottoms and a top that exposed her cleavage. She wanted him. Else she'd have a stake at the ready.

"If you think a few broken roses are romantic, you've got another think coming."

He spread his arms wide. "What does it take to please you, woman? Where you going?"

Nikolaus pursued the fleeing witch into the small closet off the living room. A fluorescent light hung from the ceiling. But he recognized the storage area for what it was.

"Nice," he muttered as he took in the arsenal of weaponry stacked along the walls. Stainless-steel shelves and hooks held a vast array of deadly arms. There were pistols, modified rifles with scopes and GPS attachments, lasers and other things he couldn't begin to guess at. Knives and daggers of every size, curved and straight blades, with handles that varied from pearl to bone to rock-hard PVC. Throw stars looked like something a ninja would whip at a target. And crosses, from small to large, all in silver, and most with hollow points. Waiting to be filled with blood?

"Unless you want a stake through the heart, I suggest you leave, vampire."

"You're kidding. A stake? They were *just* flowers."

He shoved her against the wall of knives and kissed her. A blade slithered across another and fell, landing on the floor. Nikolaus felt it, a feather's distance from his boot.

"Flowers are meant to please the recipient," he said, "not anger her."

"You're not doing this right!"

"Doing what right? Romance? Yeah, I figured that."

Always she had to fight his advances, but always she succumbed, as if she were a flower softening in the sun and opening to receive warmth. Would that he could be her sun. The best he could offer was moonlight and rose petals.

And yet, that particular seduction ploy had not gone over well at all.

"What do you want, sweetness?" He kissed down her jaw and nuzzled into the curve of her neck. No desire to bite. Now he wanted to feel her warmth and track the rapid pace of her heartbeats pulsing aside his cheek. "You want this as much as I do. What is it that I'm doing wrong?"

"You're trusting the enemy," she said. But instead of pushing him away, she gripped his shirt. Sharp black fingernails dug into his flesh.

"Do you know what you have done to me, little witch? I can touch logic, but I can't act on it. All I can think about is you. Pleasing you, touching you, loving you. That's not good."

"You think?"

"You don't understand. Right now, I stand on the verge of returning to Kila. When I should be thinking how best to command my men, my mind is off browsing for roses. And when I'm alone in the shower, I find myself wondering if you're safe."

He beat the wall over her head, knocking a dagger from its hook. It landed on the stainless steel counter and rattled a rack of brass-headed shotgun shells.

"Or I'm thinking I should have fixed that damned door, because someone might break in and harm you. Or earlier, when I bought those flowers, I found myself considering if you'd wear a dress. Can my tasty little witch be feminine? Would she wear red instead of her tough-girl black?"

"Whoa." Ravin put up a hand. "Buddy. Step away from the witch. You're creepin' me out."

"I'm creeping myself out! Ravin." He gripped her by the shoulders. "This is not me. I...don't bring women flowers. I don't show up at the door—"

"I wouldn't call breaking it down actually showing up."

"I want to know how to romance you, Ravin. I want to know you better. Is that too much to ask?"

"Yes. Oh! I don't know what I want. I want you. I hate you. I need you. I wish you were dead."

"Been there, done that. What do you say we start a new story, eh?"

A palm to her chest told him her heartbeats scurried like a frightened rabbit. She had nothing to fear from him. What had become of the vicious vampire slayer?

For that matter, what had become of the tough phoenix vampire who wouldn't think twice about doing everything in his power to take down a slayer?

This damned spell! Nikolaus could easily see himself hauling the witch over his shoulder to carry outside. Build a pyre, and let her burn.

He could see that, but the brain was telling his heart to intervene. To see beyond the label of *witch*, and to accept her as the gorgeous, intriguing woman she was. And so he did.

"I can accept that you're a tough, unfeeling witch who wants the world to leave her alone. I get that. And you're pissed at me."

"More than pissed—utterly freaked. Nikolaus, you...you said you loved me."

"And I do."

"No, you don't!"

"I know that!" Pounding his frustration out on the wall over her head knocked down more knives. One landed on a wood counter, tip first.

"Ravin, give me what I need right now. Let me give you pleasure. Let's have sex, yes? Don't say no, sweetness." Nuzzling into her hair, Nikolaus tongued the curve of her ear. "A good orgasm should make you dizzy. I want to see you all woozy and smiling like you do after you've come."

"Nik—"

"I understand what's going on—that my actions are dictated by an artificial means—but I can't fight the attraction. I don't want to." He breathed by her ear. "It feels too good standing in your arms right now, your body crushed against mine. You make the world go away, Ravin. So work with me. It's the least you can do after putting this spell on me."

"I never thought of it that way." She pulled back and pressed a palm over his heart. "I did this to you. Which means I...owe you. I need to make up for putting you in this position. I just..."

"Isn't there a part of you that can move beyond our differences and know that what we both want we can both give?"

She shifted from one leg to the other. The movement pushed her groin against his thigh. Nikolaus slid his leg between hers, pressing hard against her mons. It stirred up a moan from her that sang like a dark angel in his dreams.

"Tell me what you want, Ravin," he growled deeply. Fitting his hands behind her hips, he pushed harder, working his thigh in minute lifts, knowing he massaged her sex through the thin black silk. "Do you want me to touch you?"

She managed a mumbled *mmpf*. Fighting the seduction. Yet her hands gripped at his forearms, keeping him close to her.

The *clink* of knife blades reminded Nikolaus of the precarious danger their actions teased.

"Where?" He trailed a breath across her throat. Peeling the

thin satin strap from the pajamas from her shoulder, he twisted it around his forefinger and tugged until it broke from the stitches. "Tell me where you want me to touch you."

"Just…"

His cock hard against her belly, he crushed it against her straining muscles, stoking the energy of his imminent climax.

Sliding his hand inside the silk bottoms, he glided over the soft hairs trimmed into a neat rectangle. He loved it when a woman did that to her body. Because it wasn't just for her, was it? She wanted to be looked at, to be admired—whether or not the witch could admit that.

"Here?"

Her reply, reluctant, yet desperate, hissed against his neck. "Yes."

Swollen and moist beneath his forefinger, her sex was ready. A firm glide up and down, not too far, not too hard, concentrating on the key to her arousal.

It wasn't long before her body began to arch up against his chest, and she gripped behind her for support.

Blood spotted his forearm.

"Watch the knives," he hissed, and flung her around against the doorframe. "This could turn into a twisted sideshow real fast if we're not careful. I don't want you to get hurt."

"I trust you would never harm me."

"You do?"

"I can't believe I just said that. I…*trust* you."

Smiling into her hair, Nikolaus decided an answer wasn't necessary. But man, did it make him feel good to hear that confession.

"You're so creamy," he whispered. "Come for me, lover."

He shoved down her pants with his free hand, while not stopping his patient exploration of her nub. She made quick work of his pants. When she reached the pinnacle he felt it in

the tremor of her body against his—completely uncontrolled
and richly mad with the shimmy of climax.

As she cried out, Nikolaus slid his cock up to the hilt. She
was almost too small for him. Almost. Instead, she hugged
him tightly, her body greedily holding him. It was all he
needed to match her tremors with his own.

*You can become the man you once were. Someone who
cared, who did not stalk the night.*

With the help of a witch?

No, you've accepted your life. It doesn't need changing. But
his empty world could use a companion. Someone to love.
Someone to love forever? To make his bride? What of family?

It could happen. And it would be good.

Ravin woke to the sound of rustling. Systematic sliding
of…things. She turned over on the bed, where their frenzied
coupling had finally landed them. "What the hell?"

Nikolaus turned around with a small leather box in hand.
"Morning, sweetness."

"What are you doing?" She scrambled to the edge of the
bed and grabbed the box from him. He'd found it on the book-
shelf, snooping, no doubt.

"Just browsing." He turned his back to her and tapped a few
book spines. Hair darker than the devil's eyes fell to the center
of his back, covering the tattoos and drawing her eyes to his
firm ass. "Trying to get a bead on you. Figure you out. You
can learn a lot about a person by—"

"Going through their things?"

"You bet. You got something special in that box?"

"No."

"You're clasping on to it as if the crown jewels are inside
and I'm a cat burglar."

"It's none of your business. Quit going through my things."

"I'm just reading book titles. *The Girl's Guide to Getting It On. The Witching Hour. The Ultimate Musketeer.*"

"D'Artagnan was my grandmother's lover."

"Thought he was a fictional character?"

"Based on a real man."

"You've got a lot on France here." He noted she still clung to the box. "Sorry. Didn't mean to make you get your angry face on."

She dropped the tension and the frown she hadn't realized she wore. The tough slayer chick costume was ingrained. A very conscious move was required to *not* be that Ravin.

Who else is there to be? Do you really believe you can ever get your balance back now that you've involved yourself with a vampire?

She glanced to the window shades. Sunlight beamed in brightly around the edges. One dash. Lift the shades. Dead vampire. He wouldn't even see it coming.

Like all your kills? Stalk them and catch them unaware? How sporting is that?

Sighing, Ravin looked aside. "What do you want to know?"

"Really?" He flashed her that charming rogue smile and slid onto the bed, cupping her chin to kiss her.

It was futile to resist. And if she was honest with herself— no, she didn't want to be honest. The truth was too hard to deal with. She could continue to have great sex and ignore the white elephant, no problem.

"If your grandmother was romping around with musketeers, then it makes a guy wonder how long you've been on this earth. You've got some old books there. And that box of yours has the date 1682 inscribed on it."

Possessive of the few things she had from her past, Ravin slid the box behind her and under the pillow, while distracting Nikolaus with a kiss. "It's my grandmother's. I was born in 1790. In Bulgaria."

He whistled. "I thought you were an exotic breed. More than two centuries old. How does a woman like you survive so long and keep the anger so strong?"

"What do you mean?"

He shrugged. "Let me guess. You like to take out any vampire you lay eyes on, right?"

"It's what I do."

"Right. Because, what...? A vampire harmed someone you loved?"

He was prying, and Ravin didn't like the way her heart speeded up and the warmth behind her eyes threatened tears. Some buttons were not meant to be pushed.

"Your lover?" he tried. "Some vampire take him out—"

"No." She looked away.

"Your village? An attack by night, torches blazing and fangs flashing," Nikolaus confirmed, a little too dramatically for her sensitivity. "I didn't think the older vamps organized for hunts, most are loners nowadays, but—"

"My parents, all right? Three vampires killed my parents."

And get the hell out of my life, she thought. The torture was that she was sitting here naked alongside the very creature she despised, and yet she couldn't imagine not being here at this moment, with this man.

Because he'd touched something inside her, some deep buried part of her that was thoroughly enjoying its freedom.

"I'm sorry, sweetness." He lay before her, trying to capture her gaze. "It's gotta hurt to lose your parents. I can't say I can relate since both of mine are still alive."

"You're very lucky. I lost mine when I was ten. Not a lot of time to know the people who brought you into this world, but more than enough to know love."

"Do you want to tell me about it? Will you?"

In two centuries, Ravin had never been questioned about her past. After her parents were murdered she'd gone to live with her aunts; they had trained her in earth magic, and set her free after her ascension ceremony on her eighteenth birthday. Living the life she led did not make for personal conversations over coffee with the girlfriends. And there was no such thing as a witch shrink.

Even now the ache of their murders burned brightly within her. Almost as if she could clasp her fingers about it and draw it out into the light to display on her palm.

Is that why it's so easy to ignore the misbalance within you? You've got to start making changes.

"Ravin?"

Nikolaus stroked her hair. It felt good, calming, reassuring. A change did need to be made. Like confiding in someone? Opening her heart?

Do it. You want to lay it out on your palm. It could be a start to tilting the balance back toward the light.

Ravin drew a breath in through her nose and said, "I was only ten when they were murdered by your sort."

"*My* sort? The big bad vampires, I presume?"

"Nikolaus." Perhaps he hadn't the capacity to simply listen to her. "Forget it."

"No, Ravin, I'm sorry." He kissed her thigh and slid his palm along her leg. "I'll listen."

Dare she expose herself to him like this? "I'm trying. It's just a lot to get over."

Twisting, Ravin reached for the box and placed it on Nikolaus's lap. It had been carved by her grandfather and tanned and stained and shaped into a bridal gift for his bride. Ravin's grandmother had cherished the box. She'd kept an acorn in it from the first tree she and her husband had planted.

And a clear uncut ruby; the bride price her husband had paid for her hand.

The acorn and ruby were gone. But inside lived Ravin's world. A world that belonged only to her. A world both painful and joyous.

"You can look. It's all that I have. All that I value."

He touched the leather surface, tracing his fingers over the elaborate working of the Crosse family crest. On a quartered shield were her mother's family crest of moon and stars, and in the opposite corners, her father's scythe, which signified his farming history.

"You sure?" Nikolaus prompted. "I don't need to—"

"Please. I want you to."

Chapter 13

When he removed the cover, the smell of musty nutmeg filled Ravin's nostrils with lush memory. She loved the smell because it reminded her of the good times, so very long ago— before it all became bad.

Mornings spent feeding the goats and plucking still-warm eggs from the henhouse. And later, bringing her father an afternoon repast in the fields he worked relentlessly to support his family. Evenings were spent watching her mother scrye and practicing a few movement spells.

The Crosses had not been rich, but they'd had enough. And that her parents were always kissing and smiling made Ravin understand, at a young age, how rich love could be.

Nikolaus gave her a wondering glance before touching the objects inside. Carefully, he poked the small blue square, then ran his forefinger along it.

"Small pieces of fabric?" He lifted the box to give the contents a sniff. "You've quite the collection."

"Accrued over the centuries. Pockets," she said. "That one belonged to my mother. I keep it on top because it was the first I obtained. There's nine in total."

"A pocket. Huh. It's a wonder what people consider treasure. It's very old. I shouldn't handle it."

"I save them. They are fond memories of those I have loved."

Ravin took the box and carefully drew out the pocket, holding it flat on her palm. It was wool and dyed a bright wode blue. It had faded little over the years and the edges had barely frayed. She liked to believe the lack of disintegration was due to her mother's magic, still imbued within the threads.

"I ripped this from my mother's dress before the flames could get to it. It was the first night of winter, a bitter cold December evening that had cut frost onto the glass scrying ball my mother kept on a shelf near the door, far from the hearth."

"Where did you live?"

"I'm from a village in Bulgaria, about three leagues from the Black Sea. We lived in a cottage, set in the center of a vast forest the Crosse family had owned for centuries. The village is no longer there. Vampires destroyed the population within a month following the attack on my family."

She sensed from his movements Nikolaus had become uncomfortable, but he remained close to her, intent in his silence, so Ravin continued.

"We had eaten and were cleaning the dishes when the pounding at the front door sounded. My father, kind and inquisitive, called out "Enter" even as my mother grabbed me and rushed me toward the bedroom just off the main living quarters. She pushed me under the high tester bed, hissing at me to stay out of sight. She knew. And I knew the moment I looked into her eyes and saw the fear. I'd never before seen fear in my mother's eyes. I think that frightened me more than initially seeing the intruders."

Nikolaus smoothed his forefinger over the wool pocket, still laid flat on her palm. He didn't speak, yet Ravin could sense his presence holding her, supporting her. It felt tremendous.

"There were three of them. Big, like you, with blood smeared across their faces and necks. They killed my father first, who was mortal, not a witch, by drinking from him until he begged for mercy. They didn't give him any. He was a strong man—but no match for vampires—and he was quickly dispatched, his neck broken, and the beasts feeding on him like animals.

"When they dropped my father to the floor, I had to hold my hands over my mouth not to cry out. From my position under the bed I could see everything clearly, and I shook like oak leaves in a midnight storm. My father's throat had been torn open to show the muscles, and blood poured from his face and mouth and over his chest where I believe the vampires tapped right into his heart.

"I bit into my fingers to staunch my horror. I can still remember tasting my own blood, and being startled that it was so alien. Like dusty pennies—the taste of pain."

Nikolaus clasped her free hand and looked into her eyes. What Ravin saw there startled her. Compassion. It was such an unexpected expression to see on a vampire's face. Especially now, when relating the horrors of her childhood.

He didn't speak, and she couldn't stop. She'd never told anyone this. And the words wanted to be put to voice.

"The only way to kill a witch, as I'm sure you know, is to burn her. The vampires wrangled mother's hands behind her back and tied a leather strap across her mouth. No way to scratch herself, or spit blood at her attackers. Then, they lit her skirts on fire, and one of them punched her out cold. She dropped to the floor, tinder for the flame, and the vampires left.

"I laid and watched the flames begin to consume my mother's body, her hair, the hem of her skirt. The tiny stitches on her gray stockings melted and burned flesh became the prevalent smell. She…she did not cry out."

A shudder in her throat sifted out abbreviated breaths. But Ravin would not cry, she could not.

"I feared the vampires were standing outside, waiting for me to reveal I'd been hiding. But when I could bear it no longer, I crawled out and crouched over my mother. I was horrified. I screamed and wailed, but nothing could stop the fire that had now ignited the floorboards. It didn't occur to me to try to stomp out the flames. Reaching for my mother, I grabbed her pocket and tore it away."

Ravin stroked the pocket aside her cheek. "I was alone after that. I had no home, no parents, and only my unpracticed magic to get by. It was days before one of my aunts arrived from Paris and begrudgingly packed me away with her. She wasn't cruel to me, but I never knew love again, after the night of the horror."

Breathing out through her nose, Ravin closed her eyes, wishing away the visions of fire and of silent screams. She'd seen it so many times. Had woken some nights, her skin blistered with invisible flames. There was but one way to push it all away, to tame the ache.

"One thing I vowed that day was no vampire would ever look me in the eye and live."

Drawing up, Nikolaus looked her straight in the eye. Challenging her? It was different with him; she did not count him as the enemy. Not now that she'd gotten to know him better. And yet, he defied her with his sapphire stare, cutting through her pain and poking at her heart with his daring.

Ravin looked away. "I meant it."

"Even now?"

She nodded. "It is what I am, Nikolaus. You wondered why I attacked your tribe that night? It is because you exist. You are what I hate."

"No—"

"And I am what you hate. Will you ever recognize me for what I am?"

"You're my lover, sweetness. A woman who has had a hell of a time, and wears an armor of protection against her past."

"It's not just the past. Vampires are everywhere. I never wanted to be like this. It's not something I've thought about. It's just…who I am."

"The death of your parents is a tragedy, and I mean it. But our lives are constructed of the choices we make, Ravin. We are never forced into anything."

"Really? So you *asked* to become a vampire?"

"No, I was attacked. But I had a choice. I could have ended it then and there that night, destroying a future I had not chosen."

"I know it was a choice," she said. "To slay. To take revenge. I never said I regret it."

"No, but that was three vampires."

"Three demonic, evil, hateful vampires."

"And in turn, as a means to your revenge, how many vampires have you slain? Dozens?"

"Hundreds."

He sighed and nodded. The tension in his jaw pulsed twice. "Two centuries is a long time to hold a grudge. All that anger must consume you. Eats into your soul."

Ravin tucked her head between her arm and her knee. The pocket she pressed against her forehead. He had no idea what she had done with her very soul.

"Now, I know it's tough," he went on, "but that was two people. My God, your parents. They meant the world to you,

I understand that. But how long are you going to make the entire vampire nation suffer for something three bad vampires did to you?"

"What do you care?"

"I care because I love you. All I'm trying to say is, don't you think it's about time to let it go?"

"I think it's time for you to leave."

He wouldn't be pushed from her lap, so Ravin slid off the bed and marched away.

Damn it! She'd opened herself to him, only to be ridiculed for a choice that had never consciously been hers. To slay vampires? It had just *become* her. She would have never chosen a path of violence had it not been forced upon her. Who would?

Nikolaus was wrong. Sometimes a person was not given a choice. How could he believe he had not had the choice stolen from him that night he was transformed against his will?

"It's all right," Nikolaus said. "You keep your anger. It's obviously gotten you through the centuries."

"And what about yours, vampire?" Ravin challenged.

"My what? Anger?"

"You're full of it, Nikolaus. You claim peace, but you came to me with one intention."

A tilt of his head shook the hair over his shoulder. "That I did. And you, the mistress of revenge, can't understand why I wanted revenge for my near death?"

"I understand it completely. And yet, here you are, making love to the object of your revenge."

"I can't stop myself," he said, his jaw tightening. Too quickly his fingers splayed out before him. But she had seen that they'd tightened into a fist.

Was there a flash of the heartless vampire inside him that hated her so much? Could it be summoned? The man was of *the dark*. He could never stand above the call to darkness, no matter how he tried to deny it.

She took Nikolaus's hand, and placed it over her heart. "Vampire, take your revenge."

"No!" He sat up and put his feet to the floor. "Spell or not, I don't need it, witch. Vengeance doesn't feel right anymore. I cannot comprehend why it consumed me so before, but now…I just need peace."

"Is that why you stay away from your tribe? They've become the opposite of peace."

"I had to stay away while I healed. But I'm going back. Soon."

"Why?"

"Because they need me."

He could not disguise the anger he held toward the tribe. And why should he? He was only bespelled to love her; his thoughts and ideals about everything else remained the same. There was something about the tribe and his leadership that didn't sit right with Nikolaus.

"Kila seems to have survived well enough in your absence," she tossed out as bait.

"I'm the only one who can protect them!"

"Nothing and nobody can ever be completely safe." Bending before him, she put her face right up to his. *Match me, meet my anger, let it out, vampire.* "If the world is going to get you, it'll find a way!"

Surprised that she was now defending the vampires, Ravin shook out her arms and paced beside the bed. Naked, as usual, she couldn't summon a shred of modesty.

"Besides, you can't return. They'll smell me on you, and kill you for it."

"Pretty damn hard to kill me now. If there was a way, I'd be all for it."

"You don't mean that." She slid next to him on the bed, and despite herself, nestled into him. "You're not like the vampires I've killed. An animal. Beastly. Blood hungry."

"How can you know the men you kill when you shoot indiscriminately? You didn't know me before that night you attacked Kila."

Hearing the truth hurt. The Sight should have been hers long ago.

"You're right. I've been doing it so long it's...all that I know. This isn't right, you and me. The whole world has changed on me overnight."

"Maybe you need that change."

"Maybe you should take your philosophy and find someone who cares."

"I have found someone who cares." He grabbed her by the arm and tugged her onto the bed. It didn't take force to coax her to spoon into his body. Nikolaus whispered against her neck. "The trick is to make her realize she cares."

He thought he knew her? Stupid bespelled vampire.

"I have some things to do," he said. "Can I return tonight?"

"Would you stay away if I asked you to?"

"No. Sorry," he murmured. "I said I'd listen. I shouldn't have tried to suggest you did anything wrong. Love you, sweetness. I'll be back later."

Before replacing the leather box on the shelf, Ravin sorted through the pockets. There was one from her mother and a woven flax circle that had belonged to her grandmother. A slick periwinkle silk pocket from a suitor who had seduced her and stolen her virginity—but never her innocence—but five years after losing her parents.

A faery changeling's pocket of blood-red velvet held a crust of dried liquid on the corner. Absinthe, had to be. There was a small flowered cotton pocket from her friend, Virginia, who had struggled with her own devilish pact made in the late 1800s. She'd died early, at the hands of Himself. Or rather, at the influence of the demonic, for Himself never got his hands dirty. That's what minions were for.

The other pockets were from friends and lovers. People Ravin wanted to remember, but had never trusted that her memory would survive as long as she would.

A witch could live eternally, so long as the renewal ritual was performed once a century on the eve of a blue moon. In order to obtain immortality, a witch had to consume the blood from a vampire's beating heart.

Yeah, it was messy, and sickening. Ravin had done it twice now. She would continue to do it because life on this earth hadn't gotten unbearable, and she liked moving from century to century, watching the world grow up and come into its own. It had been moving remarkably fast the past few decades. There were times Ravin felt she might kneel down and dig her fingers into the earth to hang on so she didn't fall off the rapidly spinning planet.

But it was all good. Until she saw a vampire. Then the innate need for vengeance brewed, overwhelming all reason—and further tilting her balance toward the dark.

"Got to get my soul back," she murmured. "I just…have to."

If she could see her own aura, she guessed it would be a fuzzy gray with spots or lines of black streaking through it. Nasty business dealing with Himself. But because she had, she would never again slay a mortal being. And that made the deal worth it.

Nikolaus's aura was brilliant crimson. Very few spots of ash on it, as it was for most vampires. That was curious in itself, because while he came off as this ultraviolent, big bad guy, the lack of ash made her wonder if it was all a front.

She'd revealed her heart to him today. Would he do the same should she ask him?

"I want to know," she whispered as she clasped her arms over her chest and closed her eyes. "Who were you, Nikolaus Drake? And why do you care so much?"

What are you thinking? He's the enemy.

To summon the acrid feeling of hatred didn't work. She couldn't do it.

"But I don't *like* him," she tried. "I merely tolerate him. Until the spell is broken, there's not much else I can do for him."

Yes, that was it. It wasn't as though she was developing feelings for a longtooth.

Chapter 14

The human brain was a marvel, capable of directing and choreographing thousands of mindless daily tasks, assignments, workloads and entertainments without the owner of the brain even realizing it.

It was more powerful than any computer that existed, or would come into existence over the next billion years. It was forgiving to the extent of injury location, or it could devastate by merely bursting a microsized blood vessel.

It needed oxygen and knowledge to survive. It told the truth, it cued emotion, and it initiated disease. It protected through intuition, memory loss and outright deception.

It could trick a man into believing something to be truth, though it might not be. The brain could make a man feel emotion, such as fear over an imagined presence, or sadness when one guesses incorrectly over a missing loved one, though neither has occurred.

The brain was capable of inducing desire merely at the sight of a flat two-dimensional photo. It could summon want merely by smell. Passion, merely by recognizing the sound of lovers going at it while the brain's owner stood outside an open bedroom window.

And it was making Nikolaus Drake love against all reason.

His brain believed in the spell—that was all there was to it. He should be able to counter-intuit the feeling of love—but he didn't want to.

But did he not want to because of the spell, or because of his true and genuine feelings? That was the hard question.

"I don't want this to stop."

And yet he did.

For how could he successfully return to Kila while his heart was led by a witch's hands? She could not possibly respect him for the intelligent, caring person he felt himself to be. He was nothing—ash—to Ravin Crosse.

She held all the power. Not in her blood, but in her deadly kiss. For to kiss her, to fall even deeper, to not care if he wore her taint on his flesh, could only bring his death by those of his kind.

Gabriel strode into the living room, checking the plants in the corner. "You talk to Truvin yet?"

"Tomorrow night." Nikolaus tore his gaze from the reflected shore lights dancing on the river and studied his cohort. "You feeling better?"

"It was nothing." The man brushed off the nightmare with a gesture, but he wasn't so foolish as to think Nikolaus didn't know the truth. "A mistake."

"Killing is never—" Nikolaus forced back the need to admonish. He was not the man's keeper, nor was he his leader. He had no right to suggest Gabriel live his life a certain way.

A way that pleases you?

That is what you've been doing. All these years. Nikolaus could not have a surgeon's life, one that gave him God-like control over common, sickly mortals, so instead he had replaced it with a position of command. Of control over others. And he was only now realizing it.

"Nikolaus?" Gabriel prompted. "I said I was sorry."

Clamping a palm across his friend's shoulder, Nikolaus gave it a reassuring squeeze. "I will not judge you. And…I am sorry for enforcing a way of life that may have proved too constrictive. There are times I cannot look beyond my own world."

"Hey, man, don't apologize for being there for me when I most needed a supportive hand," Gabriel said. "You've taught me things and have taken care of me. The one who gave me the nightmares…she was just, well…it was jealousy. It is a very strong influence."

"Something you want to talk about?" Nikolaus wondered.

Gabriel shook his head, and wandered toward the kitchen. "Not unless you're in the mood to talk about what's been keeping you away at all hours lately."

When Nikolaus didn't answer, because he wasn't sure what to say—confession didn't feel right—his friend said he'd see him whenever he could, and left. For a night on the prowl, Nikolaus assumed.

He wanted to be forthright with Gabriel, but until he could determine whether or not he was being true to his own soul, Nikolaus decided an unmentioned liaison was not a lie, merely a safety measure.

Ravin stripped off her Kevlar vest and dropped it on the floor before the artillery closet.

She needed to put her mind back in the frame it was accustomed to. Nikolaus was preaching his peace and love to her and she'd almost fallen earlier. Almost.

This witch wasn't going to succumb to a love spell that had no control over her. It was designed to only affect the recipient, not the receiver.

Checking her twelve-gauge, she verified two blood bullets in the shotgun chamber. There were still a dozen on the shelf in the artillery closet. She wouldn't need to make more within the week, but she did need to use the bullets soon. Ten days' shelf life was max before the blood started to curdle and dry to the inside of the bullet wall.

And yet she stared down at the vest folded around her feet. This was the second time she'd taken it off in the past ten minutes. She couldn't seem to keep it on.

"You can't do it, can you, you idiot slayer."

Oh, she could. She just…felt off her game tonight. That was it. Not up for a jaunt outside. It was humid and sticky, the thermometer soaring toward an unseasonable ninety degrees. Not the right weather for leather. Firing up the street chopper didn't feel worth the expenditure of gas to stalk a prey that had become elusive of late.

"Tomorrow," she offered, knowing the lackluster promise would never be kept.

"And then what?"

Spinning at the sound of the male voice, Ravin drew her gun on aim with Nikolaus Drake's dark blue eyes. Like a piece of wool fabric she'd torn from her mother's dress, she realized now the color of the man's eyes matched perfectly.

"Go ahead." His killer charm and smile slid into position. "Love is supposed to hurt, isn't it?"

Damn him, she thought.

"You can't possibly cross my wards so easily." She shook the gun once, as if to do so would make it fire invisible bullets that would have some effect on the vampire. *Without implicating the slayer, right?* "I had a carpenter fix the bolts and hinges and I reinforced all the protection wards this afternoon. You need permission to cross a private threshold, vampire."

"We've been over this. Bonded by blood, remember?" He turned and casually strode into the kitchen, where he opened the refrigerator and scanned the contents.

Outfitted in black suede jeans this evening, and a soft gray sleeveless shirt, the man advertised sex with every flex of his muscles and in each grin he sent her way.

"I wish you were ash!"

Ravin slammed her gun onto the artillery shelf. She was still strapped up with a gun on her left thigh and a blade in her boot. She marched across the room, and when the vampire didn't acknowledge her approach, she tapped him on a big broad shoulder.

He turned around and kissed her.

While she struggled to get an audible "no" out, the urge to wrap her arms around his neck and her legs about his hips moved her limbs before she could protest.

"And speaking of the blood bond," he said. Another kiss. Ravin shuddered at the touch of his warm mouth to her neck. He grazed her with his teeth. "Check this out."

He tugged down his collar to reveal the havoc of tattoos and scars that disappeared up into his hairline—the tattoos were still there, but the scars were not.

"What the hell?" Dropping her legs to stand, Ravin tugged aside Nikolaus's hair and smoothed her fingers over the surprisingly soft skin.

"All gone. Even along my side and under my arm. I think you did this to me, sweetness. Pretty damn awesome, eh?"

"How could I—?" She stroked his neck and he tilted his head appreciatively. The flesh was soft and new as she glided along the strong muscle. "From having sex?"

"I think so. I don't know your witchy legends well, but isn't there something about a vampire gaining strength from a witch when they make love?"

"The blood sex magic," she blabbered stupidly. And then she mentally kicked herself for revealing so much.

"That's right. When a vampire has sex with a witch, and drinks her blood, he draws her magic into him. Hasn't happened for centuries because of the whole death cocktail thing."

"Right. The great Protection spell," she muttered. "Well, there was that one case, but the witch had immunity in her blood...."

"Pretty sure I'm immune to your blood. Trial by fire and rising from the ash, you know. Phoenix, that's me."

"Yes," she agreed absently. "Which is the reason we were able to make love—your immunity. Yes, the ancients once had relationships with vampires. And whenever they had sex, the witch's magic would flow into the vampire."

"Must be what's happening," Nikolaus said. "All I know is I feel damn good, as if I could wrestle a whole clan of wolves. Thank you, sweetness."

She shoved at his chest, but her heart wasn't in the protest. "It's not something I'd voluntarily give to you."

"I know. You hate me. You're the crazy vigilante witch. I hate you."

"Finally, you're beginning to talk some sense."

"But I don't. I can't imagine ever hating something so sweet and ripe as you."

Nikolaus hooked his hands under her thighs, and kissing her, carried her into the living room, where he laid her on the leather couch. All without breaking the incredible kiss.

He was completely oblivious.

"This is wrong," Ravin said—just so it was said. She wanted to get that protest out into the ether.

And then, she let it happen.

Again.

Until the night surrendered to morning.

"I love you," Nikolaus rasped against Ravin's ear.

She turned over on the bed, nestling her shoulder against his chest and pressing her buttocks to his thighs. His erection hugged the small of her back. Always hard, and always fascinating for its constant rigidity.

To hear *I love you* whispered in her ear made her happy. And whispered by a strapping, handsome, brooding man—vampire.

Of all the stupid mistakes. She'd done it again? And so many times.

Well, now she couldn't claim force or ignorance, only stupidity.

Or was it something else? Did she *want* to be with this vampire?

"Do you love me, Ravin?"

"It's a spell," she found herself mumbling. It was the simplest way to avoid her perplexing feelings. Feelings she hadn't had for years, decades, maybe even more than a century.

"So you say." He wrapped his arm across her stomach, hooking his fingers at her opposite hip, and rolled with her so she lay on top of his body, looking up at the ceiling.

"Now what?" she said on a giggle.

A giggle? *Oh, Ravin, you've got yourself into something here.*

Nikolaus pressed one fist against the small of her back. Placing another hand at her neck, he kept her head from falling back. He easily balanced her body there, above his by inches. And he lowered her onto his erection. It was like an extreme gymnast move, but Ravin went along for the ride.

Chapter 15

She handed him his shirt. He sat on the corner of the bed, unwillingly dressing. Ravin knew it was reluctance because each time she pulled a pant leg down his thigh, he kissed her and they made love. Again. For about the fourth or fifth time, surely.

Now even she was tired. And she simply stood there, arms crossed loosely across her bare stomach, watching as Nikolaus drew the soft gray jersey shirt over his arms. They were thick with muscle. But few scars remained on the underside of his left arm, mere scratches, really.

No longer did she wince. She'd hurt him. But now she was renewing him, thanks to the magic she gave him each time they made love.

Would he hate her for this when the spell was broken? Surely. *I hope not.*

Nikolaus was the forgiving sort. Yet she knew little about

him beyond that he could touch her with a smile and kill her with his body. And that he preferred peace to war.

"Tell me about your life?" The question frightened her, but she assumed a casual pose. I'm just chatting with the vampire, getting to know him better. Wasn't there a saying about keeping one's enemies close? "Has the tribe abandoned you since the attack?"

"They wait for my return. A phoenix is revered."

"Guess I'm responsible for your step up in the world, eh?"

And for creating something that vampires across the world may actually fear—if he really was indestructible.

Oh, she was definitely going to hell for this one. Good thing she knew the proprietor. Thinking of which…she had yet to receive approval for completing obligation number two a second time. Had she screwed up again?

For the welfare of her very soul she prayed she had not.

"So what does your tribe think of this? You coming to see me and having sex with me and—" Ravin swallowed "—loving me?"

"They don't know. I would be destroyed, you should know that."

"So why do you do it?"

"Because I can't *not* come to you," he said, his voice tired, but from more than exertion.

And for the first time Ravin wondered what he sacrificed because of the spell. Did it draw on his energy to comply with something so opposite his very nature? Surely he must be drained, for some inner knowing in him must comprehend it was wrong, and fight against it, even as he kissed her and made her cry out in ecstasy.

"Sooner, preferably, rather than later, the spell will be broken, and you will be free to kill me as you originally intended," she said lightly. And she deserved that death now, didn't she? Hell, yes. "Not that you don't kill me over and over every moment I'm in your arms."

"It's good, isn't it?"

He pulled her onto his lap. Stroking her hair from her face, he looked into her eyes. Nikolaus's eyes were not black as she'd originally thought that first time she had stared him down in her kitchen, but a deep, piercing blue that glinted with shards of ice. He had been through much in his lifetime. She could see it there.

"How long have you lived?"

"As a vampire? Two decades."

"So you're quite young."

"You, sweetness, have successfully robbed the cradle."

Yeah? And she'd once dated a three-hundred-year-old faery changeling, so she'd swung all the way toward robbing the grave, as well.

"What did you do before you were transformed?"

His eyes twinkled. Could she ever get enough of the charismatic rogue?

"Brain surgery."

She laughed. "Ah, but of course, the long-haired, tattooed doctor who charms people with his smile while he sucks their blood when they're not looking. But seriously."

"Seriously."

"You were a brain surgeon? An actual, real live...?"

"Four years premed, four more for my M.D., a long and illustrious five-year residency, and I had just begun my first year on the neurosurgery rotation."

"Wow. I had no idea. I mean, you sounded real smart with your comments about the brain, but I just thought... Huh. A brain surgeon."

"Master of the Universe, actually. I could save a man with a few strokes of the scalpel through his gray matter. I could poke and prod and cause pain in the quest for a cure, and the patients would grit their teeth and thank me. *Thank* me for hurting them. It was a damn heady position to be in. I was a god."

"So that's where the arrogance comes from."

"Didn't get it from med school, sweetness. Always had it. Of course, I don't think I—or any man—could poke around inside a person's skull without a healthy dose of arrogance."

"I suppose. I'm guessing you didn't give it up willingly. Brain surgeons make the big bucks, don't they?"

"Yep. And my career was proving very lucrative. Paid off my student loans within a few years. Bought me a nice house on Lake Minnetonka. All the big electronic toys and gadgets— you know like Atari and a CB radio."

"The seventies, eh?"

"You know it. Can't imagine what I'd have spent my money on had I been in med school this century. The gadgets keep getting smaller and fancier, and more expensive every year. Anyway, I was happy. I even had a fiancée."

"You did?" Ravin felt a plummeting sensation in her chest.

Not a confession she'd been expecting to hear. He'd... loved before? Of course he had. A man as gorgeous and compassionate as Nikolaus Drake would not live alone, even if he tried.

He nodded. "I loved her, too."

"I see." Suddenly her nakedness felt very stark. She couldn't tug up the sheet because Nikolaus sat on them.

"Don't worry, sweetness, it was twenty years ago. I was a normal mortal man with a normal life, and a pretty girlfriend, but she wasn't in it for the long haul."

"Meaning?"

"Meaning, when I got the brain tumor things went downhill, including our relationship."

"*You* had a brain tumor? But that's so..."

"Ironic? That was my first thought." He stretched his arms behind his head, unashamed of his near-nudity, and why should he be? And there was that erection, ever hard, and always wanting attention.

Nikolaus crossed his legs and nudged Ravin's thigh with a knee. She knew he was giving her the wink. A look she knew meant "let's do it".

"Tell me more," she said. "Then sex."

"Deal. I spent more than a dozen years in medical school studying how to take a tumor out of a man's skull, then the bloody tumor shows up in my head."

"What did you do?"

"Had it taken out by one of the best neurosurgeons at the Mayo clinic. A man who had been my mentor for a dozen years of my life. The tumor was completely removed, but, well…the scalpel slipped."

"It *slipped?*"

"Happens sometimes. In the seventies, we didn't have the stereostatic technique they use nowadays. Tumors had to be excised with a surgeon's intuition as guide."

"You mean he was going at your brain with a knife, blind?"

"Not exactly, though it made it difficult to determine the edge of the tumor from healthy brain tissue. I couldn't hold a grudge against the surgeon—we all had it happen at some time or other. We believe we are God, but the truth is, no one is perfect. Suffered some serious complications because of that slip."

"What sort of complications?"

"Lost motor control on my left side due to the tumor hugging the motor cortex. I couldn't walk without swerving, nor could I use my hands properly. I looked like a drunken old bastard who spends his days in the bar and his nights staking out the liquor store. Made it impossible to ever operate again.

"Julie, my fiancée, left me after I started emulating that drunken old bastard by drinking and teasing danger. I had a death wish. Hell, I'd survived brain surgery, but the Big Guy had decided I didn't need to use my hard-earned skills to survive anymore. That was irony at its most cutting."

"So that's why you're so smart. Twelve years of medical school?"

He traced his mouth over her elbow, nipping it with the sharpened points of his canines, but not drawing blood. "Doesn't take smarts to be a brain surgeon, sweetness, just a steady hand. Had I been smarter I wouldn't have succumbed to a reckless life. After the surgery I was pissed at the world."

"Is that when you got the tattoos?"

"Yep. Went bald for a year. The tattoos were meant to scream at the world and keep it at a distance. Worked."

"Must have been awful to lose so prestigious a job."

"Hell, yes. On the other hand, I no longer had the outrageous malpractice insurance bills. Those cut deep into a doctor's profit, let me tell you. Though it wasn't half so bad in the seventies as I hear it is nowadays."

"People expect miracles. And if they don't get them, they want compensation of some sort."

"Exactly," Nikolaus agreed. "We may act like gods, but doctors are no more powerful than the common man. We are taught a means to attempt to change or save lives, but ultimately it is the patient's own God who determines whether a particular crap shot will win or lose."

He flexed both his hands before him. Ravin clasped her fingers through his left. He squeezed reassuringly. "It seems you can use them both now."

"Vampirism has been very very good to me."

"I've heard that—that the transformation fixes even genetic

defects. So what if you would have been transformed *before* the operation to remove the tumor?"

"Huh." Nikolaus nudged up the pillow to prop his head. "In all these years that is one question I have never asked myself. What if?"

"So…what if?"

"Well, I might be an old man still cutting into people's brains right now if vampirism could have sucked out the tumor the way I suck blood from people's necks. Nah, I'd still be a vampire. I could never be a surgeon around all that blood."

"Maybe a little blood sex magic would have done the trick?"

"You would have never done that for me. Even if I wasn't a vampire at the time."

"Oh, you never know. You do have a certain charm…."

"Ravin, are you coming over to the dark side?"

"Already there, Drake. Been walking the dark for two centuries. I know witches call vamps *the dark* and themselves *the light*, but trust me, you can't get any darker than I am."

"I suppose dealing with the devil has something to do with that. You've seen a lot, I'm sure."

"Yes, but I don't understand it. It's such a twisty thing that brought us together."

"I like the way you put that. Brought us together. We. Us. We're together. A couple." He slid his hand down her stomach and Ravin parted her legs to allow him entry. "Tell me you love me, Ravin. It's all I live for."

It shimmered right there, in her belly, and at her core. The threat of bliss. The overwhelming release of power, surrender to the enemy.

Happiness.

But as he teased her to the edge of surrender, Ravin couldn't stop the words that spilled from her lips, "I…can't."

Chapter 16

Hard to believe, after having sex with the woman for nearly a week straight, it could actually continue to get better.

"So tell me," Ravin said, rolling to her back and looking up. "Where do you go after you've been with me? Home? Back to your tribe?"

"Why?"

"I've invested a certain amount of emotion into…us. I need some details."

Briefly, the thought that she was gathering information for her own needs—like the hunt of his kind—paused Nikolaus. But he knew better. The witch had come around.

"When I leave here I go home. Home is my tribe, but I live separately from them."

"The Kila tribe has been stirring up a lot of trouble lately."

"It's Truvin Stone. He's taken them in a completely opposite direction to where I have always steered them. We don't raise trouble or tread wolf territory merely for the thrill of it. I teach my men that we must learn to get along with everyone. We are the minority. Mortals have the upper hand."

"And the wolves?"

He smirked, revealing a wickedly gleeful side of him. "Werewolves are lesser than the vamps, but I won't begrudge them their territory. We can all exist peaceably. It's not that difficult. It simply requires respect."

"Your men must have great respect for you."

"They did. Once." He shrugged. "Now? I'm not sure what to expect upon my return. Gabriel reports the tribe is eager to see me. It's mostly curiosity over my being a phoenix. But Truvin…"

"You expect Stone to make your return difficult?"

"Truvin is respected, but for all the wrong reasons. He's powerful, and I know he won't step down from leadership without a fight. I'm ready for it." He smacked a fist into his palm. The punch actually stung.

"You just surprised yourself, didn't you?" Ravin took his palm and opened it to trace the residual sting. "Strong one, aren't you?"

"I'm getting stronger. Every day now, it's like I exert so little energy to do what once taxed me."

"It's the sex magic."

"Does this mean I'm bewitched?"

"I believe so. Which makes you a rarity." She kissed his collarbone and traced a finger down the center of his ribs. "Only the ancient vampires are bewitched. And perhaps one or two who have been successful in gaining immunity to a witch's blood. I know of one other modern vampire who is immune and also bewitched. He's a rock star."

"A rock star?"

"Yep, he lives his life before the public, and in the shadows he loves a witch, one of my good friends."

"Well, I'll be. What's his name? Just so I can know to walk carefully around him."

"He's not violent. He sings for The Fallen. You heard of Michael Lynsay?"

"Don't follow the rock 'n' roll bands. I prefer orchestral arrangements myself. Mozart is my favorite. Guitar stuff is good, too, if it has a bit of a hard edge to it."

"So you know about Sebastian DelaCourte? The man was once a star on the rock 'n' roll scene, a solo guitar player whose roots are in flamenco. And also a vampire."

"Didn't know that, either. But good to start a list. How can they live such public lives and still protect their secret? And what's the draw to stand in the spotlight?"

"You're young yet. And wise. You understand the need for privacy and will, no doubt, survive for centuries because of it." She leaned in and kissed him. "I admire your strength, Nikolaus. And your impeccable values."

"I'm not sure they're impeccable."

"You won't stand for murder. You would never harm another—"

"Without provocation."

"Yes, without provocation," she murmured the words he'd used days earlier. *Why did you attack us? Without provocation?*

She had been doing this far too long. And now she felt it. And while she could justify murder in the name of all the witches of the world, and all the innocent mortals, she could no longer justify it in the name of her parents.

The balance, it had to shift.

"I'm sorry, Nikolaus."

"What for, sweetness? For making me love you? I'm over it. Slide up here and snuggle against me. There. That's good. You smell like…mmm, snow in the summer."

"Is that a good thing?"

"I love snow. Wish it was here all year long. I've got a shed full of snowmobiles and four-wheelers that I love to take up north to the Boundary Waters come snowfall. So yes, it's a very good thing. Know what else?"

"What?" Ravin felt a hot teardrop slide down her cheek as he moved to fit his body to hers.

"I can feel you running through my veins. It's like molecules of witch coursing along with the white and red blood cells. My whole arterial system tingles every time I think of you."

Please don't let it be the spell talking.

"I'm sorry for what I did to you and your tribe," she said. "It wasn't right. I need to take a step back and learn to think before reacting. I don't know everything, though you'd think a few centuries would have taught me a bit. Hell, age does not for wisdom make."

"It is who you are, Ravin. And while you look at it from mortal standards it may seem a harsh and reckless life, from our point of view—that of *the dark* and *the light*—well, I suppose someone has to do it."

Nikolaus traced the slash marks on her chest. "Tell me how a gorgeous witch like you got involved with the devil?"

"It's not as if I went looking for Himself. No one ever does." Ravin pushed up to sit with the pillows propped behind her. "He came to me. Have you ever had a chat with Himself?"

"Can't say I have. Though, would I know?"

"You can't miss the smell of brimstone that fills the air when he's near. But he only manifests as your greatest temptation, which is a hell of a kicker."

"You mean he looks like someone you want to get busy with?"

"Exactly."

Though, thankfully, Ravin couldn't summon an ounce of desire for Johnny Depp anymore. Good. And not good. First, her favorite movie star had been ruined for her. No more *Pirates of the Caribbean* for her. Second, she wouldn't know to recognize Himself when next he showed. And she knew she hadn't seen the last of him.

She tapped the lines above her bellybutton. "Three strikes and I'm out, that's the deal."

"So you've to do three tasks for the devil, then you're free of him?"

"Exactly. Except Himself calls them obligations. Three obligations, and my soul is once again mine."

"And for that you got...?"

"The Sight."

"You couldn't see before?"

"Vampires. I know them on sight now."

Nikolaus made a gesture toward himself as if to say, "Well, here I am, what's the deal?"

"You know a vampire could stand right next to a mortal, witch, elf, faery, what-have-you, and none of them would be the wiser. Your own kind can only tell one another by the shimmer." The shimmer was a tingling sensation a vampire felt when touched by another of his kind. "But unless you flash your fangs, the rest of us never know. Until it's too late."

"And yet, you stalk us as prey. What makes you believe you're always getting your vampire?"

"Well, there you go. I've always followed the tribes, and have known who the members are. But when I strike, I kill everything in sight. Trouble is, the tribes have their mortal supplicants that they either haven't yet turned, or are just toying with."

"Cory."

"Yes." She remembered him telling her how he'd been forced to feed on Kila's mortal supplicant to survive.

He'd gone dark and quiet. Ravin knew not to push, because

she had been the reason for his need to survive. She had killed a mortal that night.

"That's the thing, see," she said softly. "Himself was able to tell me that in all my strikes over two centuries, I've actually killed five innocent mortals. I don't like those numbers, but what can I do? Himself offered me the ability to See vampires. I jumped at the chance. I don't like to kill innocents. I'm not that cold-blooded."

"Your blood is actually very warm. So what does a vampire look like to you? How are they different from anything else when you're standing there with your gun raised and hell in your eyes?"

"I see their auras. A vampire aura is like rubies and ash. Kinda cool, actually, for longtooths."

"You say that as if we're the lowest things to walk the earth."

"You are," she said, too quickly. But it was the truth, to Ravin. And until a week earlier she would have labeled Nikolaus the same, and in the same hateful tone. Not now. "Except you."

He pulled away. "Now you're backtracking. You meant it when you said we all are. Me included."

"I've had a change of heart about you."

"Why?"

"Because I know you. I've spent time with you. You, Nikolaus, mean…"

"Mean what? You can't say it. You can't say you love me because you don't."

"That's the thing. I don't think I can ever love. *Love* is some fairy tale word for mortals and princesses and schoolgirl dreams. Life is much more complicated."

"It doesn't have to be." He leaned in and kissed her.

Why had this poor vampire chosen her apartment to burst into on the night she had concocted that idiot love spell!

"Your parents loved you," he murmured.

The slide of his body, his rough, masterful warmth, over her bare arms and chest and stomach, stirred the desire back to the surface. But now he'd put the image of her parents into her mind, and Ravin pressed her fists to her eyes and let out a repressed scream.

"What's wrong?" His breaths gasped near her ear.

She didn't want to look at him. She didn't want to know him. She didn't want to have to remember. They had loved her. The only two people in this world who had ever touched her so gently, and kissed her every night, and whispered how much they loved her.

He drew her into his arms and smoothed his hand over the back of her head. And though Ravin wished to push away and run and bury her face in her hands and cry, she clung to his giving openness and opened her mouth to sob.

"I understand," he said. "It's what you know. And I still love you."

His confession broke open a flood of tears, and Ravin cried into the night against her lover's shoulder.

"I don't want to do this anymore. Do you think I did a bad thing making that deal with Himself? I thought it was good, you know, that way I'd never again accidentally kill a mortal. I thought the balance that has so horribly bent my life out of whack would begin to be restored, but…"

He slid a hand around and spread it across her stomach. Burying his nose in her hair, he whispered softly against her ear. "Stick with me, sweetness. I'll be your compass. You want to stop? I'll do what I can to make it happen."

She turned and bracketed his face with her hands. Sniffing away a tear, she touched his lips with a finger. "Nothing can change until I complete the final obligation."

"What is it?"
"Don't know, but will you help me?"
"Yes, I promise."

Chapter 17

Rock music blasted from the living room where Gabriel sat watching music videos. The sun had set. Nikolaus had risen hours earlier. After a session of weight lifting, he'd showered and slipped on some casual jersey pants and padded out barefoot to see what held his friend's interest. They were really making some salacious videos these days.

"Haven't seen much of you lately," Gabriel said. "Not that I'm your keeper, but, ah—I thought so."

Nikolaus straightened his lips from an irrepressible smile. "What?"

"You've been smiling a lot lately. You don't do that, man. So I figure you must have found yourself a girl. Am I right?"

Nikolaus shrugged, but the smile leapt to the fore and no amount of trying would push it back.

"Well, it's about time the old man got his game on." Gabriel jumped up and followed Nikolaus into the kitchen. "All it took was ridding your life of that witch, and now you're back to your old self. What does she look like? Gorgeous is a given, but is she sexy?"

Nikolaus wondered about sexy. Ravin was the epitome of all that attracted him, but she was more rough and tough than soft and slinky. He decided less description would serve her better, and made a motion before him with his hands to outline her curvy shape.

"Nice." Gabriel flicked on the tap and bent over it to slurp up some water. He emerged, water drooling down his mouth and hair pulled back with one hand. "Must be a pleaser, 'cause you're gone all the time."

"I don't kiss and tell."

"What? Like me?"

Gabriel did like to give details. Hair color, breast size and how many times she came. The man always kept a count.

Nikolaus had lost count of how many times Ravin had come. But each time, it was all good.

"You know it's not wise for any vampire to get too attached," Nikolaus said. And he wasn't, was he? Not when it was a spell. "I'm just having fun, man."

"I understand. So, I never asked, how did it go with the witch?"

Turning his face away from his friend, Nikolaus tightened his jaw. Still discussing the same woman, one he logically knew he had no right going near, let alone making love to. Maybe that forbidden element was what turned him on?

"Er…"

"Don't tell me you haven't toasted her yet? You've waited so long for this. All you've been able to think about these past few months was either getting better or burning the witch. Do you need help? 'Cause I'm your man. Just say the word."

"I've staked her out. Got an eye on her. But I need to wait for the opportune moment."

"Oh. Sure."

Gabriel was right. Those first weeks during the healing process, as he watched the flesh grow back over his ribs to conceal his organs, Nikolaus had thought of nothing more than burning the witch and listening to her screams in the process.

What had happened to change that?

The spell. And how powerful it was to completely change his thought process. He should be hungry for the smell of Ravin's burning flesh.

Why couldn't he be that monster?

You've never been a monster.

"So you got sidetracked?" Gabriel delved. "I can understand. It's been a long time since you've had a woman."

"Gabriel."

"I'm cool. But don't let the witch run loose much longer. You want to have her taken care of before returning to Kila."

"I will. I…will."

"You feeling all right, old man? How's the burns? Still tight?"

"Actually, they're getting better every day. I can swing my arm." He did so and noted Gabriel's surprise.

"Whatever that chick is doing to you, let her continue, man. That is incredible."

A row of empty bullets sat on the counter. Glass shell tips glistened under the overhead lights. A syringe sat next to them, waiting for blood to be injected into the gel slugs fitted into the glass tip.

Ravin swallowed and spun around on the bar stool, putting her back to the preparation assortment. She'd told Nikolaus she didn't want to do this anymore.

So why had she gone through the motions to get the equipment out in the first place?

You've become a mindless machine. You kill without thought or remorse.

No, she kept mortals and witches safe from the vampire threat. If she did not, who would?

How could Nikolaus love someone like her?

"Stupid witch. You know that's not the real Nikolaus who holds you in his arms and makes you believe you are loved. And who's the one who is really bewitched?"

If she would have just staked him that first night...

"And then what?"

Continued on with life as she always had? Blindly staking vamps and returning home as if nothing ever happened, and filling bullets for her next murderous rampage?

How long are you going to make the entire vampire nation suffer for something three bad vampires did two centuries ago?

That a vampire was now making her question her entire history made the hair on Ravin's arms prickle. Had the past two centuries truly been so coldhearted and intent on murder?

She killed vampires because they had killed her parents. An eye for an eye.

Yet, she had lost only two people. And in turn, she had taken hundreds of vampires from this world.

Not a bad thing, when all things were considered. Vampires were the scum of the world. One less vampire stalking the streets meant one less mortal victim. Or two, or dozens of mortal victims, now she thought on it.

Not all vamps were as conscientious as Nikolaus, leaving their victims with a healing wound and taking the memory of the bite from their minds. Most were left half dead, possible vampires themselves, or completely dead with a broken neck or drained so close to death that their feeble mortal hearts burst.

What was so wrong with cleaning up a mortal plague?

What was wrong was one of those vampires had grabbed her by the heart and forced her to look at reality. And there, in Nikolaus's dark, soul-filled eyes she saw the man behind the creature. A neurosurgeon, for cripe's sake. Someone who had once saved peoples' lives. A man capable of loving and caring.

Because you bespelled him.

Right. But beyond the forced love, Ravin had to consider that the physical gentleness and concern really were Nikolaus. He had the capacity for kindness; that was all that truly mattered.

"I wonder if there's a spell to make spells last forever? Oh!"

Spinning around, she swiped her forearm across the waiting bullets, sending them scattering. A man stood in her kitchen. He always entered with no sound, and without disturbing her wards.

"I wish I knew how you can invade my wards," Ravin muttered.

"Don't ask me, I just open the door and walk in. So you want the spell to last forever?"

Nikolaus had been standing there long enough to hear Ravin's confession. It should feel wonderful—to know she wanted him to love her forever—but instead, it stabbed him deep inside.

Because he'd never been naive of the truth.

She wanted to keep him bespelled and under her control forever? Isn't that just like a woman, to want to be in control. And after he'd given her so much?

Now Nikolaus swept his gaze over the scattered glass bullets. A syringe teetered on the edge of the granite counter. The clear body of the thing glinted red under the hanging kitchen lights. She'd been preparing death cocktail bullets. To kill vampires.

She'd promised him last night she wanted to stop. Empty words, obviously.

And he loved this woman?

Why couldn't he think beyond the spell and simply turn and walk away from his enemy? He would just begin to think how cruel she was and wish her dead for her actions, and then the thought was quickly replaced by the need to wrap her in his arms.

Which Nikolaus did.

"I just meant," she said as she nuzzled her face into the crook of his elbow, "that...I don't know. I want you here as much as you wish to be."

"Forever?" he rasped, finding he meant it more than it being a question about her words. He kissed her forehead. She smelled like cloves and cherries and musk.

She slid off the stool to fit herself to his body. "I wish you hadn't heard me say that. I was babbling."

"I came here out of anger, I'll have you know."

"You did?"

"I was speaking to Gabriel earlier."

"Gabriel is your vampire friend, yes?"

"He's my right-hand man. I've told you about him. He lives with me."

"That explains why you never take me home with you."

"You want me to? Ravin, you're confusing the hell out of me. I thought you wanted to put a bullet in my brain."

"As if that would have an effect." Her smile was too brief. "I've changed my mind about a few things since meeting you."

She bowed her head, fitting it to his arm, and absently bit into the muscle, following with a long press of her lips. Considering? Forming words that wouldn't offend him? Brewing a clever chant to bewitch him even further?

"What if you *can* make the spell last forever?"

She shook her head effusively. "No. I'm torn as it is over what I've done to you. I've no right to dabble with your very soul as I have. Maybe it's because mine is not my own any more."

"Out on loan." And then it occurred to him. "That's why your blood didn't satisfy me."

"What?"

"After I first bit you, the hunger remained. I was still empty. But it's because I'd drank soulless blood."

"You need it to have a soul?"

"Hell, yes, you can't feed off the dead or get fulfilled with stuff from the blood bank. Just doesn't work that way. It is the vampires' curse that we must touch our warm, thinking victims and struggle with them to gain nourishment."

"Makes—"

The kiss was so sudden and desperate, Ravin didn't protest its intense desire to argue against her words. A physical denial that sucked away her defenses and reduced her to someone who wanted only to be taken, and to receive.

Nikolaus drew in a breath and smiled against her mouth.

"You take the breath from me, Nikolaus. Draw it right out and make me feel as if I'm drowning in your life."

"Better than your blood. Should I stop?"

"No. Take it all. Kiss me breathless."

"Love you," he murmured into her mouth, and kissed her hard.

Don't want to love you, she thought. Hate myself. Tired of running away from it, though. Want it.

Need it.

"Oh, Nikolaus, why can't you hate me?" She bowed her head onto his mouth. He kissed her forehead. "Why can't you set the building ablaze and be done with it? I—" She bracketed his face with her hands. "I need you to be the vampire and to see me as a witch."

"I know what we are to each other. Don't you think I struggle?"

"I think you can't struggle as much as you wish because of the spell. If you had control of your emotions, you'd push me away."

She got up and paced the floor, wandering near the scattered glass bullets. "I was preparing bullets to kill your fellow tribe members," she said. The lie would never be discovered. "Doesn't that make you angry?"

"Makes me want to rage."

"Oh? You rage so sweetly, lover. Care for some posies with your anger?"

He gripped her by the arm and spun her about and into his arms. Rage did flare, briefly. His fangs descended. Sharp as pins and perfect white. Ravin lowered her hand before she could reach up to touch.

He leaned in and licked her bottom lip. "You want me to hurt you? Then I'll hurt you."

He dove to her neck and bit into her. She didn't cry out, but instead pulled herself against his body and wrapped her arms around him.

"Yes, hurt me," she cried as the intrusion of his teeth sparked pain up and down her neck. Muscles tore and any movement made it ache all the more.

Supporting her head with both hands, Nikolaus drew out his teeth and began to feed upon her. Ravin felt the blood flow out of her veins. As if summoned from her heart, she could feel it gush upward toward her neck, racing for release.

She clawed into Nikolaus's back, not to injure, but to keep herself firmly affixed to her lover. This beautiful man who took not only her breath, but her very life into him. A communion of blood and desire.

Gasping at the rush of fire her blood had become, Ravin

closed her eyes, sinking into his embrace. He held her. He would not let her fall.

"I trust you, Nikolaus. I…"

The swoon scurried through her veins and dizzied her thoughts. So powerful, the vampire's bite, and capable of summoning orgasm.

And she was there, climaxing, convulsing in his arms, releasing her breath, her blood, her bliss into the one man she trusted beyond all reason.

The hands gripping her head and shoulders suddenly let go. Slowly aware that he had slipped into his own swoon, Ravin melted down her lover's torso, her head sliding across his hips and then catching herself to kneel before him.

Nikolaus spread out his arms attempting to balance, to find his way up from the delirious swoon. A rich concoction of satisfaction and blood and desire and orgasm.

"This," he gasped, "it isn't right. I should not…love the enemy. Ravin," he cried. "Kill me, please."

"Never." She unzipped his jeans, and began to worship him as he desired. "I am yours until the spell is broken."

Chapter 18

Time to get his thoughts in order. In two days, Nikolaus would walk before the tribe and retake the leadership. He sensed Truvin would throw down the gauntlet. Tonight he would meet him at Cue for whatever it was Truvin had in mind. A brawl? A meeting of the minds?

Whatever. Nikolaus did not intend to allow Truvin to continue his reign of violence. He was ready, both in mind and body, to stand up to the elder vampire.

Physically, Nikolaus had completely recovered. Thanks to the blood sex magic, his scars were but shadows on his flesh. As well, his strength had returned. He could grip a mortal and squeeze him breathless in seconds. But a fellow vampire? He was up for the challenge.

But he had no intention of fighting. Rational, calm discussion was what was required. And who knew? Perhaps Truvin wouldn't act as expected.

And witches' blood was not poisonous to vamps.

Pummeling the punching bag suspended before the living room window that overlooked the Mississippi, Nikolaus moved around it, light on his feet. He'd worked up a sweat, which was a challenge for his kind. Going at it for more than an hour tended to do that. Forcing his fists into the bag kept his mind from other distractions.

Like her.

He had to keep away from the gorgeous, seductive witch for the rest of the day, else he would never be able to keep their relationship a secret from Truvin. When he stood before the tribe, they would know at a glance that he was not the staunch leader they had once known, and instead, had fallen in love with their worst enemy.

Ravin walked into the living room, spied Nikolaus lingering near the window and raced into his arms. She didn't argue that he was always entering without permission. If there was one man in this crazy world who could permeate her wards, then let him be the tall, dark vampire who had stolen her heart.

Yeah, she could admit that in her thoughts. The man had gotten to her, he'd looked beneath the hard veneer and had touched her with his sexy smile and tender concern. He'd taken from her. And she was in no hurry to claim her heart back from him.

He held her tightly, kissing her and loudly moaning his pleasure.

"Oh, Ravin," he murmured dramatically.

A little odd… And in that moment of wonder, Ravin's senses kicked in. An awful scent filled her nostrils.

She pushed away from the leering vampire. "Oh, hell no."

"Oh?" Nikolaus scampered across the room to peer into the floor-length mirror hanging on the wall in the foyer. "Oh, yes!"

"No. Way." Turning to the counter, Ravin gripped it, fighting the rise of bile in her throat.

Brimstone. She smelled it clearly now. But not quick enough to have prevented a tongue-dance with the devil Himself.

She should have expected this to happen. *Really?* Because if she had expected it, then that meant—did that mean she was *in love* with Nikolaus?

No. She wasn't in love with Johnny Depp, she just found him a gorgeous, tempting man. That is the guise Himself wore, that of temptation.

"I am your Nikolaus Drake!" Himself announced gleefully. He tripped over to Ravin, and when he tried to wrangle her into an embrace, she kneed him in the gut. He took the punch with little dissuasion. "Now, is that any way to treat your lover?"

"You sick bastard!"

"That's me. Hee, hee. You've fallen for a bloodsucker, you idiot witch."

"Have not!"

"Then why my ugly costume this day? Oh, now this explains the bite mark on your ass." He smirked at Nikolaus's reflection in the mirror. "Those dark eyes. So…violent."

"They're not violent, they're caring—oh! I suppose horns and a pitchfork are more your style?"

"A ridiculous commercial image." The figment of Nikolaus dusted at nonexistent lint on his shoulder. He wore Nikolaus's gray jersey shirt and snug-fitted black jeans. He even stood at a lanky tilt as Nikolaus did. "You want to see my true self?"

"Been there, done that. Not interested in replaying the video."

Ravin had seen Himself in all his wicked glory once at the turn of the twentieth century. It was not a vision she cared to stomach again, because the death of a cherished friend accompanied that return to memory.

"What are you here for? Haven't you enough souls to torture that you can manage time away for me?"

"Sweetness, you wound me. Torture is not my forte." Himself plopped onto the sofa, putting his legs—Nikolaus's long, muscled legs—onto the coffee table and stretched his arms across the couch back. "I prefer temptation, you should know that."

"Don't do that!" Ravin stalked into the kitchen to avoid the sight. The perfectly appealing, smolderingly sensual visage of a man she wanted to climb onto and ride into the night.

She'd kissed the devil! And he'd called her sweetness. That was just wrong.

"Give us a kiss," Himself called, pursing Nikolaus's mouth. "And then we'll discuss business."

Ravin slammed her arms over her chest. Nikolaus sat on her couch, his eyes closed and his lips pursed in wait of her surrender.

A momentary uncertainty coaxed her one step forward.

It's Nikolaus. *Your lover. You can't get enough of the man's kisses, his masculine smell, that easy manner he has of bringing you to orgasm with but a few flicks of his fingers...*

Nikolaus opened his eyes. An overlarge grin appeared where Ravin usually saw a charming smile. The bastard's eyes gleamed with twisted anticipation.

"Damn you." She settled to a crouch, her back to the side of the kitchen counter, and cast her best glower at the devil. "What do you want?"

"No kisses?"

"You've not enough mints in hell to mask your brimstone breath."

"Catty."

"Horrified."

"Really? Excellent!" he declared with a triumphant clap of hands. "My work is such a joy. The mortals have got it all wrong, you know. I'm not all about doom and gloom. It's the shadows between the doom and the gloom that I so enjoy. Temptation. Disappointment. Struggle. Horrific wonder. Dismay."

"Yes, yes, we are so proud for you. To the point, please?"

"Ah, yes, to business." He leaned forward and tapped Nikolaus's strong fingers upon the coffee table. "Obligation number three."

About time. And then she was out of this bastard's radar for good. One soul returned to its owner. At least until true death arrived.

Ravin had no misgivings that Hell would be her final destination. Bring it on. Maybe then she could face those she had murdered—no, *don't think about it*. She'd avoid Hell as long as possible—with soul intact.

She stood and bent at the waist, propping her palms on her knees. "I still haven't gotten credit for redoing number two."

"Right, then." Himself-as-Nikolaus made a sweeping gesture with his arm.

Pain immersed Ravin in a dizzy whirr. She was flung bodily through the air, and landed at the base of the stainless-steel fridge, her back taking the brunt. Icy prickles radiated up and down her spine. But that pain was nothing to the burn scouring her ribs. Flesh parted and sizzled, the stench of burning witch smacked her with a foreboding punch.

Punishment for her sins. For loaning out her soul. For murdering innocents. A punishment she would take and cry to the heavens so the angels would know her voice and fear her for all the right reasons.

And it was done. She fell forward, landing on the floor on all fours, panting against the pain, but managing to smile, because she knew she'd received a slash across the second tally mark.

"Happy?" Himself inquired gleefully.

"You know it."

She settled backward and fitted herself against the fridge, propping her elbows on her knees. Wheezing, she drew in oxygen, restoring balance to her dizzied senses.

Balance. It was all about bringing stability back to her life. One obligation to go, and then Ravin Crosse was on the way to that goal.

"So what's the final job?"

"You're going to love this one," Himself said, with a wink and a glide of his palm over Nikolaus's long glossy hair.

And Ravin knew, without doubt, that she would not like a single thing about obligation number three.

"You know of Truvin Stone?"

"Of course. Interim leader of tribe Kila while its former leader—"

"The indomitable—and rather sexy, if I do say so myself— Nikolaus Drake."

"—er, takes a break to recover—"

"From your devious handiwork. Such a twisted mess your world has become, Ravianna Crosse."

"Don't call me that."

"Just so. Though…" He danced over to the mirror again and tore aside the collar of Nikolaus's shirt to study what lay beneath. "I must say the flesh shows little sign of damage. Shall I account that to blood sex magic?"

"What about Truvin?" she insisted hotly. No way was Himself going to get any more out of her about what went on behind closed doors—albeit broken, wardless doors—with Nikolaus Drake.

"Oh, nothing. Just wondered if you knew Stone."

Ravin lifted a brow and grit her teeth. "The obligation?"

"I do adore the direction Mr. Stone has taken tribe Kila.

They've become more like the animals their kind are, don't you agree?"

Of course she agreed. Vampires. Animals. Same thing. Except Nikolaus. That man provided a perfect example of not succumbing to societal expectations.

"You don't want Nikolaus to return to the leadership?" she wondered.

"Do you?"

Now, that was a question she hadn't seen coming. Ravin considered all that she wanted, and all that she could not control.

If Nikolaus did return to Kila in his present bespelled state, it could prove disastrous for the vampire leader. His tribe mates would smell the witch on Nikolaus and they would *know*. And phoenix or not, Ravin wasn't sure how well the tribe would receive a witch lover. She could guess. The result would be violent, aggressive. He would not survive. And if he did, he would be ostracized.

The kicker would be if the spell *were* broken before Nikolaus returned. Because she wouldn't be around to care one way or another for what became of him—the vampire would finish what he'd set out to do—kill the witch.

Did she believe that is what would happen? She had to at least consider it.

On the other hand, if Nikolaus did return and successfully took over leadership, she suspected a war between Nikolaus and Truvin would ignite. Such a clash could only assist her in reducing the vampire numbers.

Do you want them reduced now?

"I have no opinion," she offered.

"That's not true," Himself argued. "You have a world of angst exploding inside that delightfully plump bosom."

"Eyes off my body, asshole."

"Difficult not to notice something that's always *there*. Anyway!" Himself clapped so loudly Ravin winced at the clobbering to her eardrums.

He picked up a stray blood bullet from the floor, inspected it, and then crushed the glass. Ravin's blood dripped over his fingers—Nikolaus's fingers.

Himself licked the crimson liquid languorously. When he looked to her, blood painted Nikolaus's lips. "Girl, you do like to play with fire. I like that about you. You're unpredictable. Falling in love with a vampire?"

"I have not."

"Have, too." He stood and filled the space before her without so much as a step forward. Nikolaus's dark eyes peered deep into her absent soul. His hands bracketed her face, drawing her to stand in a ghostly sinuous move that orchestrated her limbs without her volition.

He leaned in, ready to kiss. "Tell me you love me, Ravin. Be true. No one is ever true nowadays. Surprise me with some honesty."

He even smelled like Nikolaus. Dark leather and raw aggression, sweetened with desire. And touched like him, gently, so gently his fingertips caressed her jaw.

Ravin eased forward, touching the man's mouth with her parted lips. "I do," she whispered. "I am true to you, Nikolaus."

He kissed her away from the world. Into herself she coiled and once there, she spread out her arms and released it all. So easily he touched that spot that reacted with a pleasurable scream.

Ravin gasped back the climax before it could completely be born. Fleetingly, she realized her faux pas. Too late. Hot moisture between her thighs. Orgasm rushed through her. She gripped Nikolaus's shoulders and cried out.

With but a kiss. From the darkest evil to ever touch her soul.

"That was spectacular, sweetness." He patted her on the

head even as the shudders softened in her limbs and she began to cringe away from Himself. "Good little naughty girl. You shall be a treat."

"I…" Loose and melty, her limbs would not support her. Ravin clutched the granite countertop, falling forward onto it.

Oh, wretched witch. To what further depths will you descend? Can you plunge any deeper? Forget balance, you need to surface and paddle for your life.

Sinking to the floor, Ravin spread her legs before her and slammed her head against the wood counter. "What's the damn obligation?"

Himself preened the sleeves of Nikolaus's shirt. "I want your firstborn."

"What?"

"You heard me. Firstborn. It's mine, no matter the sex, though I prefer a boy."

Yes, she had heard him. What sort of ridiculous obligation was that?

"Are you nuts? This is not medieval times. People don't promise their firstborn to the devil anymore."

"How do you know?"

"They do?"

"Happens all the time. Please, take my baby in exchange for more of that lovely drug that will destroy my life. What do they call it? Meth! There are times I simply must refuse, because who needs another rug rat to corrupt? Oh, not that I physically take the child. I leave the social services to that. But it's all the same.

"There are only so many souls to be darkened, battered and abused. And there is the whole equilibrium thing. I can't have them all. The world would be a bore without a healthy balance of good and evil, corrupt and pious, et cetera, et cetera."

"But my firstborn? That's not even an obligation, it's a…

Sorry, can't do it. I don't want kids. And even if I did want them, I'd have to find…"

"The right one? If that's how you want to play it. Doesn't matter to me how you go about getting things done. Nor is time of concern."

"But it is to me. I want to get you off my chest!"

"Such a lovely one it is. Have I mentioned that?"

Ravin growled and stomped across the room. "I want my soul back!"

"You know the rules."

"Give me something different to do."

"'Fraid not. I want your firstborn. And, since you're not the motherly sort, you'll have no problem handing over a child. It'll be such a joy to see what results from a witch and a vampire. I wait with anticipation!"

Have a baby with Nikolaus? The thought intrigued more than it should. Ravin quickly looked away from the image of her lover as he bent and caught her silent stare.

"You're thinking about it already," Himself stated with a gleeful glint to his sapphire eyes. "Perfect!"

Her firstborn. But when she really thought on it… There had been the miscarriage. So technically… Hmm…

"I do that for you, and my debt is paid?"

"Third slash mark is yours. Now, don't overthink it. And like I said, I've all the time in the world. But I don't think I'll need so much as you believe. Ta!"

The air held a mist of brimstone. The devil had left.

She had allowed the devil to bring her to… Raven raced to the kitchen sink, and her stomach gave up the bile.

Chapter 19

Nikolaus walked to the Cue restaurant just down the street from his building. No one could miss the sensuously curved lapis lazuli Guthrie Theater that curved along the Mississippi's shore.

When Nikolaus had first met Truvin, the ancient vampire—created in the eighteenth century—was tired of doing things on his own. He had seen the world many times over, had grown weary of all it offered, and felt a compulsion to create family. To put down roots and invite others into his world.

Nikolaus had immediately taken to the suave man-about-the-world. They both enjoyed fine wine, expensive toys such as cars and suits, and discussing the evolution of science and, yes, gorgeous women. Though he'd had to overlook the man's apparent disregard for mortal life, Nikolaus had firmly laid down Kila's rules—that no one in the tribe killed or needed to kill.

Truvin had reluctantly left behind his bloodthirsty ways, but Nikolaus had seen an immediate change in the man.

He'd made him his right-hand man after a surprise attack by wolves had found Truvin and Nikolaus cornered. The elder vampire was strong and fearless. He'd had his throat ripped open by a wolf, and yet had stood back to back with Nikolaus, fighting until the remaining wolf had scampered away, its tail between its legs. Werewolves did not frequent the metro areas, but when they did, it was as a pack and on a quest for blood.

The fight had gleamed in Truvin's eyes, invigorating him, and Nikolaus knew then he'd always have to keep an eye on the vampire, lest he slip into his old ways.

And yet, Nikolaus would preach to no man. If Kila was not the right place for Truvin, if he found it too restrictive, then he could leave any time. But he had not.

The restaurant was crowded, and Truvin was already seated at a table near a floor-to-ceiling curved window that looked out over the sidewalk. With a welcome slap of handshake the two vampires then sat quietly, reading the menus, then ordering immediately. They were each summing the other up. It was an expected ritual.

Nikolaus suggested a bottle of pinot gris, which was served at the perfect temperature, not too chilled, not lukewarm.

"You're looking good," Truvin said after the waiter had left them alone. "I expected to see a scarred shell of the man you once were."

"Doesn't Gabriel keep you updated?"

Resting with a casual shrug against the chair back, Truvin drank his wine. "He's most faithful to you. I watch him carefully. Doesn't like to follow the tribe, and usually stays away when we're out stalking butterflies."

Butterflies are what Truvin termed his gorgeous victims. Nikolaus had never warmed to the euphemism.

"Gabriel avoids confrontation. Nothing wrong with that."

"He's become quite bold recently."

Nikolaus recalled watching Gabriel suffer the *danse macabre*. Bold, indeed.

The waiter returned to take their menus after they politely declined a meal.

Distracted by two particular women at the blue glass–tiled bar, Nikolaus studied them. Both slid interested glances over to his table. Lipstick-kissed wineglasses tilted back more than he felt they should be drinking. But they were gorgeous and had legs that wouldn't stop. Spiky black high heels were one of his weaknesses. Interesting to find them at the subdued theater. Couldn't be here for a play.

"Gabriel tells me of your intention to return to the tribe this weekend," Truvin said. "We welcome you, of course. It has been a long time."

"You'll welcome me?" Not unexpected, but to judge Truvin's tone, not completely honest, either. "But not as the leader."

A sigh lifted Truvin's broad shoulders. The suit must have set him back several thousand, though Nikolaus had stopped concerning himself with brand names after his medical career had tanked.

Nikolaus noted the women whispering to each other. One broke into an open-mouthed sigh at the sight of Truvin splaying his fingers back through his short thick hair.

"Is it fair," Truvin began, "that you deem to merely step back into a role you abandoned?"

"Abandoned? I had no choice!" Checking his voice, Nikolaus swallowed the remainder of his wine, then poured another full glass. Why he was allowing Truvin to strum him like this was beyond him. "I touched death. My heart had stopped beating, I didn't abandon a thing; I was given no choice."

And there—he'd just played hypocrite to his own convictions, after trying to convince Ravin that everyone had a choice.

"Yes, a phoenix," Truvin presented wondrously.

And what did Truvin know of the phoenix legend? He had been on this earth two centuries; surely he had met one? He could hold knowledge that Nikolaus craved.

It didn't feel right to ask. Weak.

"Certainly, you had no choice. And without a leader to watch over the flock, I stepped in."

"It was a moment you dreamed of, Stone. You were the first to abandon rank during the attack; don't think I didn't notice that."

Truvin leaned over the table and, measuring the tone of his voice, hissed, "It is every man for himself when a witch attacks. That is an unwritten rule."

"Yes, and…" Nikolaus sighed.

Anger was completely counter-productive at a time like this. Nothing would come of aggression. And Truvin would delight too much in watching him blow his top.

"I don't blame you, Truvin. I'm glad you had the sense to protect yourself. One less notch for the witch's belt. And truly, you were the obvious choice to step up in my absence. You've a certain commanding presence. The tribe members respect you."

It was true, Truvin did command respect. But there were many kinds of respect, twisted and misaligned being just a few of the sort that fit Stone to a T.

"I will happily hand over the reins to you," Truvin announced, "if you can prove yourself fit and able, my friend."

"If?"

"Do you expect anything less? If you were in my position, I should demand the same caution. I can't, as a leader, step back and hand over control to one unworthy, or physically incapable—"

"What means of proof do you require? An Olympic trial of sorts to test my strength?"

Tracing the stem of the wine goblet, Truvin said, "There

won't be tests. I must know you are mentally capable of leading my men—"

To have his intellect challenged stung far more than a physical boast of prowess and strength.

"I am capable, and I will lead *my* men. But trust me when I say they will not continue to follow the path you have taken them on. Why have you done it, Truvin? You know I prided myself on Kila's peacefulness. We do not need to kill," he stressed, then checked his voice.

The women at the bar had left. The table next to the two of them was content on laughing over the play they'd just seen. All about them, the world lived, loved and laughed, oblivious to the dangers lurking in their presence.

"I understand," Nikolaus added. "You have been on this earth a long time."

"And don't forget that, youngling," Truvin sneered. "Born in the eighteenth century, and changed on my twenty-fifth birthday. I have seen it all. War, plague, injustice. Greed, desire and the fall of humanity to material wealth. What right have you to command me to do anything?"

"Don't forget, you joined Kila voluntarily. No one forced you. You knew what we were like then, and agreed to the terms we offered in exchange for family."

"Yes, and you knew what I was like. But I've come to learn family is vastly overrated. I have endured for years, living your ridiculous rules—"

"It is not ridiculous to value human life!"

Both men sat back in their chairs as the waiter appeared. Truvin ordered another bottle of the two-hundred-and-fifty-dollar wine.

Nikolaus glanced to the potential butterflies, lingering at the front of the restaurant. Flutter away, he thought. He could influence them from here, subtly persuade their compliance—

"I do adore you when you have the tribe staring up at you as if you were a god."

Nikolaus pressed back in his chair.

"*I* feel you are a god," the elder vampire offered. "But I've never had religion, as you well know."

Yes, and the glint of the gold cross at Truvin's neck was a defiant warning to all the baptized vampires who would challenge his lack of belief.

"I don't know how to conform," Truvin continued. "It's so tight. It itches."

Many times Nikolaus had considered that Truvin might have already touched madness. He certainly killed often enough, and those kills were tainted by the *danse macabre.* How many nightmares could a vampire live through before madness altered him?

Outside, the moon was visible between two buildings, and just above the river, which flowed behind the theater. Was she at home looking at the same moon right now? His lover.

I love her so much.

But you hate her.

"We are of a particular nature," Truvin said around a swallow of wine, "that requires the sort of extracurricular activities the tribe engages in."

Nikolaus could but shake his head at the inane explanation to stalking a victim and then killing him for no reason other than partaking of a long deadly drink. Truvin had once explained such a deadly kiss eliminated the need to worry over creating another vampire. Ridiculous. Self-control was all that was required.

"It's not that I desire control," Truvin added.

"I believe that." And for some reason, he did.

The waiter reappeared with the wine, and a business card, which he dutifully explained was from the two ladies by the door.

Truvin spun about to spy the women, who stood at the doorway, waving. "They're leaving?" he asked the waiter.

"Headed to the gift shop, I've been informed," the waiter offered with a knowing grin. "Said they'd be around for another half an hour."

"Thanks." Truvin took the card and tucked it into his coat pocket. He nodded to the girls.

"So, let's wrap this up, shall we?" Truvin poured another full goblet of wine. "We've dessert waiting for us after all."

"You can have them," Nikolaus said. "I'm not into blondes."

"Since when?"

"Since…just take them."

"You look the same, Nikolaus, but you're not." Truvin tilted his head, studying him over the wine goblet. "Gabriel tells me you killed the witch who did this to you?"

"Yes." The answer came easily. And Nikolaus maintained eye contact with Truvin.

"Then we should celebrate your kill upon your return. One less witch walking the earth is a day to rejoice. Difficult to take out?"

"Nothing a little fire couldn't handle." The one method to kill a witch. If he'd said anything else, Truvin might suspect.

"I would have loved to hear her death screams."

"That's the difference between you and me, Stone. You live for the dread in your victim's eyes, and the kill spilled all over your pristine thousand dollar suits."

"Armani," he added. "This one set me back a couple thousand."

Nikolaus shook his head at the waste. Not the material waste, but the manner in which Truvin brushed off the lost life of the innocent. "I prefer to walk away, keeping my soul as clean as possible."

"You're so high and mighty. We're all headed to hell in our final days. Don't pretend you're going anywhere higher."

"I agree. But I'm tainted enough by this condition, why make it any worse?"

"Condition? Ha! You've much to learn, Drake. And so many centuries in which to learn it. If you survive that long." He touched the cross at his neck.

Nikolaus did not fear the holy, though there were times he wondered what his parents had stolen from his soul by not allowing him to learn the ways of the church. To at least offer the option. He'd once believed science ruled, until he'd been given the God-like power to save lives—and had learned he was unworthy. There was only one creator with the power to give and take life.

"There's something utterly wrong about you." Truvin leaned forward, studying Nikolaus. The man's eyes were an indeterminate smear of gray and amber and blue. Eerie. But capable of disguising the blood lust when on the hunt. "I will figure it."

"I have survived death," Nikolaus offered. "That right there is utterly wrong." He swallowed the last of his wine and gestured toward the door, in hopes of distracting Truvin's inspection. "You shouldn't delay."

"Yes. I suppose." He signed the bill and grabbed the wine bottle, still half full. Standing, he offered his hand to Nikolaus. "I'll be seeing you soon, before the entire tribe, then?"

Nikolaus stood and shook the vampire's hand. The shimmer scurried up his arm and burst through his system, a subtle but tingling sensation that always alerted to another of his kind. The only real way to know another vampire was by touching them. No Sight granted by Himself would ever make it easy to recognize another.

"Will you step down gracefully?" Nikolaus asked.

"Will you prove your worth to the tribe?"

"I will."

"Then I shall step down. No questions. No challenges. I give you my word. You sure you don't want to share dessert? There are two of them. And my net is large."

"I'm fine. Thanks for the meal."

"Sure." Truvin stood and detoured for the men's room.

So Nikolaus headed out to the gift shop. He sinuously gained the first woman, sliding his persuasion into her mind before she could even realize he stood too close to be put off by her strong perfume.

Go home. You are tired.

And he left as quickly as he'd entered.

Nikolaus stood at the curb, taking in the night air. He hadn't stopped at the valet stand so Truvin guessed he walked. He knew Drake lived somewhere in the area, but Nikolaus was cleverly cautious to keep his address private.

When he'd emerged from the men's room, Truvin had been disappointed, but a little suspicious, seeing the women no longer lingered. Had to have been Drake's doing.

Truvin snapped open his cell phone and contacted Zak, one of the newer Kila recruits. "Follow Drake home. Report back to me."

Now Truvin dialed his backup man, whom he'd positioned without Zak's knowledge. "Follow the new guy. He's on Drake. I'm sure he'll be discovered. Don't let Drake see you."

Chapter 20

He hadn't expected Truvin to put a man on him, but when Nikolaus sighted the tail, he immediately changed his direction. Instead of walking home and having Jake drive him to Ravin's place, he detoured for the river. From there, he followed the river's edge a few miles north.

He had no intention of spending the night alone.

He needed to feel Ravin's warmth, the safety of her arms, to renew and strengthen—for his greatest challenge yet.

Ravin strode out of the bathroom, still moist from the shower, and dug through her dresser drawer. She pulled up a pair of panties and tugged a sheer pink camisole over her head. Granted, pink was not one of her colors, but she grabbed it for some inexplicable reason. It was…girlie. And that felt all right.

Since Himself had left she'd been doing a good bit of muddling. And muttering. And cursing. And sighing.

What a ridiculous obligation. It wasn't even an obligation. More like a sacrifice. She shuddered to imagine what the devil could do with a newborn. Why even consider when the decision was already made? She wasn't mother material. Having a baby was out of the question.

One soul—lost forever.

And yet, while she'd stood under the hot shower stream, she'd begun to imagine a couple, the mother holding a baby in her arms, while the father looked on proudly. She and Nikolaus. And baby makes three.

It was crazy. "Not as crazy as it should be," she muttered, pacing out to the living room.

It was late. No lights were on in her apartment, so she didn't balk to stand before the window and look down over the city. There wasn't much to see on this end of Washington Avenue. She lived on the edge of all the downtown action, though the pink neon facade of the strip joint Déjà Vu did flash at the edge of her periphery.

A baby?

Ravin knew she could get pregnant. She had never taken the pill. She'd learned a contraceptive spell centuries ago, and when invoked once a month, it kept a witch from becoming pregnant. It had worked every month she had used it—but sometimes she forgot.

She wanted her soul back. Balance could never be achieved otherwise.

And what of it? Could she have a baby and give it up? She'd meant it when she'd said she wasn't mother material. For as long she'd lived—alone and focused as a slayer—she had never once stopped to consider making room for a baby, both physically and emotionally.

Emotions. They took so much out of a person. It was difficult enough dealing with a vampire who loved her. It was as if she had to…love him back. And that took work. It didn't come naturally.

Maybe.

If it hadn't come naturally she certainly would not be returning the love to a vampire, Ravin instinctually knew that.

"So are you in love, then, you crazy witch?"

Stretching up an arm along the sill, Ravin turned her side to the window and closed her eyes.

Yeah, it felt good. Being loved by a man. And it didn't matter what he was, only how he treated her. Nikolaus was not your average vampire. And Ravin was thankful for that.

So she had fallen. And she couldn't set aside the idea of spending more time with Nikolaus, maybe enough time to have a child.

But a child born of love was not something she could even conceive of handing over to Himself. And she could imagine Nikolaus's reaction should he learn the future of his child. "Hey, honey, I'm pregnant." "Oh, sweetness, I love you." "Great. We'll be sending it to hell instead of baptizing it. You cool with that?"

"Can't do it with him. Just…can't hurt him that way."

But it needed to be done. Unless… She had wondered about the miscarriage. Officially, that pregnancy could be counted as her firstborn.

"Gotta think on this. There must be some way…"

"Some way to what?"

Ravin spun around to find Nikolaus standing ten feet from her. He looked positively vogue, having exchanged his leathers for stylish black trousers, with pristine white shirt lapels peeking out above the buttoned suit coat.

"How do you do that? You always enter my house without a sound, and without alerting my wards."

"You want me to go back and knock? Do the whole 'permission to enter' thing?"

"No. Come here."

It felt so good wrapped against Nikolaus's hard frame. Loved. Safe.

Family. She couldn't stop thinking about it. It would be so good.

"Why the suit?"

"I had a meeting with Truvin. It was at a nice restaurant, and I didn't want to attract attention. So what were you thinking about just now?" he whispered. "It looked like you were daydreaming. You know you shouldn't stand in the window like that. I don't like rivals."

"They can't see in."

"I could see perfectly fine as I approached from the end of the block."

"You're kidding me. Oh, now I am embarrassed."

"I didn't think you could be embarrassed."

"I think I'm—" she touched his jaw, tracing the smooth skin he must have shaved to go along with the not-drawing-attention costume "—softening. Does that sound strange?"

"Miss Vampire Slayer in pink panties soft? Nah. I wager you've an arsenal of blood bullets prepared for your next patrol."

"I do not. I couldn't go out last time. I didn't want to. Nikolaus, you've changed me."

"I didn't try to."

"I know. And that's the strange thing. It just happened. I keep thinking about what you said about me making the entire vampire nation suffer for my parents' deaths. I don't want to be hard anymore. I want to step back and start thinking. I want to return to the light."

"Sounds good to me, sweetness." He led her into the bedroom and tugged off his suit coat. Sitting on the bed, he swept an arm around her waist, tugging her onto him. "Ravin, these past days have been all good. I wouldn't have had it any other way. I know when I say I love you that I mean it."

She began to work on the pearl buttons at his neck. "Even beyond the spell?"

"Yes."

"You can't know that."

"Yes, I can. I feel it in my heart." Clasping her hand, he stopped her halfway down the shirt. "It's like nothing I've ever known before."

"Even when you had a fiancée?"

"Even then."

"But I thought you said the brain is tricky? Don't abandon logic on me now, Nikolaus. You're not supposed to like my kind."

"That's spin bullshit manufactured by a bunch of ancient witches and vampires."

"Yeah, well…you *are* a vampire."

"You hate us that much?"

"Nikolaus." She crawled onto his lap and kissed him. "Truth?"

Something devastating glimmered in her eyes. So obvious, Nikolaus felt the prick to his own heart. "Go ahead."

"I hate the vampire that is you." Another kiss bruised his mouth the way he liked it. Hard and urgent. "But…" Her eyes swept back up to his. "I admire the man that you are. You're kind and generous. You seek peace. It confuses me. Twists my morals and makes me want to punch something."

He lifted her fist. Yes, it was tight and ready to punch. "Did you just say, in some roundabout way, that you love me?"

She shook her head, defeated and yet glowing with honesty. "I—don't push, Nikolaus. It's just me and you right now. And I plan on taking all the kisses, sex and love I can get from you before you burn me at the stake."

"I will never hurt you, Ravin, I promise you."

"Nikolaus Drake can make that promise. But the vampire, the man who desires to once again lead Kila, won't honor that promise. It is the way of the world, and I accept that."

She snuggled against his chest, drawing up her knees and gliding a palm through his dark hair. "I've always known I'd die at the hands of those who destroyed my family. I just never thought it would be my lover who delivered the killing spark."

"Don't say things like that. I mean it. Ravin, I could spend the rest of my days with you."

And have children?

Closing her eyes, Ravin rolled off Nikolaus and spread her arms across the bed. "You're talking as if you're whipped."

"Completely."

"That's not a good thing."

"Shut up and kiss me, witch."

"You think so, eh?"

She knelt over him, placing a knee to either side of his hips, and glided a palm up her stomach. Drawing up the pink camisole exposed the underside of her breasts. She liked the way he looked at her. Worshipful. Hungry. As if she were the only woman on the earth, and not a witch, at that.

In fact, the whole scenario was just so alien that it turned her on. When had she ever sat upon the lap of a man in a suit, looking so rich and business-like? He appeared the furthest thing from a vampire. The closest thing to a normal life of domesticity she'd ever touched.

"Higher," Nikolaus said. "Let me see it all."

The glide of silk over her hard nipples curled a wicked grin onto her face. Displaying herself, she reveled in the way such teasing exposure made her feel. Sexy. Free of her darkest worries. She'd seduced men before, but always with an ulterior motive in mind—getting her own pleasure.

This time she'd change the goal a bit.

"Oh, no," she said. "Don't touch, Nikolaus."

"You playing hard-to-get tonight?" He leaned back on his elbows. A tilt of his head signaled he was ready for this play. "Then give me a show, sweetness. Make not touching worth it."

"You're on."

She licked her fingertips then swirled them over a nipple. Her nerve endings reacted with a shiver that shimmied all the way down to her groin. Tossing back her head, Ravin slid her hand down her stomach and under the lacy band of her panties. She could satisfy herself anytime, but turning on her lover was all she was about right now.

Grinding her hips over Nikolaus's erection filled the room with his tight but appreciative moan.

"Don't know if I can *not* touch," he murmured.

"I thought you liked control? Show me just how in control you can be, lover."

"A challenge, eh? All right, then. Let me see you touch yourself. Pull down your panties."

She took directions, slowly guiding the pink silk lower.

"Yes, nice and slow, that's how I like it."

"I thought you liked it rough?"

"That's good, too."

Shifting her hips forward, she pressed her mons against her fingers. Already wet and hot, she slid a finger up and down over the exquisite core of her being. The back of her hand rubbed Nikolaus's cock through the trousers. She liked the tease.

She liked the power that held her lover captivated, his eyes half lidded as he focused on her journey to release.

"Slower, sweetness. Make it last."

"Too late," she murmured.

It didn't take long to reach orgasm with a sexy man staring

her down. Throwing back her head, she clutched at his trousers, wishing they would just tear off. She sprawled upon him, kissing his neck and tracing her finger across his lips so he could taste her.

"Now I get to watch you," she whispered.

"Deal."

"Since I did get dressed for the occasion," Nikolaus said as he retrieved his shirt from the floor, "maybe you'd dress up for me?"

"You didn't dress for me tonight, you said it was for some other vampire."

"Yeah, but it's not often I do the suit thing. You got a pretty dress? Maybe we could go dancing."

"You're not serious."

"You don't dance?"

"Not in front of people. Besides, it's too late. All the bars are closed."

"I'd never bring you into a dark, smoky bar." He slid an arm through the dress shirt sleeve. "How about we make it something special. You got roof access?"

Intrigued, Ravin curled forward to distract him from buttoning the shirt. "I do."

"I'll give you an hour while I run out for some champagne. Meet you up top for a dance, then?"

The idea, silly as it sounded, was the best offer Ravin had had…ever.

"An hour," she said. "I'll be waiting, lover."

Gabriel stood between two new members of tribe Kila. They looked deliberately tough, with punked-out attitudes and nose rings, along with studded leather gloves and biker boots.

Before him, and leaning against a black granite office desk, which contained records and files for the tribes' possessions, Truvin Stone stood, arms crossed over his chest. The man had instilled a certain fear in the tribe members.

He must know. About her.

"You wanted to see me?" Gabriel asked. He couldn't help but feel the hairs on the back of his neck poke out. Something wasn't right. Why the two on either side of him?

"I need you to take a message to Nikolaus Drake."

Maybe he doesn't know.

"Didn't you see him tonight?"

"I did. A few hours ago. The wine was exquisite and the women were—well, that's of no import. But I've received some disturbing news about our former leader. News that will not allow me to accept him back into the fold with open arms."

"He's good for Kila," Gabriel insisted. "He's a sense of decency that—" *You don't have* was not spoken.

And why not? Was he so afraid of this bastard that he feared his backlash?

"That decent vampire," Truvin said slowly and succinctly, "has lied to you and to all of us."

"He doesn't lie."

"I know differently. You will return to him with this message." Truvin took a step forward.

Gabriel sensed the danger, could feel it in his veins and smell it stalking closer. He fisted his hands, but the men to his sides clasped his arms. He struggled. They held firm.

Truvin lifted a cross before him. The solid gold piece was six inches long and about four inches wide. Before Gabriel could beg mercy he felt the burn of the holy object eat through his flesh as Truvin pressed it high on his chest.

"Go with blessings, and whatever the rest of that holy crap is." Truvin grinned widely.

Gabriel dropped to the floor and passed out.

* * *

He would return soon.

Ravin dug to the back of her closet. She knew she owned a dress. It had been a long time since she'd worn it, and it hadn't been taken out since she'd moved to Minneapolis.

Half buried in her closet, and surrounded by the musty scent of leather—she really did own too much leather—she groped toward the back. Something soft shivered across her wrist. She grabbed the fabric and it fell off the hanger. Pulling it out, she stroked the red silk across her cheek.

A giddy giggle escaped.

Ravin twirled and landed on the bed, kicking up her feet and landing with the red silk dress splayed across her belly.

He made her feel beautiful. And tonight she wanted to be beautiful for him. It was so silly, she laughed again.

Chapter 21

A gentle mist glittered black diamonds across the tar rooftop. It was well into early morning, and the streets below were quiet. A police siren wailed in the distance, but here, time had stopped.

Red silk drifted across Ravin's body, clinging at her breasts and floating near her knees. This feeling of utter femininity lightened her, made her forget to worry about the darkness in her life.

All she wanted to do was revel in the feel of the soft silk as it shimmered across her flesh. And to bask in the admiration coming from her lover's eyes.

Nikolaus had found a red rosebud for his suit lapel. Swoonworthy, his look. And Ravin had swooned right into his arms.

Now they stood at the center of the rooftop, swaying to music they heard only in their heads. A naive dance of testing one against the other. Did he wish to move? She couldn't resist the sway. So long as he held her it didn't matter if they moved or stood still until the sun rose.

Scratch that. She'd be sure to get her lover inside before the first ray of light burst across the horizon. This phoenix had survived much, but it was questionable whether or not sunlight was still his enemy.

Could he survive her?

Once already Nikolaus had risen from the wake of her destruction. And while Ravin believed him when he declared his love toward her, she knew that was false. *It had to be.* He was fighting another of her cruel tricks. Which is why she'd chosen not to tell him about the third obligation.

Have Nikolaus's baby? She could go there.

But, she must not.

Maybe?

Never.

And yet, it was the only thing that would set her soul free. So what to do?

Count on the loophole. Said loophole being that her miscarriage was actually her firstborn.

And, not give it another thought, at least for tonight. Tonight she wanted to concentrate exclusively on her and Nikolaus.

"Can you fly?" he suddenly whispered. Breaking the tight hold, Nikolaus led her to the roof edge by one hand. There the cinder blocks built up to shin level formed a half-foot-high precipice around the rooftop. "I've never known if witches can fly on their own, or if they need a broomstick."

"We do not do broomsticks." Ravin hugged him from behind. The breeze listed Nikolaus's mist-tipped hair across her lips. "But with the proper training we can fly. One has to master the element of air first. Unfortunately, I've only mastered earth and water."

"Difficult studies?"

"Yes. Earth magic took me almost a century to master. But it's the most valuable and necessary. A witch will never starve if she masters the earth and all the riches it gives up from a few seeds pressed into soil."

"So you control the earth? Can you make an earthquake?"

"That's wizard stuff. I can feed a village from a single field with a touch of magic. I can move the earth to dig a foundation or rescue a child from a deep well. But nothing so spectacular as earthquakes."

"And water?"

"Water was easy, and another valuable skill, for a witch who masters water need never fear a drowning chair."

She caught his wince.

"Obviously some of the craft has been around for ages. Though there are still witch finders out there, and they do use a more diabolical form of the chair."

"Can you make the rain fall?"

She splayed out her palm to catch the tickling mist. "I can redirect it." And with a swish of her hand she sent the mist to the edge of the roof, leaving them surrounded by a shimmery fall of rain—yet not on them.

"Nice trick. But I still want to see you fly."

"Air is a tricky skill. Flying isn't necessary for survival, and I have only ever focused on the necessities."

"I wish I could fly you to the moon." Nikolaus stepped up onto the cinder-block ledge. Four stories below car headlights rushed by en route to Saturday night haunts. A precarious balance swayed him unevenly until he found his center and dropped his arms, for he didn't need to thrust them out. "I would, you know."

"I believe it."

Ravin crossed her arms and looked up to the vampire backlit by the moonlight. Long black hair rippled in the breeze. He sniffed the air. Always smelling, taking in the scent of the world. He was cerebral, feral and exquisite. A god of some mythical legend, his imposing frame and build could send mere mortals screaming. All *without* a single flash of fang. If fang were revealed, she felt sure chaos would ensue.

She rubbed a palm along her neck. Painful and pleasurable, his kiss.

I could spend forever with this man. And yes, I could have his child.

Stepping up beside her lover, Ravin stretched out her arms and closed her eyes. "I want to fly," she murmured. "It must be incredible, soaring through the clouds."

"Clouds are cold," he said. "But probably a real kick to dart in and out of."

Eyes still closed, Ravin turned to face the street, arms wavering as she tilted side to side.

"Hold my hand," he said.

She did, and began to walk along the brick ledge. Daring to tilt outward, she trusted that he would not let her go. It was innate, the trust. He wouldn't allow her to be hurt. Damn her soul.

It was already damned.

The air breezed over her face and slithered inside her dress where it tickled between her breasts and set her nipples to a tight ruche. The silk skirt rippled out from her legs, giving her a brief death thrill, to stand so boldly defiant of gravity.

"Hold my other hand."

An unspoken dare rang in the clap of their palms. *You want to do this?*

Oh, yeah.

Stepping down onto the roof, Nikolaus leaned backward and used his weight to counterbalance Ravin's tilt. She hung over the street, her hair and clothing listing freely, as if she were a medieval banner declaring one's fealty to a cause. Her cause was bold red love.

From above, the moon beamed a cold caress upon her face. "This is incredible. Do you think the moon will tell?"

"If she does, I'll take a bite out of her."

Ravin laughed and thrust back her head. If she tilted farther, she could see the building across the street once used to sell architectural antiques. The wall of rain just misted her forehead.

The stretch of her limbs felt exhilarating. The utter freedom made her want to begin her air studies. To fly would be awesome, not so unnatural as she'd once thought.

"If you mastered air," Nikolaus said, "and I keep having sex with you, I'd take that air magic into me. I could fly, as well."

"Then I'll start my studies tomorrow," Ravin declared. "So we can fly to the moon together. Nikolaus!"

"What?"

And she did it—she simply reacted. "I love you."

A pulse moved through her system. It was deep and basso and ominous. The feeling of love? Of finally letting go and accepting, come what may?

She'd snatch it, let no one attempt to destroy this moment of happiness.

Once again a pulse quickened her heartbeat, but it felt…bigger, not a simple part of her. In fact, it didn't feel like something she owned at all.

A vibration shuddered through the buildings and street below. It radiated a clear wave across the landscape, moving everything by a fraction, as if the world were suddenly displaced a quarter of an inch.

"What is that?" Still clutching his hands, Ravin looked up and into the eyes of her lover.

Nikolaus stood upon the ledge, his feet to either side of hers. He held her with ease. His eyes had changed.

"Nikolaus?"

"Witch," he growled.

And in the next second, Ravin knew the spell had been broken.

Nikolaus's hands opened up, his fingers sliding free of hers.

Arms flailing out and behind her, Ravin groped for a way to stop the imminent collision of bone to hard sidewalk. Instead, her fingers snagged on Nikolaus's pocket.

And as she screamed silently, her body rushed away from the vampire who crouched above, snarling at her.

Chapter 22

"Soften," Ravin chanted furiously as she felt the gush of chill air beat at her shoulders and hips and thighs. She couldn't see where she was headed. Not a bad thing at a time like this.

"Goddess, protect me."

For a witch without air skills she could not slow her speed or make the air caress her fall. So she'd have to concentrate on the earth, the hard, cement sidewalk.

The earth was ancient, the giver of life, and capable of destruction. It took so many forms....

Cement was formed of powdered limestone and clay and small pebbles before being mixed with water and allowed to harden. She just had to focus on its initial state...and make it deep enough....

Above her the vampire glared down, a dark demon whose eyes captured the moonlight and flashed silver. A vampire who had been forced to play love slave to a witch for weeks.

He waited for the crash. Fragile witch splattered into a mass of blood and guts. Quite a feast for a hungry vampire.

"Dissolve!" she invoked forcefully.

Impact stretched out so long, Ravin wondered if her soul hadn't leapt from her body to stand beside the accident, watching it all.

No, her soul was out on loan.

She could hear the eulogy now. *She was not a perceptive person; could never see the good in people until it was too late. She betrayed the craft by loving a vampire. Bury her deep. Welcome to hell.*

She may be soulless, but she was immortal and it was going to take nothing less than fire to do her in.

Impact flashed a brilliant white aura behind her closed eyelids. She felt every spiking stab of pain. Cartilage crunched. Her brain jumped inside her skull. Lungs compressed. Extremities flailed.

Yet, even as she tallied her injuries, she knew the softening spell had worked. She had hit at full impact, but cement dust spumed about her.

She choked on a throat full of blood. Didn't hurt overmuch to move her arm. A monster of a headache buzzed her brain. Her fingers clasped something like fabric.

Soft Italian wool. His pocket. She'd claimed a piece of her lover.

And her heart ached for his loss more than broken bones ever would.

Above, the vampire leapt. Like a predator descending upon its prey, Nikolaus landed on the pavement with the grace of a cat, and the snarl of a caged lion set free. His long hair streamed out like a death flag, whipping in the wind. Fingers clenched before him. He beat the air and roared.

Gorgeous long fingers. Stroke me gently, lover. Please…

He slapped her face. Impact loosened a stream of copper blood down the back of her throat. But Ravin wasn't about to argue after having survived the fall.

Now, she just had to survive the vampire.

"What have you done to me?" he growled. "Witch! You cursed me to…to…"

He couldn't speak the word—*love*. Oh, she knew his revenge would be horrendous.

Ravin wanted to scream at him. *Yes, kill me now. The fall didn't do it, but you certainly can.* She could but swallow back her own blood. Lungs wheezed and she choked on her breaths.

He gripped her chin roughly. "You will pay for this, witch." A gnash of his fangs preceded a toothy snarl. Never had she seen Nikolaus so animalistic. Her lover, the man who had whispered softly in her ear as he'd made her come over and over between the sheets.

She loved this man—this vampire!

His shoe stomped the dusty ground near her ear. "You had better hide, witch, because I will come for you. And it won't be with flowers in hand or kisses for your foul lips. Do you understand?"

She tried to nod, but a weary darkness toyed with her conscious.

He dropped her head and stepped over her. Ravin lay there on the sidewalk, arms spread out and legs crooked one over the other.

And the vampire strode away. Her lover.

Her destroyer.

Ripping the red rosebud from his lapel, Nikolaus crushed it and flung it aside.

He stalked down the street, away from the sprawled body

of the witch—*a witch!* Just moments ago he'd been standing on the rooftop *dancing* with her.

It hurt him in the chest to consider he'd been romancing her. His breath, it was difficult to find. She'd taken it away. The very witch who had once tried to kill him.

How had she…?

Nikolaus gasped, summoning his breath. It gushed up in a wave, exploding in a choking spasm. She'd bespelled him!

A spell she had claimed not to have purposefully put upon him, but Nikolaus suspected differently. What a way to rub the salt into his already deep wounds.

Sliding a palm along his jacket, he felt the torn fabric. What had she taken away from him? His respect, his integrity. A piece of his soul?

He spat to the side and glanced back over his shoulder. Already, he'd put four blocks distance between them. The witch struggled to sit up.

The urge to race back to her side and break her neck had him clenching his fingers into fists. Easy and quick. The nightmare would be vanquished.

Nikolaus whipped his head back around and focused on the street. The bar crowds had all gone home and no one walked the street.

No, he'd let her suffer. She had to have sustained incredible injuries hitting the rock-hard cement like that. Though, he'd only noticed the thin trickle of blood from between her thick, red lips—

Nikolaus bellowed out a brute wail as his thoughts revisited their dangerous association.

He shivered and sloughed his palm down his opposite arm, pushing off her taint but knowing he could not completely remove her scent. Picking up his pace, he headed home.

The witch must be shucked from his skin, or he would go mad with the tingling remainder of her essence.

She must have lain on the sidewalk behind the apartment building for an hour. The mist had not stopped, and it stirred the cement dust into a foul gray mud.

Not a soul walked by. This alley was quiet, rarely used except by a lost driver who used it to turn around and head back in the right direction. Residents parked in an underground lot—where she kept the chopper—or across the street on a ramp.

As the second hour began to tick by, Ravin rolled to her stomach, wincing at the lingering pain. She did not cry out, for her injuries were slight. Nothing broken, she knew that intuitively. The real damage had been to her heart.

Crunching the wool pocket square into her fist, she drew herself to her knees in the pebble-riddled slush of cement dust and rain, and then stood. Wobbling a bit, she stabilized with a balance of her hands out from her body. The red silk dress was coated with gray mud. Thick wodges ran down her thighs and fell in clods to the ground.

A glance to the rooftop did not spy a gorgeous vampire perched like a stone deity. *An angry warrior*, she thought, *just released from captivity*.

Wistful, she then made her way inside and up to her apartment.

Relief over arriving in her own home, a place that had once provided sanctity, loosened Ravin's tension. A tension she'd not realized tightened her muscles, until her body decided to let go. As her neck relaxed, her head dropped. Knees shaking, she rushed forward, aiming for the bedroom to collapse on the bed.

But when she reached the bedroom, her stomach pushed up its contents, and she veered into the bathroom.

Settling against the bathtub and slinking down to rest her

head against the outer edge of it, she began to cry. Hell, a fall like that would make anyone sick.

But Ravin suspected something far more dreadful to be the cause of her nausea.

Streams of water poured over his head and shoulders. The water bit into him, so hot the temperature, but Nikolaus wanted to ensure no trace of Ravin Crosse remained on his flesh.

Manic with his own rage and struggling against the fact he'd allowed himself to fall to the witch's bidding—when rationally he knew what she was to him—he snarled and intermittently beat a fist against the slick black glass-tile walls.

"What kind of leader falls to such idiocy?" he muttered, and then twisted off the water.

His flesh was red and sensitive to the cool air in the loft. He walked from the shower, dripping across the marble-tiled floor, and stepped onto the hardwood floor in his bedroom, not bothering to dry off with a towel.

Stalking the room from bed to windows, Nikolaus struggled with the imminent resolution of his crimes.

He could not allow the tribe to discover his indiscretions. The evidence threatened—that he was a witch lover—and it was false. It must not be used against him, because he'd been out of his head. Bespelled!

His own brain had tricked him into believing a lie. Pity he'd not been able to excise the spell as if it were a tumor.

He must slay the witch and put this nasty business behind him before returning to Kila. Which meant he had to go after her today. Sunrise neared. Tonight he would act, after the sun had set.

But why not test his indestructibility? Should not a phoenix survive the sun? He had no intention of waiting around when action was required.

Damn the witch. Those dark evil eyes had once focused on him and fired a blood bullet. Soulless brown eyes. He couldn't imagine looking into them again. Peering deep into the centers and feeling the plunge as his heart slipped a little and succumbed to—

"It was a spell!" He cursed his thoughts, and the need to return to that one pesky little word he'd not muttered to a woman for decades. *Love*. "False and premeditated. I was not in control of my senses."

Nikolaus paused over the pile of clothing he'd stripped off upon arriving home. Clothes the witch had touched. He'd have to burn them, for he wanted no evidence of her presence, anywhere.

Squatting, he gathered the pants and shirt and—a scruff of torn fabric slid across his palm. The pocket from the front of his suit trousers was missing.

I save them. They are fond memories of those I have loved.

"She took something from me."

Beyond his pride, beyond his humility and the outer layer of sanity that had been shredded and scuffed decades earlier, rose a vicious, boiling anger.

With a piece of his clothing a witch could stir up a spell, cast an awful curse, or do all number of crazy things to him.

"I have to get that back. I must cleanse her home of my scent and all I have left there. With fire," he said, remembering. "Yes. And then…I will burn the witch at the stake."

So much for the peace-loving Nikolaus Drake. This vampire had been pushed too far and he would not stand for it.

Chapter 23

The mindless drone of the television flickered in and out of Ravin's thoughts. She sat on the couch, legs spread, head bent before her work on the coffee table. Images of army tanks and crying children flashed in her periphery. Some CNN news program.

After mixing up a potion to heal her torn muscles and mend any possible bone fractures, she'd slept the entire morning. This afternoon she felt creaky and her joints twinged with sudden movement, but nothing was broken. A few more days and she'd be at the top of her game. Physically.

Mentally, well that was another story. A book she didn't want to study too closely, because the outcome would make her cry.

Yes, cry. That bastard vampire had done things to her. Made her remember what it had been like to actually care about another person. To know that to open one's heart didn't always bring pain. Happiness had proved a heady elixir, and she had become blind to the past and to the future she'd once believed would play out as had her past.

Everything had changed. The balance she'd thought so tilted toward the dark? Nikolaus had pressed a finger to the scale, bringing it closer to the light. Amazing.

She wanted life to return to what it had been like before she'd blasted Nikolaus Drake with her blood. Easier that way.

Or was it? With the memory of love so fresh, she had to wonder if it was even possible to go back.

She glanced to the television and recognized a familiar face. A gorgeous titian-haired female walked on the arm of a blond rock star at some award ceremony. The announcer reported the singer, Michael Lynsay, and his group The Fallen, were in Los Angeles for a homecoming concert.

"Jane Renan," Ravin muttered, remembering her old and dear friend.

The montage of the singer and his band moved from a practice session to the stage. Raven studied each shot of the singer closely with her new eyes. She could see him. As she had never seen him before.

"She always told me she'd never date a vampire, or a witch."

Though, now she thought on it, if Jane had seen goodness in a vampire, then why couldn't others?

Ravin mouthed the name of the vampire who had declared his love to her. It felt like sacrilege to say it out loud, so she would not. The powers of invocation were not to be trifled with. But the way her mouth had to move to utter his name felt so good. As if he was sitting next to her, his strong, masculine scent overwhelming and seeping into her being. So gentle a man for his size. She still couldn't understand the ease he'd had with her when, by rights, he could have snapped her in two with but a flick of his wrist.

I love you, Ravin.

And now he did not. Because he *should* not.

The world had been made right again. Vampires hated witches, and witches would continue to prove deadly to vampires.

But what did she feel?

The idea of getting dressed in her leathers and buckling on her weapons, and then psyching herself up to mindlessly seek and destroy—well, it just felt so wrong. While the urge to destroy a vampire filled her veins with a familiar rush, the *need* wasn't as strong.

How long are you going to make the entire vampire nation suffer for something three vamps did to your family?

In all her decades, Ravin had never once had such a thought. Nikolaus had uttered it as if it were the most obvious conclusion. Surely the debt to her very soul had been paid by now?

She mouthed his name again. Closed her eyes. The trace of his lips gliding over her eyelids made her smile.

"Again," he'd whispered, so many times. And again and again she'd given herself to him, as he'd given himself to her.

She had always chosen a man for what he could do for her, how he could make her feel. Now, with wisdom, she'd grown picky. She sought the confidence of the warrior vampire, the independence. One who could listen to her, and wasn't afraid to ask her what it was that she wanted.

He gives you all of that.

Ravin sat upright, the motion so quick it eradicated her sleepy, wanting mood. A pinch at the base of her spine reminded her of her fall from the vampire's trust.

"Don't think about it. Sex is not love. It's over. It's...you'll never see him again."

At least, not in the mind-set she wanted to see him. If ever Ravin saw Nikolaus, it would be as he was—a vampire with vengeance in his heart for the witch who had once killed him.

"Aren't you the weepy Wanda this evening?"

That voice. She knew it.

Ravin swung up and around. Standing in her kitchen, his arm propped casually upon the counter, her lover smirked. "Nikolaus?"

The dark-haired man tilted a moue at her. Long, gorgeous hair shone blue in the beams of summer sunlight. The strokes of color glinted and matched the blue T-shirt he wore, the sleeves straining across thick biceps and a hard, toned chest. No scars. Not a single mark that claimed her violence toward him.

She had given him that with the blood sex magic.

And he deserved it, if only for the enslavement her spell had forced upon him.

He strode past her and into her bedroom, a casual meander, completely oblivious to her concern. She followed him.

He posed before the full-length mirror, studying his visage. "Now, this is telling," he said, in a voice that didn't match the voice Ravin held of him in her head.

Brimstone crept up Ravin's nostrils. Though the facade was perfection, the smell would ever give the bastard away.

Nikolaus Drake stood before her, clad in black leather and looking like the lover she could still smell on her sheets. But the devil grinned at her, exposing sharpened fangs.

"Bastard." She stalked out of the bedroom. "Why do you have to do that?"

"It's not my choice, kitten." Himself wandered out, fluffing at his hair—so not Nikolaus—and plopped onto the couch. "Can't help it. It is what you most desire."

"I don't desire him," she argued. *Oh, yes you do.*

The devil could be wrong, even if his appearance wasn't something he could control. He had to wield some control over it. What if some nut desired a freak or an animal?

"Then I appear as a robust bull or sheep. Hey, it's happened."

"Don't do that, either. Leave my thoughts alone."

"And what have you done to speak to me so? A little respect, if you will. I did grant you the power to see."

Right. Do not piss off the devil. It'll come back to bite you in the butt when you least expect. *Like when you're dancing in the moonlight with your vampire lover*.

"Of which I am most grateful," Ravin offered. "And eager to complete the third obligation so I can get you off my back."

"Seriously? You're going to get yourself knocked up?"

Ravin could not suppress a shiver. She clasped her arms across her chest and closed her eyes. Nikolaus's husky baritone shivered up her neck and planted itself in her breast. *Hold me now, lover*.

"Oh, yes, the witch does prefer the complete package. A vampire. Delicious spectacle. I can screw like him, too, if you wish. Won't be as satisfying as if I gave it to you in my true form, I warn you."

"I don't understand why he can breach my wards so easily. Is it because we've a blood bond?"

"It is because he is a phoenix, idiot."

"Yes, but the bond we have—"

"All the witches' blood in the world couldn't keep that vampire back now. He has survived death. He has taken the blood from generations of witches into his veins. As well, your magic. You, Ravin dear, have been successful in creating one of the most powerful vampires to ever exist. The phoenix."

"But I—"

"Had no idea? Ha! Well, that is what he is. Though I wager the fool hasn't realized his full potential so sick with love he is over you, eh?"

She plopped onto a bar stool. The world sat upon her shoulders. "I just wanted them to pay."

"Your parents' deaths were avenged that first time you

took down the six vampires riding the high roads of France with your crossbow and blade. You relished the kill. I was quite proud of you."

Six vampires, but not the ones who had actually murdered her parents. Would she ever find those three? Did they even exist?

When would she stop reaching for excuses?

"Let's get back to what's important," Himself said. "You're willing to hand over your firstborn, and I'm willing to play matchmaker."

Ravin put up a blocking palm and squinted as if a severe migraine had attacked her sinuses. "No, thanks. I can handle the matchmaking by myself. And it most certainly will not be Nikolaus Drake."

Would a sperm clinic be her best bet? No, if she were going to do this, then she was damned determined to enjoy it, at least for the few moments it took to perform the obligation.

An obligation. Having the devil's baby.

"Now, there is an idea," not-Nikolaus drawled. "Let's do it!" He moved up to sit on the arm of the couch, Nikolaus's long legs bending before him. "The two of us, getting it on. We'd make such a delightfully twisted rug rat."

"I may have done some nasty things in my lifetime, but I will never sleep with the devil."

He mocked a pout, fingers to his broad chest. "You wound me."

"You'll get over it."

"As I already have. So!" Leaping up, he strode across the living room, too grandly for anyone but the lord of hell. "Do give me a holler when the blessed event is to occur. Will you have one of those baby parties? What do they call them?"

"A shower?"

"Yes, I'd like to send a pram and perhaps a rattle carved of werewolf bone. Wouldn't that be precious?"

So precious she wanted to get sick right now. Ravin leaned over the kitchen counter and swallowed back her bile. She'd been getting sick regularly of late.

"Just go. Please. I'm sure you'll be the first to know if, and when, I've gotten myself into this horrible obligation."

"Indeed," whispered right at her side.

He stood behind her, Nikolaus's hands moving across her shoulders. Brushing aside her hair, he leaned in, the tip of his nose stirring up a shiver as it nudged her ear. "The vampire was exquisite, wasn't he? And now he wants to burn your bones and dance about your ashes. Do keep a lookout for Nikolaus Drake, will you? And be safe. I'd hate to have the phoenix destroy my precious future in a flight of frenzied rage. Ta."

Sinking to her knees in the center of her empty kitchen, Ravin choked back her rising bile and began a cry that segued to a wail.

Chapter 24

He stood behind the roof door. It was cracked open to reveal the brilliant morning sun. Though he'd heard Gabriel coming up the stairs as he was walking the hall to the access door, Nikolaus had kept going

He was decided. Nothing could keep him back.

If he was supposed to be so powerful, then this would be the test.

Drawing back the door completely, Nikolaus stood in the cool shadows of the tiny access cupola. He lifted a hand, considering—palm, or just a few fingers?

But then Nikolaus Drake stretched up tall, proud and ready. He had once saved lives, made the sick well, given hope to the hopeless. He had been a god.

Could he have that power now?

"Don't need it," he muttered, and stepped outside.

* * *

He'd stood there an hour, maybe longer. It had been twenty years since Nikolaus had felt the sun on his face.

Sweet. Warm. Like home with his family during hot summers at the lake.

Tears had come to his eyes. The phoenix had risen, and nothing could take him down now.

But the delight simmered, and he stalked back down to his loft. There were things to do. He had a witch to hunt. Today.

Kicking in the door to his loft, Nikolaus smirked when he noticed the cracked Sheetrock from the doorknob hitting it so often. So he was taking out his anger on inanimate objects. The witch would appreciate his release of excess energy when he returned to finish the angry pummeling she deserved. All the pummeling in the world would have no effect, though— he needed but a matchstick to bring her down.

He peeled his dress shirt from his arms and shoulders, then balled it up and tossed it into the laundry room as he passed by. The shades were set in the living room. The house was cool and dark. Quiet. As it should be in the morning.

He flicked open the shades, then quickly closed them. Gabriel could still be burned. But wouldn't his friend be amazed to learn Nikolaus could not get a tan?

What was that?

Following the soft echo of whimpers, Nikolaus stopped before Gabriel's bedroom door. He was about to knock, but the sounds of pain were all too familiar. Charging inside, Nikolaus choked on a gasp at the sight of his friend splayed on the bed, clenching his stomach in pain.

He was clad in jeans, his thickly veined bare feet dug into the sheets, pushing up a mountain of comforter. His white T-shirt, though he'd apparently not removed it, had literally melted over his chest to fall away in a bloody slush.

"How recent?" Nikolaus asked as he inspected the wound. "An hour? Two?"

"This morning," Gabriel managed to say. "Maybe three or four."

"But you just got here. I—" Had heard him arrive. Hours ago. He'd stood in the sun—while his friend had lain below suffering.

The open wound high on Gabriel's chest was wider than Nikolaus's hand, perfectly shaped from the tip of the cross and out to the crossbars. Flesh bubbled and bloody seepage spilled down Gabriel's sides. Nikolaus recognized the sweet chemical smell. Infection.

"It hurts like nothing I've ever known," Gabriel said on a whisper.

"Hold tight, my friend. I'll be right back."

Racing to the bathroom, Nikolaus searched the closet for alcohol and some gauze. They had plenty of medical supplies, thanks to Gabriel's tending Nikolaus's burns for months, and what doctor—albeit formerly—could go without a complete first-aid kit?

He grabbed the plastic bottle of alcohol, but there were no medical dressings. Towels would serve, so he grabbed a stack.

Pausing before entering Gabriel's bedroom, Nikolaus winced. A wound inflicted by a holy object meant death to any vampire who had been baptized—and Gabriel had been baptized. There was no easy healing. The wound could not be stopped from burning into the vampire and eventually eating him alive.

Gabriel let out a moan when Nikolaus poured the alcohol over his chest.

"Are you trying to kill me?" his friend cried. "That burns worse than the cross did."

Obviously, Gabriel wasn't aware of the consequences of his injury.

"It's infected. I need to do what I can." Nikolaus sopped over the wound with the towel, pressing the alcohol deep into the disaster. He stifled the ingrained reaction to order a nurse to slap a forceps and suture needle in his hand so he could begin stitching the wound. "Did the witch do this to you?"

"Haven't seen the vigilant slayer for months. Just let me die, will you?"

"Suck it up, man."

"*You're* going to save me? You don't do wounds, you were a brain surgeon."

"Who tended wounds on the skull, brain, spinal column and everywhere else during internship and residency."

Just because he'd had a specialty didn't mean he hadn't studied it all. Even a monkey could bandage a simple wound. But there was nothing simple about this preternatural havoc burned into his friend's body.

"I don't know—ah!" On the verge of passing out, Gabriel fluttered his eyelids. His fingers dug into the sheets, but he didn't try to push Nikolaus away. "Is there anything you can do to stop it from eating into my chest?"

Nikolaus sighed and tossed a blood-soaked towel to the floor. "I don't know. It needs to be…"

Cut out? He didn't know how to fix this. If he cut it out before it crept too deeply into Gabriel's chest, would that stop it?

His mentor's joking warning abruptly sounded in his brain: *If the patient isn't dead, you can always make it worse if you try hard enough.* To peer through the muscle and charred flesh, he did not see the lungs or heart. Yet. It hadn't infiltrated organs.

Utterly helpless, Nikolaus felt his heart sink. Just moments ago he'd rejoiced in the sunlight, completely oblivious to Gabriel's suffering. He should have known, have sensed his pain. He should have been there for him, leading him away from this— What *was* this?

Instinct raged to the surface in an animal growl. "If not the witch, then who did this to you?"

"T-Truvin. He wanted to send a message to you."

Truvin Stone. The name ripped at Nikolaus's intestines and tightened his fists. If the bastard had a problem with him then he should have come directly to him.

"I'm going after him."

"You can't!"

Slamming a fist against the door frame succeeded in splintering the hard maple. Nikolaus didn't turn back to Gabriel.

What had come of Truvin's promise to hand over the reigns without question? He'd asked for proof of Nikolaus's alliances—which he intended to show them all.

"He said," Gabriel gasped, "that you lied. That you hadn't killed the witch. But you told me you did. Did you…"

He'd thought to be so careful when he'd discovered he was being followed. Damn.

"She's as good as dead," Nikolaus answered, hating himself for the original lie. And look what that lie had done to Gabriel.

"Stone said you were…screwing her. I laughed. You would never…"

"Just be quiet, Gabriel. You need…"

He needed…? Nikolaus wasn't sure what the man required to heal. Blood and lots of it? His best bet was the blood from a fellow vampire.

For a moment he knew what he must do.

Nikolaus lifted a wrist to his mouth, willing his fangs to descend.

"You've powerful blood, my friend," Gabriel offered.

Powerful, yes. Enhanced by blood sex magic.

Nikolaus removed his wrist from his mouth, unbitten. He couldn't do this. His veins flowed with witch's blood. One drop and he'd write Gabriel's death sentence.

"What's wrong?"

He couldn't tell Gabriel he'd been playing moon-eyes to a witch the past few weeks. But what excuse to deny him the elixir Gabriel felt would help him?

"I've an idea. I'll be back."

"You can't go out…it's daytime!"

And Nikolaus walked out, abandoning his friend, his hand held out and pleading.

The digital code to enter the warehouse had been changed. No surprise. Nikolaus searched his memory for the six-digit code Gabriel had given him, and then punched it in.

The warehouse near the university was quiet, packed to the rafters with treasures collected, won or earned over the years and centuries by fellow tribe members. It was a safe for valuables, and a storage facility for belongings those who lived far too long wished to hang on to, but no longer had the room for. The tribe didn't "hang out" here, they merely met, discussed any news, problems or issues with their constant rivals—the wolves—then parted ways.

There were no windows, all original window frames were fit with steel plates, so it was occasionally used as a safe house for those too far from home, and too close to sunrise.

Nikolaus's boots cracked across the scuffed hardwood floor. In the file cabinet across the floor were ancient texts, grimoires stolen from witches, and rites of the vampire nation. Could there be something written down that may help Gabriel?

He was not alone. The smell of blood invaded his senses. Rich, fresh, perhaps splattered on clothing so that the molecules traveled the air. Who hadn't made it home last night?

"I come in peace," Nikolaus offered, so he wouldn't alert a fellow tribe member.

"I accept the concession."

Truvin sat in a beam of light, perched on the cream satin arm of a Louis XV divine, his own possession. A gaudy reminder to Nikolaus that the man was of a completely different generation than he. In essence, a different realm.

Head up and blood scent piercing the murky darkness, the smile in Truvin's dark eyes hit Nikolaus right in the heart—as if a stake or misdirected spray from a blood bullet.

"I'll assume you got my gauntlet," Truvin said.

He stood and hooked his hands at his hips. His frame equaled Nikolaus's broad shoulders and height, though he hid his brawn with the Italian suit. The two had once been a match in strength.

Nikolaus rushed the vampire, shoving him against the wall and pinning him by the shoulders. "You had no right! This is between you and me, Stone, it always has been. Gabriel should have never been—"

"Killed?"

Fisting his knuckles up under Truvin's rib cage, Nikolaus took sweet pleasure feeling the resistance of his organs as they took on the brunt of his anger. Yes, he had lifted Truvin with ease, as if he were a child. If he wished, he could push a fist through his ribs, reach in and rip out his heart.

At such a macabre thought, Nikolaus dropped the man and paced away, but kept his awareness keen.

"Gabriel is not dead." But he didn't say "yet," because they both knew death was inevitable. Smacking a fist into his palm, he swung around. "Let's get this done with right now. You want control of Kila? You're going to have to kill me first."

"I—" Truvin spread out his arms in mock savior pose "—will allow the tribe members to decide. I've no desire to fight you, Nikolaus." He flicked nonexistent dust from his shoulder "You must be working out, eh?"

Nikolaus fisted his open palm; the loud smack rang in the large room.

"Jake drop you off?"

"No, I walked."

Truvin rolled that one over awhile.

"Got a tan," Nikolaus taunted.

"You're kidding me."

"Shall we walk out and test your disbelief? Oh, what's that? You're stuck here until sundown?"

"I have my driver—"

"Enough small talk." Nikolaus lunged for another attack, but this time Truvin dodged.

A kidney punch to his left forced Nikolaus against the wall. It hurt—for two seconds. He swung out and grabbed Truvin by the throat. They went to the floor, fists connecting with flesh and bone and animal growls enforcing their lacking humanity over the other.

Truvin gasped. "You are stronger, Nikolaus."

The vampire was surprised. Good. Let him wonder what it was a phoenix truly took back with him from the shadows of the grave.

"So legend holds true? Strength, and immunity to the burning sun?"

"Believe it." But did he believe it himself? Time to begin. "You are serious about allowing the tribe to decide who will lead them?" Nikolaus rolled away from Truvin and spat out blood.

"Of course I am." Truvin knelt on all fours, huffing. His tousled brown hair obscured his face, but Nikolaus felt his ever-present smirk. "It is what is fair. After all, I was never officially declared leader after you left."

"You left me," Nikolaus spat. And then he regretted the accusation.

He could take care of himself. He would have done the same in the situation had it been reversed. All vampires knew when there was a witch around that fleeing was the only option.

And yet, if only someone would have reached out for him. Shown him a sign of compassion.

You've softened because of the witch. Don't be a fool, vampire.

"Whomever the tribe chooses to lead, I shall abide." Truvin stood and thumbed the edge of his mouth, removing his own blood. He walked to the center of the warehouse and turned to face Nikolaus. "I am not your enemy, Nikolaus. I want what is best for all."

"You want death."

"I want an impartial leader who has not become mired in humanity. Of course, I'm ever after the witches. Why has no vampire ever organized against them? Hmm? A simple bite, and they spit on us, and it is a cruel way to die. Through the centuries witches have aggressively hunted us. And yet, has a vampire ever hunted a witch?"

"Too dangerous. We usually hire someone capable," Nikolaus said. The confession felt like a cop-out.

"Did you just hear what you said? We need to hire a capable party to do our dirty work. We are not capable of bringing down a witch? That pitiful bit of a thing who stalks this city alone, riding her big black chopper with an attitude that's all show and no merit. There are no others. Just her. And we flee like rodents at her presence."

"Until the Protection spell is lifted we must be cautious," Nikolaus offered. "All predators have their own predator."

"That has changed," Truvin stated. "We've developed a means to capture witches. Myself and some new members of the tribe. You'll meet them tomorrow. And that, my friend, is what I intend to concentrate on after you have returned to Kila."

"Witch hunting. Sounds intriguing." He could not allow Truvin to know he was against it.

But was he? He wanted the bloody witch dead, as well. But

an organized hunt? Seemed medieval and against all he wished for Kila.

"A vampire as powerful as you should be a prime player in the hunt. You can now stalk the enemy when she least expects—during the day. You up for it?"

"I'm…behind anything that'll bring down a witch," Nikolaus said.

So why the reluctance?

"I should think so." Truvin tilted his head, perusing Nikolaus's face and neck. "Remarkable recovery."

Nikolaus bowed his head. He was wasting time. "You deserve death for Gabriel's death."

"He's been your eyes when you've been away. And I do respect him, if for the fact he is a close ally of yours. But…he challenged me."

"Gabriel is not aggressive. He has no reason to challenge—"

"He's been with my woman."

"Oh, come on, Stone."

"Gabriel is the sort, you know it."

He couldn't argue that. The vampire did go through women like wealthy men went through Cristal.

"Yes, but since when have you ever cared so much about a woman that you couldn't drop her as quickly as your pants? It's an excuse, and you know it. Your violence against Gabriel was willful and unnecessary."

"And what of you, Nikolaus?" Truvin approached, blood creased at the corner of his mouth and a smear of crimson at his brow where his face had hit the stone wall. "Have you never had a woman that you would do anything for?"

"No." Nikolaus drew himself up straight. He would not reveal his mistake in a blink or a sudden flash of enlarged pupil. Enough of this. "Until tomorrow night."

"I wait with eagerness," Stone called to Nikolaus's retreating back. "Kiss her goodbye before you come, will you?"

Eerie foreboding trickled up Nikolaus's neck. Truvin knew nothing about his love life. He was merely summoning guesses, trying to make him falter. There was no woman who would ever sway him from his path. No one.

As he charged out into the bright afternoon, Nikolaus hissed. She was not a woman, but a witch. Two very different things.

Briefly, he'd been bespelled.

His mind was his own now.

And yet, he could claim to be as the ancients—bewitched—thanks to the infusion of her blood and the blood sex magic.

Bewitched.

But only in body, never…his heart.

Chapter 25

There was one other place he could try before returning to Gabriel. Nikolaus knew of someone who might be able to help, or at the very least, set him in the right direction.

The Dungeon was a Goth bar that featured live bands, yet dead-looking patrons. It wasn't tops on Nikolaus's list of entertainments, but it was the only known recreation for the snitch he sought.

Seating himself at the black-rubber bar between two pale-faced females who found sudden interest in the new patron, Nikolaus ordered a Guinness, to make it look good, but knew he'd no more than sip at it. Sure, he could take in liquids without getting a foul stomach—but he wasn't much for beer.

Blood suited him fine. And oh, the marvelous, pulsing, pumping, gushing receptacles that sat in this establishment. Each one hot and so unaware. He hadn't drunk human blood for weeks, and the taste of nasty witch's blood still lived at the back of his throat.

Before he left this bar, he would find a hearty meal to slake his needs.

Shouting at the end of the long, sweeping bar resulted in one skinny fellow, limbs flailing and mouth slapping, being hauled from his stool and punched.

It was never difficult to locate Memori.

A fight put up Nikolaus's hackles. The last thing he needed was aggression in the air. How easy it would be to lash out and join the fray. To beat out his anger upon the delicate bones and flesh of a mortal.

Some vicarious aggression was what he most needed. Either that, or he'd haul off and kill someone. But the idiot was doing a good-enough job all by himself. He was like a snake, slipping from one defensive set of punches and wrangling arms to the next. He was loving it, snapping back with infuriating comebacks, and taking his punches with a laugh and a sneer.

Finally the bartender's shout got through to him. Surrounded by a bunch of huffing, stone-eyed Goths, the snake slithered away. Aggression salted the air. Nikolaus took a hearty swallow of beer to redirect his senses.

The snake's shirt had been tugged up to his pits, and as he walked toward Nikolaus, trying to get it untucked, the marks on his chest were visible. Three lines, each with a slash through them.

Nikolaus had seen those marks before—on the witch. Himself got around.

Resuming worship over his foamy pint, Nikolaus drew in the hostile scent of the snake as he slid onto a stool next to him and slammed a fiver on the bar. "More!"

The bartender rolled his eyes but was obviously pleased to

have the cash. He snatched the bill and replaced it with a murky beer. A drunken giggle preceded the snake dunking back the entire glass in one gulp.

"Impressive," Nikolaus muttered.

"That ain't so much," the man slurred. "I can down a gallon in the same swallow."

"I meant that you're still upright. You've blood running down your chin." Nikolaus pushed a black cocktail napkin toward him. The scent of the blood didn't tempt him, because he knew this thing sitting next to him was tainted with some nasty essence. Sallow flesh and red eyes marked him inhuman; he could very likely be a demon.

The man wiped himself clean and tossed the napkin to the floor. "I'm ready for round two if you're itchin'"

"I prefer to watch…Memori."

"Not many know my name, mister." The man tilted his head, viewing Nikolaus at a horizontal. "I haven't got the Sight, but I'm guessing I know what you are."

Both glanced about the room. Not wise to put it out there, and neither would. The man sobered instantly and huffed a breath through his nose.

"You know everything that goes on, up or down in this city, I'm told."

"You've been told right. 'Course, I don't give out nothing for free."

Nikolaus drew up a roll of hundreds from his leather jacket. He placed two on the bar behind the empty beer glass. "Do you know of cures, spells or concoctions to help the wounded?"

"Just so." Memori slid the cash into a pocket. "If I don't have something to help you, I can point you in the right direction. 'Course, your kind should heal on their own. Must be something nasty."

"A holy wound. From a cross."

"Baptized?"

"Yes."

Nikolaus wondered now how long Gabriel had. It had been but an hour since he'd left him alone, and dying. He should be home at his friend's side, just…being there, offering his presence.

"There's no reversing a holy wound," Memori said in a low tone, his eyes constantly darting about the crowd. "Unless…"

Nikolaus shifted his arm along the bar and he placed his face right before Memori's. He knew he looked imposing, and he was not against a warning growl.

Memori's lower lip shook. He sucked it in and spread his gaze across Nikolaus's neck. "Not many vamps have tattoos."

Rarely did a vampire wear tattoos, unless they'd come by them *before* the transformation. Wasted pain.

"Keep your voice down. How do I reverse the wound?"

"That'll be Himself you need to talk to. He's the only one who can reverse the power of the holy on a vamp. He'll be askin' for a trade, of course."

"Like those marks on your chest?"

"Precious, aren't they?" The man spat onto the floor beneath the bar. "From Himself."

Memori sucked back the remainder of his beer and slammed the mug on the bar to get the bartender's attention. "Another!" He nodded toward Nikolaus. "He's paying."

"For performing three obligations?" Nikolaus wondered. He'd seen such markings twice now, and to see them in so short a time period? Curiosity made him ask, "Are you free of Himself now?"

"Ha! Free? I wish. The devil's imp, I am." The man slammed his palm onto the bar and shot Nikolaus a poisonous look. "Three strikes and I thought I was free. But no! Now I'm the bastard's familiar for the rest o' eternity. Kill me now, will you? Just haul out and slap my head from my shoulders. That'll do it good. That'll teach Himself."

Nikolaus shook his head. "You performed three obligations for the devil, and after, he rewarded you by making you his familiar? Shouldn't you have gotten your soul back?"

"Yes, well, the concept of reward is quite another thing when it comes to Himself and his rules, eh? Once you sign away your soul, it ain't never gonna be returned, loan or no. 'Course, who would want it after where it's been, eh?"

He slugged back another swallow. "What do you care, vampire? You thinking of forming an alliance with Himself? I'll tell you right now, just run. Don't look at the bastard, don't fall for that sexy Pamela Anderson pouty-lips come-on, don't even think of what turns you on when you get a whiff of brimstone, cause, buddy, that will be the end of you."

"Yet here you are. Walking the mortal realm. Very obviously…free."

"If you consider calling in lost souls and tracking vicious killers free, well then…" Memori lifted his mug and slugged back another round. He followed with a loud belch and a swipe of his shirt across his mouth. "That all you wanted, buddy?"

"Yes." Nikolaus stood and took out another hundred dollar bill. He laid it on the bar and walked away.

Three strikes and Ravin Crosse would not be out, but forever indebted to the Old Lad Himself.

Nikolaus couldn't decide which would be more satisfying, to know she had become the devil's familiar, or to kill her himself, and feel her life wilt away in his own hands.

The moment she heard the crash, Ravin knew it was her front door. "A girl should just put in a revolving door."

She stomped out from the kitchen to spy the tall, dark vampire standing upon the flattened door.

The urge to continue her pace, right into the man's arms, was stalled by a sudden wariness. Nikolaus or Himself? She didn't scent brimstone. Usually Himself appeared without the fanfare.

"We need to talk, witch." Nikolaus stomped off the door and right up to her.

By the time he'd pinned her to the kitchen wall, Ravin knew it was the real Nikolaus Drake, likely come to end her days—as promised.

"Talk?" she squeaked out. His grip about her neck compressed it painfully.

"Talk first—" his sapphire eyes roved over her face. No hint of compassion in them, only a dark curiosity that belonged in the eyes of a predator before it lunges for the attack "—then death."

"Ah. For a second there I thought you'd forgotten. Set me down, will you?"

His grip tightened. Ravin choked and kicked out. She managed to heel him on the knee, but he didn't flinch. The vampire growled and gnashed his fangs in anger. His hair shook about him like a beast's mane.

Ravin closed her eyes, for all she could wish for was another bite. A long, deep bite that would tease her into a mindless, wanting oblivion.

One last time. Please, lover, give me back your gorgeous, deadly bite.

"You know of holy wounds?" Nikolaus asked in a demanding, deep voice. "Look at me, witch!"

Ravin met his vicious urgency with her own defiant stare.

Nikolaus blinked, lowered his gaze and his grip loosened. He dropped her and spun around to pace away and out into the living room.

"There is little time," he said. "I need your help. A friend of mine has been burned with a cross."

Must have been hard, if not impossible for him to ask her for help. "A vampire?"

"Of course."

"Gabriel?"

He turned and his eyes briefly touched hers, before slanting away. Could he not look at her? Did he understand how difficult it was for her to stand before him and *not* run into his arms?

"He was wounded five, maybe six hours ago. The wound grows deeper. I must help him."

"A holy wound is irreversible." She shrugged up the sleeves of her low-neck shirt, and while wanting to step up to Nikolaus and wrap her arms about him, Ravin maintained a ten-foot perimeter away from him.

He showed no sign he had ever once loved her. And he *had* mentioned he was here for her death. But while she instinctively knew her fate, her body responded to his presence of its own accord.

Crossing her arms over her hardened nipples, Ravin searched the floor, hiding her own needs. "The vampire is a loss. There's nothing you can do."

"You must have a spell," he insisted. His vehemence made Ravin flinch. "Bring out your book. The one I know you keep above the stove. Get it!"

He demanded so intensely, Ravin moved as if on autopilot to retrieve the grimoire. She set it on the counter and began to page through it. Though she knew there was nothing inside on holy wounds, she would show Nikolaus that she was willing.

More than willing. How to make him understand she would do anything for him?

Yes, damn it, she loved this vampire.

Heartbeat pounding, Ravin turned another page. Aware Nikolaus had moved in to stand behind her, peering over her shoulder, she suppressed the shudder that shimmied up her spine and tickled across her breasts.

His breath upon her hair. His scent surrounding her. His very presence…

"Nikolaus, I…" Closing her mouth, she swallowed back the urge to bellow out a weeping insistence to his touching her. "Do you remember nothing of the past few weeks?" she whispered.

His fist slammed the counter next to the book, setting the hanging plants overhead to a titter.

"I remember your betrayal, witch. I remember—"

"That you loved me," she quickly murmured, so quiet, perhaps he would not hear. No, she wanted him to hear, to *know*.

Another animal-like huff sounded at her left ear. Nikolaus pushed away from the counter and the sound of his boot kicking the fridge made her wonder if the stainless-steel appliance wasn't now dented.

"Have you no spell?" he demanded.

"No, Nikolaus, I'm sorry, it's not possible."

"Then you will arrange for me to speak with Himself. Now."

Now she did turn and clutched the counter behind her. "What do you want to speak to the devil for?"

"I will ask him for a reversal of the holy wound. I know that bastard can do it."

"For a trade! Three obligations, Nikolaus." She lifted her shirt and thumped her chest. "You know the sacrifice."

"You think you know the sacrifice," he corrected. "Out on loan?" His smirk ended in a muted chuckle.

"My soul will be mine—someday," she said, choking on the last word. "But you! Even when you do get your soul back, you will forever know you served Himself. How can you live with that?"

"Oh, I know my soul will be gone, witch. You think you are free with your final obligation?" He shook his head, and as he bowed before her his hair veiled over half of his face. When he looked back up, a rarity of emotion shimmered in his rich jewel eyes. "Three strikes and you're his, sweetness. You've been lied to. That is what Himself does so well, isn't it? Lie?"

Ravin clutched her throat. She attempted to process what he'd said, but she couldn't get past the word *sweetness*. He'd called her by the pet name he'd used only when he had loved her.

But what he'd just said. It could not be true. Her soul. Gone. Forever?

"No, you're—" He always spoke the truth. The man's integrity had never been questionable.

Her knees felt like noodles. Breaths came quickly. Ravin reached out—and fell into Nikolaus's arms.

Quickly he set her down and stepped aside, their contact brief, but everywhere he had touched her, Ravin's skin flamed, crying out for a more lengthy connection.

"It's true," he said, pacing from the end of the counter to the couch and back. "I've spoken to another who was given three obligations, for which, he believed, was merely a loan of his soul."

"But he promised," Ravin managed to say. And then it all made so much sense. Of course the devil had lied, he was the great tempter, the master of deception. "So when I complete the third…?"

One she wasn't keen on in the first place, but when she'd thought to get Himself off her back, well then… And there was the plan that maybe she could slide by on a technicality because of the miscarriage.

"You become his familiar. Enslaved for eternity. I assume the three obligations are more an admissions test than loan repayment." Nikolaus hiked a foot up onto the couch arm and leaned over to look down where she sat sprawled against the counter. "Not that I give a crap what happens to a witch, you understand."

"Of course not." Or did he? He'd called her— No, it had been a slip. "This friend of yours is so important to you that you'd ransom your soul?"

"Yes."

He stood tall, drawing his neck straight and thrusting back his shoulders. A warrior for the battlefield. Fit him with black armor and a broadsword and he would command denizens, taking down all who would dare approach with challenge.

A warrior who had mastered her heart. Damn him.

Damn Himself for breaking the spell.

Damn herself for allowing the mistake to happen in the first place. She was completely responsible for this mess she found herself in. And nothing she said could ever change the vampire's hatred for her now.

But she knew his anger, and wouldn't allow him to slip farther into the darkness that he'd so deftly avoided for decades.

"No." Ravin pushed up against the counter. "I won't do it."

The vampire's fingers coiled into fists, gearing up for the attack.

"I have principles," Ravin rushed out. "I won't allow you to sink to such depths."

"Principles?" he spat.

Bounding backward, he spun and rushed to the arsenal. He ripped the door off the hinges and slammed it to the floor. Reaching inside, he drew out knives and tossed them to the floor. Guns were slammed down without concern for the danger.

He pulled out a glass-tipped knife. "This is what you call principles?"

"Be careful, Nikolaus! It's tipped with holy water."

"Bah!" He flung it toward her. It landed on the floor, but inches from her feet, the glass breaking to leak out the inert water that would have smoked and sizzled upon contact with the flesh of a baptized vampire.

"Who are you to claim principles?" He stalked up to her and bent down to get in her face. "You have murdered so many."

She winced at his declaration of her ugly, awful truths. He knew she wanted to change. *Could* he remember how close they had become?

"You kill gleefully," he continued, "without regard for family, home or alliance. You have even murdered innocent mortals, and you toss out that word is if you've a right to own it?"

She wanted to sink into a sniveling ball, to cast him away with a simple deportation spell—if only she was up on such a spell—but Ravin knew Nikolaus would only listen to one who could match him fire for fire. And where had hers gone?

You gave it to him. Each time you had sex with him, you fed him your fire. And she didn't want it back.

Splaying out a hand to encompass the scattered weapons, she said, "It's not right, I know that now. I won't harm another soul, I promise. If only you will…"

"I will what, witch?"

Hold me. Kiss me. Love me.

Her body now shaking, Ravin could not fight back the relentless tears that took their leave with repulsive precision.

"You cannot make me summon Himself," she murmured, lowering her head to avoid his vicious gaze. "I won't. Besides, he does not come to anyone's bidding but his own."

The stroke of his hand across her hair momentarily stopped the world. Sound ceased. Ravin's tears suspended at the corners of her eyes. Her heartbeats slowed to a drowsy pace.

He touched her. It was not a hard or pinching grip. Nikolaus stroked his palm over her hair, softly, sensuously. A lover's regard, a lazy summation.

And then he gripped a shank of her hair and the world revved back to the manic horror of reality.

"Time is of the essence," he hissed into her face. "You will not refuse me, witch, because you do not want me to haunt you daily should my friend die. It will be a painful, atrocious haunting that will see you raw and bleeding. And yet I will not kill you, because that would prove a mercy I don't have for witches."

He had not an ounce of love for her remaining.

And yet, to imagine Nikolaus Drake haunting her ever after—no matter the pain—could only staunch Ravin's determination. "So be it, vampire."

"Fool!" He pushed away from her.

"Did someone call my name?"

"Oh, hell," she muttered.

"That's me!"

Standing in the doorway, the exact duplicate of Nikolaus Drake held out his arms in grand display. The devil had arrived.

Now the chaos would begin.

Chapter 26

Taken aback, Nikolaus looked over the woman standing on the fallen front door. Raven-haired and clad in black leathers; at her waist and thighs silver weapons glinted. Biker boots laced up her ankles. Looked as though she'd just stepped off the rumbling street chopper.

He switched his gaze to the witch in the kitchen. Same face, same hair, killer curves and determined expression.

Back to the door. They were both...Ravin Crosse.

Impossible.

"What sort of witchcraft are you working now?" Nikolaus flashed a look to the Ravin in the kitchen. "I've had enough of your black magic!"

"I didn't do a thing," Ravin answered.

The other Ravin stepped forward in a weird jaunty trot. Not the real Ravin's sensual, confident stride. She shimmied over to Nikolaus and traced her fingers up his chest, summoning an unwanted flush of desire to the surface.

He recalled the witch once telling him the devil appeared to others in the guise of their greatest... *No*.

Nikolaus shoved her away.

"Now, now," the new Ravin chided, "that's no way to treat a lady. Or so I assume. Ah! I must see about this one." She traipsed over to the mirror by the doorway and preened before it. "Now, *this* is delicious."

"You are Himself?" Nikolaus asked.

The second Ravin turned and performed a curtsy. "In the flesh of your greatest desire."

"You lie and trick," Nikolaus spat.

"That is my trade," the smirking creature agreed. "But I've no control over my appearance, unless I wish to take on my usual form."

"Then do so!" Nikolaus demanded.

The newest Ravin marched up to him and gripped him by the collar. "Do not order me, boy. I can strip your soul from your body if I choose and toss the husk to my minions to peel out the veins, all while you live to suffer the agony. Shall we give it a go?"

"I've no time right now," Nikolaus replied. "Maybe later?"

Himself turned to the real Ravin. "Oh, I like him."

"He's a vampire," Ravin said. "You should regard anything he says with prudence."

"Silence," Nikolaus hissed at the witch—the real witch.

He turned back to Himself, who batted long dark lashes at him in a distressing come-on. The fact he saw the witch disturbed him, but he hadn't the luxury of time to question the meaning of it.

"I need a holy wound reversed," he said to Himself. "Can you do that?"

"I can do anything for a price," Himself answered. She perused Nikolaus from head to toe and paused for an uncomfortable age at his crotch. "Wanna get laid, big boy?"

Gnashing his teeth, Nikolaus fought against his rising rage. He would not touch the hideous being that taunted him. No boon was worth lying with the devil.

"Not much on screwing the dark lord, eh?" Himself shrugged. "Always so difficult to convince you earthly souls of the exquisite ride. Ah well. Your friend is almost dead. You've not seen him this past hour. The wound burrows deep into his internal organs to chew away his life."

He should not be here…wasting time. Gabriel needed him. "But you can fix that?"

Another shrug. The fake Ravin tugged out a glass-tipped blade from her thigh belt and made a show of tossing it up and catching it. "I can stop the desiccation at this moment. But if that's what you desire…"

"Save him now."

Himself tipped the blade against her plump lips. "For three obligations?"

"Yes—"

"No!" Ravin dashed into the room and gripped Himself by the arm. "Take me instead. Use it as my final obligation."

Himself shook Ravin off. "I already have you, witch."

Watching the two Ravins right next to each other was a confusing thing. But knowing Gabriel lay dying was vital. Did he have the right to save him, knowing he would be preserved in such a damaged state?

Nikolaus had faced this decision many a time in his career as a surgeon. Yes, we can operate on your child, Mr. and Mrs. So-and-So, but she'll never open her eyes again and will depend on a respirator to breathe for the rest of her life. It was always similar. An operation to relieve pain, but it could never help to restore lifestyle. Nikolaus had relied on the decisions of the family, sometimes regretting he hadn't encouraged them to simply pull the plug. But it hadn't been his choice.

Was it now his choice?

"You lied to me!" Ravin shouted at Himself's matching feminine face. "You told me I would be free after three obligations."

"I never said that. Three strikes and your debt is paid is how it goes. But that doesn't mean you're free. Your soul is mine, sweetness."

"Don't—" she put up a hand before her twin "—call me that." Casting a fleeting glance over Nikolaus, she paced away from them and squared her shoulders. "So even if I do complete the third…" Her brown eyes pleaded woefully.

Nikolaus felt his heart lunge in a gulp. He understood her pain, and wanted to…

Take it away.

Because she wasn't what she should be. A vicious, vampire-hating witch. She was—damn it—he cared for her in a manner he didn't want to label, but could not put off from his thoughts.

Seeing Himself in Ravin's form meant only that he was still attracted to her, it did not mean he loved her.

It had not been real.

Part of it was. That part that still clings to your soul.

A soul you can bargain with.

"Her freedom for my soul," Nikolaus said quickly.

Himself lifted a brow, perusing the offer.

"No!"

Nikolaus pushed back the real Ravin from her double. "This is not for you to decide, sweetness."

She settled, whispering the endearment as she looked up at him, her eyes wide and glossy with tears.

He'd called her sweetness. Something he'd called her when he'd…loved her.

Nikolaus fell into Ravin's soft, watery gaze. *Did* he still love this woman? This witch?

That was impossible. She had killed him. She had bespelled him to love her. He couldn't have possibly… fallen—

A spell can influence the brain, but logic is always your own. You acted of your own volition after being given a shove. You know that is true!

Christ. He did care. And right now, he wanted to take away her pain, and Gabriel's, and make the world right.

"One obligation is all I require to wipe the witch's slate clean and return her soul intact," Himself stated.

"What of Gabriel?"

"Eh. I'll toss that in as a freebie. Can you do one thing for me, vampire?"

"Of course I can," Nikolaus answered.

Ravin didn't deserve to lose her soul. She was changing. Had changed. And Nikolaus knew the feeling. It made a person have hope. And she should have that after two centuries of bleakness and the kill. He would give her that freedom as his last act of compassion toward her.

"You want my soul?" he asked Himself.

"Mmm, something a bit more valuable."

"Than my soul? Save Gabriel, and take away Ravin's debt, and you can chose your boon. What do you want from me?"

"Your firstborn."

"No!" Ravin shouted.

But a glance from Himself set her back against the wall, hands spreading for support.

"My…?"

A ridiculous notion. Nikolaus would never— Well, he had

once dreamed to be a father. It couldn't happen now. Vampires did not PTA-attending daddies make.

Will you help me? Ravin had asked him to help with her final obligation. And he had promised he would.

"Done," Nikolaus said, knowing one more wasted moment would only see Gabriel further deranged from the wound.

"Excellent." Himself cast Ravin a wink, and then he was gone.

Nikolaus shoved his hands in his pockets. He'd gotten Gabriel's life. He had secured Ravin's soul. And if he was lucky, it would be a long time coming before he had to contend with the devil's due.

Not that he'd shirk a bargain, but he had no intention of ever marrying and starting a family. What kind of bizarre circus freak would he father? And if the kid were lucky enough to be born normal, look at the old man. Not a good example for any kid.

"No." Ravin sank to her knees. "He knows!"

"Knows what?" Stalking across the room, Nikolaus picked up the front door and propped it against the wall.

For some reason he felt…empty. Empty of anger, of the heady violence that had charged him to a rage earlier. Empty of vengeance.

And open to whatever might come his way.

Had making a deal with the devil brought him to such a place? A feeling of peace, for now his most pressing worries had been solved.

He looked over at the witch, kneeling on the floor, swaying back and forth.

You called her sweetness. You know you meant it.

So many times he'd held her gently, taking from her, giving to her, bringing her to orgasm, quietly sharing their pain.

And yet he had never shown her his hopes. He did have them. Did she?

He knelt before her and stroked the glossy hair spilling over her shoulder. Hate had emptied from him, as well. He wasn't sure what he felt toward the witch right now, but negative violent feelings no longer resided in his heart.

"Knows what, Ravin? What does Himself know?"

Ravin curled forward, shaping her body into a ball, and pressed her forehead to the floor. "Nikolaus, I think I'm pregnant."

Chapter 27

"You have to go," Ravin said, still coiled forward onto the floor.

After her confession she did not want to look into the vampire's eyes. She sensed she had guessed right—that she was pregnant—but she hadn't proof. Instinctually, she knew. And while she used the birth control spell religiously, it was certainly only as effective as an over-the-counter product. Wasn't there like a two-percent failure rate?

"Gabriel will need you," she said. "Please, just go to him."

Nikolaus wrenched up her head by a shank of her hair. It didn't hurt and he supported her now by the back of the head. Squatting, he lowered his gaze to hers. The sapphire irises pierced Ravin with reluctant wonder.

"Why did you say you are pregnant? Do you think to win me back? Why would you…?"

Want me back? were the words Ravin sensed he couldn't put to voice.

"We'll talk about this later." She clasped a hand over his wrist, which caused him to pull away. Rejection. Utter indifference. "It's just an intuition. I tried to stop you from making a deal with Himself."

"That was my choice. When he would not take my soul, I jumped at the option that I knew might never have to be repaid—at least not in this century."

"Nothing in this world is free. I thought to fool Himself when he asked for my firstborn as the final obligation. If you do not pay, then Gabriel should die."

He turned a sneer down upon her. "It's not as if I do not intend to make good on the bargain, it'll just be a cold day in hell before it ever happens."

"I think…" Ravin murmured, "Himself knows. Oh, damn—he *does* know. He must have orchestrated this from the start. The love spell—oh!"

Suddenly racked with pain, Ravin felt her muscles tighten and she strained against the razor ice that ate across her chest. Slow, precise, the slash marks felt as though an invisible hand were peeling them from her body, lifting up flesh and muscle to do so.

She slapped a palm over her chest; the sting of that act ended the immediate pain. Beneath her fingers she felt smooth flesh.

And her body arched, bending upward. Pinpricks stung her from head to toe. Something entered her through those pricks of pain. And Ravin collapsed, gasping but smiling.

It was back. Her soul.

"What the hell was that all about?"

Smiling, she closed her eyes and lifted her fingers to reveal her rib cage to Nikolaus.

"I'm pleased for you," he said.

She was about to ask "Are you really?" but the vampire stalked toward the door and lifted it to set it aside. "Gabriel needs me."

Ravin turned her cheek against her knee to watch as he pressed his palm against the frame. He stood there for a moment, looking over the door, and when she saw him turn his head, she tucked hers facedown into her lap.

"Yes, we will discuss this. Later," he said in a husky growl. "Goodbye…sweetness."

And that single word struck Ravin in her heart and dredged up a soulful sobbing. He'd said it again, purposefully. He'd wanted her to have that.

Could he still love her?

He had expected to find Gabriel lying in bed, alive. Instead, Nikolaus charged through his front door to find the decimated form of his best friend standing in the center of the living room, the shades open to the rosy warning of twilight.

The stench of Gabriel's wound assaulted Nikolaus, but it was nothing he had not experienced before. He did not waver as he approached his friend. Only when he saw the silver stake in the man's trembling hand did he stop, but a stride away.

"I feel…" Gabriel said. "…as if the wound has stopped eating at me." His voice had been reduced to a slithery whisper, racked with pain. "Isn't that odd?"

A curious smile traced Gabriel's lips, but they were thin, stretched in pain. He'd suffered greatly. It appeared a monumental task merely to stand upright.

"You will not die now," Nikolaus offered. Jaw tight, he swallowed. What had he done? This was no life for any man! "I've…seen to your survival."

"Have you," Gabriel muttered, a reluctant acceptance.

"Please, my friend, hand me the stake?"

Gabriel clutched the weapon tighter and wobbled. When Nikolaus reached to steady him, he stumbled backward and put up his free hand, the shaking fingers coated in blood from his wound. And there, though he had pulled a clean brown T-shirt on, the shape of a distorted cross soaked through. It was so large.

Would he walk endlessly after with the seeping wound to remind him of the death he had cheated? A death Nikolaus had *decided* Gabriel must cheat.

Had he the opportunity to ask Gabriel before if it was what he wanted, would he have chosen as Nikolaus wished?

"You must…kill me," Gabriel said.

"No."

"Do you wish me to live like this?"

He lifted up the shirt to reveal agonizing havoc. His heart had been exposed and pulsed at the corner of one of the cross armatures. Other organs Nikolaus felt sure he could identify if he were in the cold confines of a lab doing an autopsy, showed as well.

"I…" What could he do to rescue his friend? It was he who had wasted the time in getting the wound stopped. He, who had sentenced Gabriel to this undying hell—with no means to change it.

Could he perform surgery to close up the wound? Skin grafts?

Ridiculous. The man needed organs and body fat and muscle and…sanity.

"I am so sorry" was all Nikolaus could offer. "This is all my fault. Had I not led you to believe I had killed the witch…"

Pregnant? With his child?

Yet another blow. One that should lift him to rejoice, and yet…if she was pregnant, he'd just sold his unborn child to the devil.

This was not as he'd intended his life to go. Everything was wrong. How to make it as right as it had been but days earlier?

"My God." Nikolaus bowed his head.

It had been right with her.

"I blame you for nothing...but kindness," Gabriel wheezed. He waved the silver stake between them. "You have been good to me...for years. So much you have taught me. Restraint. Pride. Compassion."

Nikolaus winced.

"Now. Continue that kindness."

The stake wobbled in his trembling grasp, but it was directed toward Nikolaus. *Put me from misery.*

To kill. To purposely take a life, and not because of some medical mistake, or because he had tried for hours to clamp off an intracerebral hemorrhage to no avail.

Since he'd become a vampire, Nikolaus had killed twice. Both times, an accident. When first he'd been transformed he had not known how much blood to take, that if he stole too much from his victims they would arrest and die in his arms. A harsh lesson to learn, but learn it he had.

Not since then had he killed.

But you did consider it weeks ago.

Yes, the witch. A revenge killing. A means to cleanse his soul of the anger that had brewed within him for the months following her attack.

And what had his assassin done to him? She'd opened Nikolaus's wanting heart and thrust in her hand, caressing, massaging, making him soften and gentling him.

And he had—*did*—love her for that.

I love the witch. I love Ravin Crosse.

And that love would destroy him.

Does she truly carry my child?

"Nikolaus, please."

Brought back to the moment, Nikolaus straightened his focus on the vampire standing before him.

Gabriel had suffered for his indiscretions. Perhaps the devil would be served his due by taking his child, as punishment for what he must now do for all the wrongs he had committed against others.

Stepping forward, Nikolaus grasped the cool silver stake. Heavy, it weighed a good pound or two. Designed for maximum thrust and pointed to glide easily through flesh and blood. Why did Gabriel, a vampire, possess such a thing?

It was too late to ask. Macabre wonders must be set aside. The longer he stood, indecisive, the longer Gabriel would be made to suffer.

"You must know," Nikolaus began, swallowing regret and forcing himself to be true, for that is what Gabriel deserved. "She is still alive. I could not kill the witch."

Gabriel nodded, the weight of his head hanging heavily.

"I believe I may…love her."

A thin smile cracked Gabriel's face. "She's been good for you, then. You are bewitched, Nikolaus. And a phoenix. You are probably one of the most powerful vampires to walk the earth now."

"I have not told you. I…can walk in the sunlight."

Briefly, a joyous smile stretched Gabriel's mouth and his eyes closed. "The sun. So warm. You are truly blessed, my friend."

"It means nothing without my friends at my side."

Gabriel smirked and shrugged away the joy. "We are creatures. Not meant for this world in the first place. You must know I welcome death. And it is deserved."

"No, Gabriel. No man deserves death." Or witch, for that matter. "Ever."

"A man cannot prevent who his heart will grow attached to. I…fell in love with Rebecca, Truvin's girl. I killed her in a fit of jealousy. I didn't tell you, because you've been so busy with your own woman. A witch." He snickered. "Only you,

Nikolaus, have the capacity to see beyond your enemy's darkness and offer love. Only you."

"I am not so magnanimous."

"We are, none of us, stellar citizens. You should…fight for her."

As he had not fought quicker and harder for Gabriel? A tear escaped his eyes. Nikolaus grabbed his friend by the shoulders.

"I have loved you, my friend," Nikolaus said. "You have been the one to share kindness with me, and in turn, teach me things that the darkness might have fouled."

"I love you, Nikolaus. Now, do this quickly. The pain has become so great, I am numb."

Endorphins, thank God for that.

"Go in peace, Gabriel Rossum. May the heavens forgive you the dark that was never your choice."

And he stabbed the stake through Gabriel's chest. The doomed vampire spread back his arms and called out to the fickle heavens.

For a moment, a luminous aura surrounded Gabriel, pale and silver and twinkling with the midnight stars. And then his form cracked and dispersed to fine dust that fell from the air, but did not touch mortal objects, for it did not land before disintegrating. No speck of him remained.

Nikolaus dropped the stake and fell to his knees. He had not sobbed for decades. Now the tears came easily.

Was he right to allow the tribe to choose a leader?

Truvin Stone tapped his beringed thumb on the black granite desktop. He'd been spending a ridiculous amount of time here at the warehouse, where centuries of collected treasures watched silently from their dusty perches as he worked out ideas, plans, and struggled with expectations.

He expected Kila would pick him to continue to lead, but he could not be confident that would be the case.

Daily, he heard the whispers from his men. Their desire to see Drake return, to look upon the all-powerful phoenix, was imminent. Wouldn't that be something? To be led by one rumored to now be indestructible? To follow a man who had *not* been defeated by a witch?

Yet, what would they whisper if they knew the truth of Nikolaus Drake? Did he wish to expose him, the one person who had only offered him kindness over the years?

Truvin despised the no-kill policy, but he had survived it, nonetheless. And he could continue to do so should Nikolaus reign.

But he did not care to be told what to do, or how to live his life. Did he not deserve some respect for his wisdom, for having walked this earth ten times longer than Drake?

True, he wasn't keen on leading and the responsibility that came with it, but he was serious about forming a crew of vampires who would not back away from a witch. Strong, fearless vampires who could stand defiantly before any who would think to slay their kind.

He was ready. He'd developed a method, a tactical process— as well as outfitting his crew with safety armor. But to do so, he must make an example of his former colleague. For Nikolaus had broken the one unwritten rule that no vampire would ever dare break.

He had allied himself with a witch.

Chapter 28

The alley was dark. A streetlight on the corner had been busted days earlier. Surprisingly it hadn't been replaced. The city was usually quite careful about things like that.

Didn't matter, Ravin could see vamps on a moonless dark night thanks to her deal with Himself.

Your soul will never be yours.

Fool, that she had thought for even the flicker of a moment that she could deal with the devil and emerge unscathed.

And now her soul *was* hers. And yet… "I will never have the balance I seek."

Her debt was paid.

Ravin closed her eyes. Nikolaus could not have known Himself had asked the same of her—for her firstborn.

Himself knew.

"Who was it really for?" she muttered now, thinking of that damned love spell. She hadn't asked, hadn't thought it her place to ask, nor had she wanted to know. When preparing the spell, she'd even considered that Himself had wanted to play one enemy against the other.

It made such twisted sense. A child born of a phoenix—who was also a bewitched vampire—and a witch could become a very powerful being. Himself had orchestrated this masterfully.

"What a fool I have been."

It was time to get out of this city. Head south for a while. Hell, Europe sounded good. Sure, there were a lot fewer vamps across the Atlantic, even fewer that ran in tribes, for the tribes were an American thing. But that was all good. Because she'd abandoned the slayer costume. Maybe.

Ravin wasn't going to start philosophizing on her changing morals. They were there. Somewhere. And those morals no longer wanted to see vamps turn to ash.

It was time to stand aside from the carnage and begin to view the future through new eyes. The vampire nation had suffered enough for her parents' deaths. Truly, the debt had been paid. She would move on, if only to honor Nikolaus for his sacrifice for her.

And to make a better life for the child.

The scent of blood carried through the evening air. Curious. Ravin had expected Kila to gather in the upper warehouse as they usually did on Sundays. But they never risked taking a victim when their numbers were so large.

She did a scan up and down the alley. Maybe some mongrel alley cat, fresh from a claw match, shuddered behind a pile of refuse licking its wounds.

Tonight was Solstice. She wasn't sure if Nikolaus would show, or perhaps he already had. Had he retaken his position as leader?

She had to see him. Just to know that his friend had been saved. To know his sacrifice had not been futile.

His sacrifice is yours.

But was she really pregnant?

Ravin ran her palm across her flat belly. She had survived for centuries, had taken many lovers without becoming pregnant. Save the one time, which proved the birth control spell wasn't entirely fail-safe.

A child conceived of a faery and a witch. The match seemed no crazier than that of a vampire and a witch. But she'd miscarried in her third month. She had been slightly relieved at the time, but her sadness had been equal, for then she had allowed herself to indulge in the fantasy of family, even knowing full well Dominique had loved his dead wife and his absinthe, and might have never been able to love a child. The miscarriage had been for the best.

Still she tried to convince her empty soul of that.

Now, when she had committed the gravest betrayal to her kind—and Nikolaus to his kind—would she be punished?

Was it a punishment to bring a child into this world, fathered by a man she loved? It didn't sound so awful. But knowing that a child could never be hers was.

What have I done?

Pounding her forehead against the brick wall gave her a brisk slap. Now was no time to go soft. Nikolaus hated her. He'd as easily hand over their child as biting a mortal for lunch. She meant nothing to him. A child created by a witch could mean less than nothing.

He called you sweetness.

Habit, nothing more.

She had looked into his eyes and felt his anger radiate from his pores and into her newly returned soul.

She heard footsteps and swung to look down the alley. A wide hand slapped over her mouth, the other hand going for the dagger she'd tucked at the back of her waist. Pinned effectively against the wall, Ravin didn't struggle, because she saw her attacker's face.

"What the hell do you think you're doing, witch?"

Nikolaus's hand was clamped over her mouth so tightly, did he actually expect she could answer?

"Is this tipped with your blood, witch?"

She nodded.

"I thought you wanted to stop?"

Still couldn't speak. But what did he care if she carried it now out of self-defense instead of anger?

"Go home. Better yet, get out of town. You're not wanted here."

She scissored her legs but couldn't summon enough leverage for a good kick. Nikolaus pressed his weight solidly against her frame, forcing air from her lungs with the action.

"I'm giving you a free one this time," he said. Pressing his nose against her ear, he breathed. Or did he sniff? "I'm going to take my hand from your mouth. If you scream, the entire tribe will be upon you. And I won't be taking a witch's side, not on the night of my return, I promise you that."

He took his hand away and Ravin stretched her jaw. Remembrance of his gentle touch felt so distant. "I'm here to see you."

"You've seen me. Now go. Quickly."

"Not until I know about Gabriel. How is he?"

Nikolaus sucked in a breath, his body bending against hers. For a moment he pressed his lips to her forehead. A stroke of his thumb glided along her cheek. Was he…?

Ravin felt he distinctly showed her gentleness. But… *He hated her*.

He pushed from her body and turned his shoulder to her, looking out over the alleyway. "Gabriel is dead."

"But—"

"He was alive when I returned home, Himself kept the bargain. But he was in no condition to thrive. The wound had taken too much from him, changed him. It was a mercy killing."

Ravin sucked in a breath. It made perfect sense that Gabriel would be so wounded life would not be worth it. And that Nikolaus had had to take his friend's life? "I'm so sorry."

"Think on it no more. I will not."

And he looked at her, face-to-face, not a blink, and no anger in his eyes. It penetrated deeply. Now she had a soul inside her, Ravin felt it sigh, and wanted to grab out for it all. Anything he would give to her, she would take.

"What was that?" she dared. "Just now. You…touched me. Nikolaus?"

"Go," he rasped. He shoved the dagger against her stomach until she took it. "Just…go."

"No. Look at me again. Deep into my soul, like you just did. Nikolaus—"

"Please! Do not say my name. It—" he kicked the base of the brick wall "—hurts my heart. I can't handle more pain today. I just…"

She hung suspended in an instant. Nikolaus held her with one hand, under the neck, her shoulders to the wall, feet dangling. She would not draw the blade.

"Are you sure?" he asked. Raspy and deep. The tone of it calmed her.

"Sure of what? That I love you? Yes."

"No, you cannot— I…you said you were…" He set her down gently, and his long fingers stroked her stomach.

Ravin placed a hand over his, wishing the contact to never stop. A part of him did not completely despise her, she felt it. And there, in her belly, she felt the swirl of awakening, her body responding to his touch she so desperately desired.

"No, I'm not sure. Like I said before, it's a feeling. I've been sick a few times. Didn't think anything of it. Just intuition. But I could be wrong."

"You should see a doctor."

"I know of a witch doctor in St. Paul."

"A—" he nodded, understanding "—doctor for witches. Yes. Do it quickly. I need to know if—"

If he had consigned their child to hell.

Oh, Nikolaus, I will love you even for our horrible decisions and desperate acts of love.

"Now, get out of here before we're seen together."

"I'll go," she said.

She wobbled forward, and it took some balancing to avoid touching him. Though she wanted to. Desperately. *Just kiss me*, she wanted to cry. *Make me feel the way I did a few days ago. Bring me into you and push away the world.*

And then she did ask. "I'll go if you kiss me."

"Have you lost your marbles, witch?" He lowered his voice and leaned in again, so close, their noses nudged. "I'm no longer under some idiot love spell. I despise you. I hate the smell of you. I—"

He was lying. She felt it. Intuition again; it was never wrong.

So she would see for herself. Ravin went up on tiptoes and planted a kiss to Nikolaus's mouth. He shoved at her; she held on. And for five seconds, he kissed her back. It was all she needed.

Breaking the kiss, Ravin stepped back immediately to avoid his anger. But it did not come. Turning, she strode down the alley to the parked chopper.

She had felt it. He'd kissed her back.

Fingers pressed to the brick wall, Nikolaus kept his eyes closed tight. She shuffled away, her boots clodding down the

street. He kept them closed even when he heard her fire up
the street chopper and rumble off.

Only then did he dare open his eyes—to the truth.

He'd kissed her. He hadn't shoved her away at the offense.
He had taken the kiss from her and given back.

"What the hell?"

Heartbeat pounding, he gasped, trying for breath, as if he'd
run a few laps, pre-vamp condition. His entire system raced,
frenzied by her touch.

The smell of her. Cherries, cloves and musk.

The feel of her mouth upon his. He traced his lower lip with
his tongue. The taste of her—dark and lush.

"No!" Nikolaus slammed the wall with his fist. "I can't be.
It was a spell. Is it still there, affecting me?"

He knew better. He knew that night the spell had been broken,
as he'd stood on the rooftop watching her plummet to the dusty
cement sidewalk, that he'd felt instant hate for the witch.

And now? It was different. He hated her for what she'd
done, enslaving him.

But for who she was as a person?

I hate the vampire, but I love the man.

Did he really feel something for Ravin Crosse?

He searched the street for a trace of her, but the chopper
had turned and rumbled off. "Come back to me, Ravin."

The moon crept out from behind the clouds as Ravin parked
her chopper in the garage below the apartment building.

She was in quite the mood since leaving Nikolaus in the
alleyway.

"He doesn't hate me," she whispered. "He kissed me back."

Hooking a hand behind her waist to tug out the dagger that
was beginning to rub against her spine, she suddenly paused.

Oil and gas fumes misted the air. A row of silent cars

parked along the north wall. To her right, an ominous black van sat. No one in this building owned a van.

Swinging to her right, Ravin instinctively dodged as the rope lariat sailed over her head, missing its target. A dark figure wearing a full-head black mask with goggles reeled back the rope.

She heard motion behind her and swung, wielding the dagger, but the glass tip did not cut through flesh, instead slipped over the black fabric. Kevlar, she guessed.

And there was another figure, making three, surrounding her. Clad in Kevlar, and wearing goggles that lit their eyes with a soft amber light, not an inch of flesh or hair showed. Looked like ninjas, but she knew differently.

Their auras were crimson, shadowed with dark ashy speckles. Vampires.

Biting her lip, Ravin spat, and one of them dodged.

Struck from behind, Ravin went down, landing on her elbows and moving into a roll. She blocked a punch, but felt her legs being pulled straight. The attacker sat on her knees so she could not kick, and began to wrap the rope about her ankles.

Groping over the Kevlar, she managed to hook her fingers over the rim of the goggles. Spitting directly in the man's now-exposed eyes scored her one point.

A blood-curdling yowl exploded above her. He clutched his eyes and staggered off her.

A thick block of leather was shoved into her mouth. A leather strap was secured over and around her head.

Beside her, the vampire she'd spat on dispersed to ash.

Her arms yet free, Ravin punched, but to no avail. As she was slammed forward on the tarmac, her arms were wrenched behind her and secured with more rope.

"Time to roast a witch," one of the attackers announced.

Chapter 29

Nikolaus waited on the sidewalk, his boot toes hanging over the curb. The moon was high and round, fitting for this Solstice eve. And when he should have been prepared, fired up and ready to step back into his position as leader, now he could but stand in the sky and close his eyes to the soft breeze that dusted his eyelids.

What had he done?

What had *she* done?

"Do I love her?"

Vampires did not love witches.

Never had he been one to discriminate against those who did not look or think as he did. Yet now, when the rules said he should not do something, he obeyed.

Since when had he been one to follow the rules?

And that he was questioning his alliances made him realize it wasn't all black and white. *Nor should it be for Truvin, eh?*

Right. Because if the very man who sought to again lead Kila could not follow a rule ingrained in the vampiric being, then why should he expect Truvin to repress his nature?

"It's all because of the witch. She brought this on."

He had thought the spell dissolved after he'd leapt from the rooftop to look over the broken witch. End of story. He would go back to his life, she to hers.

But as he held her in the alley, his hand firm about her neck, and her body lifted so her feet had not touched ground, he had leaned into her. The scent of her had lured him. Reminding. No, her blood would never sing to him as the luscious, life-giving mortal blood did.

But her soul, ah, he had sensed the woman's soul. Her own, not out on loan to the devil Himself. And he had touched it.

As she had his. Because she could. Because he had not bargained with his soul for Gabriel's life, but rather with a soul he believed might never exist.

Clutching his chest, Nikolaus looked up to the moon. "What have I done? What if she's…?"

Pregnant. With his child. And he had sacrificed that child for the life of a man he had no right trying to preserve.

Nikolaus would sooner give his own life than see any child— especially his own—handed over to the very devil Himself.

Could he do that? Make an exchange? This whole bargaining-with-the-devil thing had never occurred to him until he'd met Ravin. And now he had used the bargain to destroy not one, but two innocent souls.

"Let it be a mistake," he murmured. "She thinks she is, but it's something else." For he could not forgive himself otherwise.

"Ravin," he whispered. To speak her name made it all so real, returned him to her arms, her hair, her body, her kisses. "Sweetness."

He had to see her again. Wrap his arms about her and pull

her in to nuzzle his nose into her coconut-scented hair. And that gorgeous perfume that summoned his desire every time he smelled it—cherries, musk, honey, and some other dark essences. The unique scent of his lover.

Yes, his lover.

Somehow, he had managed to fall in love, beyond the spell's coercion. The brain learns what it likes, and will seek it ever after, as if an addiction.

Could he walk before the tribe and present himself as their leader when his heart belonged to the vampires' greatest enemy? To guess at his intimations, Truvin had instilled in the tribe the heady ambition to hunt witches. Something he should not fault them for; it was a natural desire for their kind.

You need the control to feel alive. God-like.

He *was* alive. He didn't need the control because he had something better. Love.

He'd intended to walk the eight or nine blocks to the warehouse. Nikolaus looked down the street, not seeing beyond the huge flour factory that was currently being refabricated into luxury half-million-dollar lofts.

To back down now would show his men fear. That he wasn't up for the challenge. They needed guidance.

Do they really need to live the way you want them to?

Perhaps Truvin was right in allowing them to simply function as the creatures they were.

Nikolaus grimaced, regretting his thoughts. He thought of them as creatures? That made him a creature. One who lived on the blood taken from others. A monster in the eyes of the world.

But not in hers. She had changed. She had learned to love that which she most hated.

So why did Nikolaus still vacillate against his own changed truths?

You're not vacillating, you're trying to put a logical spin to it all. Stop that. Just accept.

A black limousine pulled up to the curb. The back door opened and Nikolaus knew immediately who it was before he even saw the smirking grin peek out from inside.

"Need a lift, Drake?"

Very conscious of the closed interior and that he could smell Truvin's spicy cologne, Nikolaus decided to let go of his anxiety. If the man recognized the witch's scent on him, then so be it.

Just accept.

"Eager?" Truvin asked. He slid a leg up to rest the ankle across his knee. His right hand, beringed with diamonds and platinum, tapped his crocodile shoe.

"Ready," Nikolaus provided. "We're going the wrong way."

"We'll get there."

"You promised we would have a vote over my return."

"With proof of your alliance to Kila," Truvin said. He strolled his gaze over Nikolaus, his nostrils flaring.

He's picked up something, Nikolaus knew.

"How's Gabriel?"

His fingers curling into tight fists, Nikolaus cut off an angry growl. If Truvin could set up his ire so instantaneously then he wasn't ready to go back. He must control his need to lash out.

You did not kill the witch. You can do this.

"Gabriel is dead."

"Sorry."

"No you're not. And it wasn't over some damned woman, that was just a convenient excuse. Why couldn't you have kept this between the two of us? Gabriel was the least harmful thing in your life."

"You're right. As usual." Truvin stretched an arm along the

back of the car and leaned into his corner, turning his body to Nikolaus. The accusing tilt of his head spoke volumes. "How could *you* do it? Is she still alive?"

"You know that she is." Nikolaus turned on the seat and looked him full on.

"I do. You've seen her recently. I can smell her on you."

"Not a sweeter scent this side of the Mississippi."

"She is the enemy!"

Nikolaus nodded, knowing he had to contain Truvin's rage and make him understand. Knowledge, that was the way to survival—for the entire tribe.

And yet, a looser rein might also be necessary.

"Not all witches walk around equipped to slay," Nikolaus said. "In fact, I'd wager less than one percent of them actually do so. She's an anomaly. We've nothing to fear from her."

"All witches must die. We cannot afford them life when they carry our death in their veins. You know this, Drake. How is it you can be so cavalier after all you have suffered because of a witch?"

"It was a spell. A love spell that forced me to love her."

Truvin chuckled and swiped his fingers across his mouth. "Now, that is rich. You lie."

"I wish I did. I knew I should hate her, even as I was screwing her."

"The witch put a spell on you? Why?"

"It wasn't her intention. It was…" Who had the spell been for? Nikolaus had never given it thought. "It was an accident. She tried to push me away, but the spell was too strong. It's broken now."

"And now you'll come groveling back to the tribe, asking forgiveness after screwing the one person who we must hide away from for fear of death?"

"I don't grovel."

Truvin countered, "Nor do I hide away in fear. So, you ready to hunt the witch?"

No. But until he had a good solid plan—and figured Truvin's intentions—Nikolaus needed to play along. "Name the time, Stone."

"I don't believe you."

"And I don't believe you'll hand over the reins, so we're even."

Truvin tugged out his cell phone, checked the screen and punched in a few keys. "Driver, turn around. Head for the warehouse."

The limo changed course and the glow of the cityscape's lights grew brighter with midnight neons and flashing bar signs.

Nikolaus exhaled. The silence cut across his ribs. He did not want to feel threatened by Truvin; the man had always been his friend. What was he not seeing?

"So tell me, Nikolaus, what sacrifice will you make to have the world as you believe it should be?"

The question could not have been worded more precisely. To have the world as he believed it should be? Was that what he was doing? Striving to take back control, to manipulate the lives of others so they coincided with his ideal for a perfect world?

How miserable your manipulations of Gabriel's life proved.

Indeed. These truths, they cut deeply, and yet he felt he should wear the scars from them ever after as a reminder. It was time to take a step back and loosen up on the control. It just might…feel right.

"You know I tried the no-killing thing, Nikolaus. Really, I gave it my best. But I believe you will never understand what it is that makes me what I am. I have been Truvin Stone for centuries. I was completely fine with my world before you walked into it."

"You were hungry for family."

"Yes, yes, I needed connection, a solid reality that would not die or leave or slip away with the world. Kila gave me that. And for that, I am grateful. But your ignorance of our very nature startles me—why, you have to take a victim once or twice a week. I can go for months without blood."

"Because you drain mortals to their deaths."

"That is what I am."

"A vampire can choose to be, or not to be, a monster, Stone. I choose not to be."

"Understood. But don't force your choice on the rest of us."

"It has never been forced!" Checking his anger, Nikolaus pressed his shoulders to the leather seat and looked out the window.

"Can we come together in some sort of agreeable communion?"

Despite his nature, Truvin Stone was not evil, nor did Nikolaus despise him—even after Gabriel's death. So many hands were involved in bringing about his macabre end.

"I mean…" Truvin shifted on the seat, leaning forward to explain. "We work together. You've the presence, the command, the clear and true ability to lead. While I have a focus that you seem to lack."

"Sounds dangerous. The two of us working together?"

"Perhaps you're right. You could never share authority. I could never live under a dictator—"

"A—what?"

"We're here."

Indeed, they had parked outside the warehouse. The street was dark because the tribe ensured the lamps were always broken. They'd also painted a graffiti of gang signs across the building facade, which kept back most curious mortals.

Nikolaus inhaled deeply and opened the car door. He was

not a dictator, and he could share authority. It would be a challenge, but he was up for it.

"It all falls on the choices a man makes," Truvin said. "Can you sacrifice for the greater good?"

To control and rule the tribe gave him a sense of accomplishment. He could no longer get that by drilling a two-inch hole in some guy's skull and cutting out a tumor. Here was his family. A weird, screwed-up, seeking family. But weren't they all?

This was the one place on the earth where he truly belonged.

And yet, a lack of control would free him of responsibility. Could he do that? The only time in his life when he'd not felt completely in control was when he'd been in love. And hadn't that been a way to fly?

Was it possible to have both at the same time—control and freedom?

He stepped out into the night sky. A tremor of recognition touched him. And Nikolaus's heart dropped.

She was inside. He could smell her fear. *Unnatural*. And she was not safe.

They'd tied her arms high above her head, secured to the overhead beams with knots worthy of a hangman's noose. Her ankles were also secured, the ropes drawn through hooks anchored into the wood floor, so she hung suspended. The strain on her shoulders and hips would break her sooner than any torture would.

Unless the faggots beneath her were lit. A low circle of tinder and logs were placed in a six-foot diameter at Ravin's feet.

The only way to kill a witch? Fire. A slow and painful death.

"Prove your alliance to Kila."

A flash of silver swept before Truvin's face. He handed the plain silver lighter to Nikolaus—and he took it.

Chapter 30

Snapping out the lighter, Nikolaus made a show of it before his men. The warehouse, stacked to the rooftops with treasure and files and safes, smelled ripe with the heady will to cause chaos, to harm—to kill. It wasn't a pleasant scent. And it toyed with his struggle to conjure a plan. Did he need one? Hadn't concealing the truth done enough to foul his life already?

You are ready for change. Face it.

Besides he and Truvin, there were seven in attendance. Nikolaus recognized five faces. Two must be new, and looking more punkish and ready to fight than David, the Frenchman with a Mohawk who worked a nightshift at La Belle Vie because he loved to cook, or Nathanial, who was young, handsome and always ready with a salacious joke.

Clad in ankle-length dusters, skinny black jeans and high-laced combat boots, the two new recruits didn't suit Truvin's style. They wore goggles perched upon their heads, and one sported a vest that appeared to be Kevlar. Of course, a vampire required protection to capture the enemy.

Ready to hunt with us?

Had he crushed Truvin at the time, this whole awful disaster might not be happening now. But violence wasn't his style.

Just over his shoulder, Ravin's breaths came heavily. Nikolaus's heart ached. The moment he'd walked into the warehouse and had seen her there, the foolishness of his quest had become real. He'd been questioning his ideals for days. Did he want to rule over men? Or did he simply wish to make a good life for himself? One that included the woman he loved, and very possibly, their child.

You love her. You never stopped.

He wanted to turn around and cut Ravin down, clutch her close and dash away with her. But he had to play this right. He was not about to back down, cower with his tail between his legs and watch while Truvin ordered Ravin's demise.

Nodding and pulling a staunch grimace onto his face, Nikolaus stalked across the warehouse floor toward Ravin.

"Are you ready to die, witch?" Truvin called as he stepped forward from the ranks.

Nikolaus felt the power inside him pushing against his flesh, eager to get out. Misdirected anger, for it was all for Truvin. And Gabriel.

He turned his back to the crew of vampires and looked at the witch, lighter still in hand.

She spat upon him. Delicious defiance, even when she could only guess her chances at survival were nil. But he couldn't risk her sensing his fear. Fear that all may not go as planned—hell, he hadn't a plan. Could he get the witch out alive? He could use her…as a weapon.

"Make it long," someone from the tribe called out. "Painful."

Nikolaus winced. In but two months his men had drastically changed. While he could grant that even when he had led them, none had held any respect for witches, this lust for death sickened him.

And what of your own lustful revenge scheme to kill the witch? You are no better than any of them. Step down, Drake. You are not a god.

"Yes, do it, vampire," Ravin murmured. "I deserve it." And then she said so softly, that none but Nikolaus heard, "For enslaving you. The spell…I had no right. It was my fault. I planned it."

Rearing back at that statement, Nikolaus checked his sudden switch to empathy. So many eyes were upon him. Shoulders stiffening, he stalked the floor before the witch.

He knew better; Himself had asked for the spell. She could have had no idea an angry vampire would knock down her door that night and upset the direction of the love spell.

Nathanial, head bowed but eyes upon him, delivered the most scathing of all looks. He had only been a vampire for two years. He was young, naive, and needed leadership if he were to walk the earth ever after and not get himself into irreversible trouble. To his side stood Gear. He had been the wildest, most difficult to keep under control, and yet the man had genuinely sought guidance and flourished under it. They were, not a single one of them, animals.

Nor was Truvin. The man pursued an innate need. He wanted to be safe. Nikolaus could fault no man for protecting himself and doing all that he must to ensure that. Kill first or be killed? An easy answer.

And then Nikolaus knew what he had to do. But he could not sacrifice a single friend to do it.

Nikolaus stepped up and put his nose right in Ravin's face. He heard her intake of breath. Those lips, so close to his. *Take my breath from me. It is yours.* Though she smelled of sweat and fear, the unique perfume of her teased at him.

Obviously, she had tried to defend herself. A flick of his tongue licked the blood from the corner of her mouth.

"Nasty stuff," he hissed so all could hear him.

Aware the tribe members took a step back, Nikolaus smiled. Not stupid, then.

"How can you…?" David started.

"He touched her blood," one of the punked-out vampires muttered. "And he's not sizzling."

Nikolaus cast a sharp grin over his shoulder. "Witch's blood? Dangerous stuff."

He swung around and splayed his hand out before him. On his fingertips glistened Ravin's blood, crimson and bold. The sight of it forced the tribe back a few steps.

"One drop will sizzle through your flesh and eat into your insides as if it were a demon on a quest for a man's soul. It does not relent. And it hurts like nothing you will ever want to experience."

A flick of his fingers sent a few droplets into the air.

"Watch it, man!"

He shook his head at their fear, but inside cursed himself for threatening his brethren. It had to be done this way. They would know his strength.

Nikolaus walked around behind Ravin. Her head fell back and he pushed it hard.

"Stay alert, witch. Can you feel it? Your life slowly seeping away. I've tasted it. A world of goodness and evil rushes through your thoughts. Did I do everything right? Why should I care? Will I be punished? Why couldn't I get away?"

Drawing out the knife he kept at the back of his waist, Nikolaus swung around in front of Ravin and slashed the blade down her wrist, drawing a six-inch line toward her elbow. The blood sprayed and he closed his eyes to receive her baptism of wicked poison upon his face.

Forgive me the pain, Ravin. It has to be done this way.

"It is ironic to stand in the bath of your life now. What once killed me now makes me stronger!" he announced.

He turned and now none stood close. And most obvious, Truvin stood back by the door.

Ravin spat upon him.

Nikolaus smirked, but did not wipe the spittle from his brow. "What makes you strong, witch?"

Now she pierced him with those witchy eyes. A smile fortified him with respect for her bravery. Her outrageous defiance.

"What makes me strong? Do you really want to know, Nikolaus?"

"Yes, speak your death speech, pretty little witch. It's a gift I give to you."

"I don't need your gifts. I have all that I need knowing I have held love in my heart. True love. Perfect love. I love you, Nikolaus—"

Nikolaus raised up his hand and angled the knife to slash. He lunged down, aiming for her neck, but at the last moment, he turned and marched across the floor, bloody blade held high.

"I've returned!" he commanded. "And I've not only the strength of a phoenix but the blood magic given to me by this witch. Know that I shall not suffer any of you to harm her, for she has made me whole and given me the strength to endure anything you and your false leader put to me."

"He is a witch lover!" Truvin shouted.

The tension tightened across the line of vampires, who stood tall, assessing, snarling, and the one on the end wearing the Kevlar stepped forward, fingers fisted.

Nikolaus stalked over to Truvin, brandishing the blade before him. Truvin's eyes never left the weapon, shining with crimson.

"You don't like my girlfriend, Stone?" Nikolaus challenged. "You don't like a lot of things I do. Like kindness and peace and keeping the relations with the wolves."

"We are not moral beings," Truvin shouted. "You cannot demand we live as bloodless creatures who refuse to answer our very nature. We need the kill!"

"We need only blood, Truvin." Nikolaus bent into the man, until their heads were but a foot apart. He snapped out the blade to cut him beneath the chin, but stopped an inch from making contact. Ravin's blood swirled upon the blade. "Care for a taste?"

Truvin smirked and forced a chuckle, but Nikolaus could feel his need to dash. "You would not. You who preaches kindness?"

"I'm no preacher. I do believe in life, though. And the only life you've power over is your own. You cannot take from others to serve your wicked, twisted wants."

"You should mark your own words, friend." Truvin inhaled and he met Nikolaus's stance, no longer wary of the bloodied blade. "You've power over your own life. Let them choose." He gestured to the vampires who had curved around behind Nikolaus. "Kila does not require a babysitter to keep watch over our actions. We merely require—"

"Wolves!"

All turned to the vampire at the door. He'd been posted outside as guard.

"A dozen of them," the guard said, frantic. "They've circled the building. Severo stands out front, and demands to speak to Kila's leader."

Truvin turned his gaze upon Nikolaus.

He would not ask for permission. With but a glance over his shoulder to ensure the witch was alive, and alone, Nikolaus then turned and stomped outside, bringing his tribe along with him.

* * *

They'd all walked out, leaving her alone. Bless the wolves for their timing.

Ravin ceased struggling against the rope bonds. Her shoulder sockets burned. No twisting or squirming was going to loosen the secure knots.

But a little air magic might do the trick.

"Gather," she began to chant. A rush of wind pushed back the air from her face, cool and tickling softly against her tormented joints. "Infuse the ropes and expand."

She felt the rope chaff around her ankles and wrists. Air crept into the tightly woven hemp, expanding the fibers. Feeling her fingers begin to tingle with the needles of aborted circulation, she closed her eyes and concentrated.

The pack leader stood at the bottom step before the warehouse as Nikolaus descended, his tribe flanking out defensively to his left and right.

Truvin skipped down the steps before him, eager to be the first to talk to Severo. Nikolaus noted there were twelve pack members to their nine vampires. Three flaming torches were held by a few; an odd step toward medieval villainy.

Severo stood proudly, shoulders thrust back, an angry snarl exposing a canine. Thick black hair sat on his head like a true wolf's mane, bristling in the wind. While he was shorter than Nikolaus and Truvin, Nikolaus knew the werewolf's physicality to be remarkable. And should he morph to complete animal form, the vamps would have quite the challenge on their hands.

But no one was changing shapes, not in this neighborhood. A scan of the nearby buildings—all warehouses—didn't spy light. But three blocks to the south sat a major freeway; a car could cruise down the street anytime.

"Severo," Nikolaus offered, steeling his need to rush back

inside the warehouse and grab Ravin. She was safe, so long as none of the tribe members went back in. And they would not with a pack of angry wolves ready to bloody their teeth on them this night. "You and the boys in town for a party, or should I be worried for the safety of stray mortals this evening?"

The wolf just behind Severo's right shoulder cracked a snarl and lifted his goatee-striped chin.

"I have no enmity toward you, Nikolaus." The black-eyed pack leader tilted his angry snarl toward Truvin. The muscles threading his neck were thick and bulging. He was close to a shape-change, Nikolaus sensed. Severo was too smart, though. He relied on intelligence to hold off the wolf's ferocity. "It is the leader of Kila who has been treading on the pack grounds I want."

"This can all be discussed—" Truvin started.

Severo let out a snarl.

And Nikolaus, checking the ranks to see the pack had closed in, could not allow the aggression to rise.

"What the hell have you done?" he asked Truvin, but then to Severo he offered, "I will make it right. We can exist closely, with respect—"

Severo spat at the ground before Truvin's feet. A toss of his head bristled back his thick hair. Moonlight flashed in his eyes, reflecting a sickly yellow mirror.

"Too late, Drake. Too little," Severo said. "You go. I know you've been away from Kila for some time. Had you been able, you might have prevented this. But as it is…"

"For Christ's sake." Truvin took a step forward. Nikolaus caught him across the chest. "You're going to let a wolf scuttle onto vampire territory and speak to us like that?"

"He is justified," Nikolaus said, "if you've been treading on theirs. And I know that all of Kila has crossed the line onto wolf territory."

"It was just a few nights!"

Severo lunged for Truvin and caught him about the neck.

The scent of musk grew strong. Nikolaus made eye contact with David and one of the new guys, who stood offensive before the pack. Arms arced at their sides and jaws tight, they were ready for action.

"This is happening," Severo ground through a toothy scowl. He lifted Truvin until the vampire's feet left the ground. "Leave, Drake."

"No!" Nikolaus plunged into Severo's chest, successfully knocking him to the ground. He met the leader's stunned obsidian eyes. "Kila is my family. You have a beef with one of us, you have a problem with me."

. He didn't have to rally the tribe to attack, for all around them it had begun. Truvin swung a punch at Severo, clocking him even as Nikolaus held the wolf by the shoulders. "Back off!" Nikolaus warned the idiot vampire.

And Truvin could not protest, for he was lifted from behind, and spun to defend himself.

Severo lashed up with a strike so fast, Nikolaus hadn't time to comprehend its speed. Claws dug through Nikolaus's cheek—but he did not release his prey.

"I don't want to be your enemy," he said. Spitting his own blood out to the side, Nikolaus then slammed Severo's shoulder into the concrete.

Rolling to his side, he then stood but was dragged back down by the wolf's powerful grip. Contact with the cement rubbed the flesh from his arm.

"You were not my enemy," Severo said. He twisted Nikolaus's arm behind his back and pressed his cheek to the sidewalk. "Until now. You want to stand with the bastards in Kila? Be my guest."

"You can put your claws and fists to me all night,"

Nikolaus growled out of the side of his crushed mouth, "I can bounce back—"

"—until dawn?" Severo laughed. "All I have to do is keep you occupied a few hours, then stand back and watch you fry, vampire."

The affront at using the term *vampire* was quite enough. Nikolaus rolled, toppling Severo, and kneed him in the kidney. The wolf yelped like a mutt put down by its master.

A glance surveyed the periphery. Two wolves down, and one vampire standing with a pack member's claws imbedded deep in his chest.

He didn't see Truvin. And the warehouse…it was on fire!

Slam! As he was punched from behind, Nikolaus's palms slid across the ground and the breath left his lungs as he was momentarily flattened.

"The building," he managed to shout. Pushing up, he elbowed Severo in the jaw, but the wolf bounced right back, swinging Nikolaus around by the shoulder and a hank of his hair. "I need to get inside," Nikolaus said.

He took the wolf's claws to his gut.

"Your precious storage burns to the ground, vampire."

"There's a woman inside."

Severo chuckled deeply and dug in his claws. "I'm surprised at you, Drake. Attempting such pitiful deception to end the match. Don't think you can last until sunrise?"

Fisting Severo in the gut, Nikolaus put all his strength behind the move. He wasn't sure, but that might be a kidney he just pushed up into the rib cage.

Severo landed on the ground, sprawled and choking blood.

Little concerned over his torn gut, Nikolaus lunged after him, gripping the wolf by the hair and stepping hard onto his chest. "There's a witch inside the warehouse. She's tied up and can't escape."

"Vampires burning witches? How original. Filthy bastards." Severo spat at Nikolaus. "You were once a vampire of integrity, Drake. I respected you. Now you've sunk to new lows."

"Believe what you wish." Nikolaus punched, and he felt Severo's jaw pop from the hinge. "I'll be right back."

Slamming the wolf against the sidewalk succeeded in knocking him out. Probably not for long. But it gave Nikolaus escape.

He dodged by a vampire bent over, spitting blood and unaware of the wolf leaping at him from behind. Nikolaus spun into a roundhouse kick and met the wolf as it soared to land on the vampire's back—but did not. The wolf yowled like a wounded puppy and tumbled away.

Had the wolves started the warehouse fire? Dashing up the steps, Nikolaus briefly wondered about Truvin. He hadn't marked him in the brawl. Had he slipped out? To set the witch on fire?

He had to trust that Truvin would not do something so cruel when the entire tribe battled for their very lives right now. A battle that Nikolaus must participate in—but not until he stopped a witch burning.

Chapter 31

The flames consumed the doorway to the warehouse. There was but this door, which led to a foyer and then another door into the main warehouse, and roof access. All the windows were shut up with steel plates. A sprinkler system had been installed years earlier, but obviously it wasn't doing the job on the outer walls.

Nikolaus hoped it had turned on inside.

Without a second thought, he walked through the doorway. Flames attached to his legs and arms and hair. The crackle of the blaze drowned out the sound of his gasping breaths. Unconcerned for his own danger, he kicked at the interior door, which fell to emit clouds of thick gray smoke.

Drinking in the smoke and choking, Nikolaus plodded blindly forward. He felt water spatter his arms. The sprinklers were working. But had they saved the witch?

Though he still could not see a thing, he knew instinctively to walk straight forward. They had tied her up in the center of the—

A body slammed into Nikolaus. "Ravin?"

"So much—" she coughed and clutched his arms; only now did Nikolaus realize his sleeves had burned away and everywhere she touched him it ached with raw flesh "—smoke."

"You're free."

"A spell. Air. It's all gone. Can't…breathe. Help…"

She collapsed and Nikolaus caught her in both arms. Overhead the ceiling showered cold water and the smoke had begun to settle.

Racing for the door, where the flames mastered the wooden frame, he paused, just under a sprinkler. Holding Ravin there for what seemed an eon, because he just wanted to get her safe, Nikolaus steeled his impatience. If her clothes did not get soaked, then she risked burning. And he wasn't sure how much flame it took to kill a witch, only that it wasn't going to touch this one.

Nikolaus stepped outside and entered the dawn. A rosy sheen painted the horizon, topped by a copper band of sky. There were no vampires to be seen, and the few wolves remaining groaned and loped about, favoring their injuries.

As he descended the steps, Ravin in his arms, he brought the attention of the six or seven wolves up to him. From the left, Severo appeared, limping, and blood dripping from his nose, but he walked straight and pushed up his chest at the sight of Nikolaus.

Stopping before the pack leader, Nikolaus stood there. Come what may, at least he had rescued the witch.

Not the witch. *Your lover.*

The woman he loved.

"You went into a burning building to save a witch?" Severo asked.

Nikolaus looked over Ravin's wet face. He wanted to see happiness curving her kiss-bruised lips and the aftereffects of orgasm softening her every muscle. Easy, sated. In love. He'd do anything to see that expression on her face one more time.

"Someone had to."

"But—" Severo swiped his mouth with a palm and rubbed the blood along the torn thigh of his jeans. "She's a witch. And you're a… And—and the sun!"

Just as if it were announced, a flash of gold touched the sky. Morning had arrived. Nikolaus felt it warm his face.

Severo backed up, a leeriness to his hunched back and sulking posture. He was unsure of Nikolaus now. And the pack followed their leader's reluctance, stepping back a few paces.

Bending his knees, Nikolaus set Ravin carefully on the sidewalk. He stroked the wet hair from her face. Two fingers to her carotid felt a strong pulse. She had inhaled a lot of smoke, but that wasn't going to kill her.

In the distance, fire sirens alerted them all.

"We need to take a hike," one of the pack said.

Nikolaus looked up to Severo, who remained quite stunned. "I love her," he offered. "She's bewitched me."

"You are bewitched? That means you've taken her blood. And…to survive?"

"It's called a phoenix. The dude's a phoenix," Severo's right-hand man offered, then stepped back. "We need to leave, Severo. I can see the fire engine down the street."

"Yes, disperse and retreat," Severo ordered.

Nikolaus gathered Ravin into his arms and followed the wolves down the block away from the scene. Before they parted, Severo turned to Nikolaus. "A phoenix?"

"You have not marked me as an enemy tonight, Severo. I give you my word." And then Nikolaus offered, "I'm sorry.

I'll hold myself personally responsible for Truvin Stone. He won't go near wolf territory. That, too, is my word."

"Your word is good," Severo said. The wolf bowed, and then with a look to Nikolaus, and after receiving a nod, he touched Ravin's hand. "We will always be allies," he said to her.

"Good to know," she said on a raspy whisper. Her voice was still weak from the smoke. "I'm taking a break from hunting vampires for a while, though."

The morning light glinted in Severo's grinning eyes. "I can guess why. Until we meet again." He turned and trotted off with his pack.

Nikolaus kicked in the door to his flat and set Ravin down. "You're big on the dramatic entrance, you know that?"

Chuckling, he bent and kissed her soundly. "You taste like smoke."

"You look like a roasted pig."

He drew out his arm and saw the red, burned flesh. Pain didn't exist when standing so close to his woman. "Doesn't hurt a bit."

"Yeah, well, it looks awful. Come on, big boy."

"Where we going?"

"Soon as I find your bedroom, we're going to do something about healing those burns." They glided down the hallway, Nikolaus shedding his tattered shirt in their wake. "We should do something about your hairstyle, as well."

"What's wrong with the hair?"

Tugging him into his bedroom, Ravin pulled Nikolaus across the room to stand before the black marble vanity. She snuggled up to him as he examined the damage in a half-circle mirror. Flames had eaten away most of his hair and did a nasty number to his entire right side, including his neck, shoulder and arm.

"You up for some blood sex magic?" she asked his reflection.

"It's going to take a long, drawn-out session of sex to take care of this mess," he said.

"I'm up for it, lover."

And that was the best offer he'd had all day.

He sat in the living room, legs crossed, head tilted back across the sofa. Gorgeous black hair spilled over his shoulders. Ravin knew it wasn't her Nikolaus, because he was in the shower, waiting for her to join him—and he'd already shaved his head bald to expose the tattoos. She liked them, and hoped he kept the look.

She'd wanted to get a drink of water, and now, on the way to the kitchen, she paused to glance over her shoulder.

"Tell me one thing," she said to Himself. To turn and face him would grant him too much respect. She rapped her fingernails across the marble countertop. "Who was the love spell for?"

Not-Nikolaus's chuckles simmered in a curl of sulfurous brimstone. "Finally figured that one out, eh, witch?"

Crossing her arms over her stomach, she leaned against the counter, studying the floor. "You planned this all along. But you couldn't know that I would get pregnant."

"Life is crazy, isn't it? Witches can fall in love with vampires, without hindrance of a spell, and vampires can be enslaved beyond their darkest nightmares. Of course, I do know everything about you—now, then and what is to come."

He spoke the truth. She had fallen in love. And it hadn't taken a spell to make it happen.

Like the wind, Himself's breath stole over her cheek. He stood right at her side, his closeness sending a million creeping corpse worms under her flesh.

"Your son will be one of the most powerful vampires to

walk this earth. He will have his father's strength and lust for blood, combined with his mother's magic. Born bewitched. I cannot wait!"

"You'll never have him." As she said the last word, she faltered. It would be a boy? "Nikolaus and I will protect him with all our resources."

"Won't matter. The child is mine. Nikolaus Drake made a deal. But you mustn't fret, dear one. I don't want the thing as a newborn. Toddlers are frustrating. And teenagers? Too much work. I'll come for the boy when it is time. And there's nothing in this realm you can use against me to stop it from happening."

And like that, Himself was gone.

And Ravin felt Nikolaus's arms embrace her even as she crumpled to the floor.

He held her close and whispered in her ear, "I'm sorry. It's done. But we will be vigilant. If we cannot prevent Himself from taking our son, the very least we can do is make him strong and resilient to the devil's influence."

"Is that possible?"

"We'll make it so."

And he kissed her, a kiss so bittersweet Ravin didn't want to think about this moment ever again. And she would not. She would look to the future—in the arms of her vampire lover.

GLOSSARY OF TERMS

adrenaline: Achieved by flashing fangs before biting, anything to produce fear. A very addictive vampire drug.

bewitched: Vampire who has achieved witch magic through the enslavement of a witch. Only a half dozen remaining ancients achieved it before the Protection.

blood child: A vampire created by another vampire.

blood sex magic: Strength and magic are gained by the vampire when he/she has sex with and/or drinks blood from a witch. (Only a vampire with immunity to witches' blood such as a phoenix, can do this.)

the dark: All vampires, excluding those few who have gained witch magic.

danse macabre: After a vampire kills a victim, the nightmares of that victim die slowly in the vampire. It can take days and involve visions and actual experience of the nightmare. Will bring eventual madness if too many kills are made.

death cocktail: A witch's blood.

donor/victim: Experiences an orgasmic form of the swoon when bitten. Will forget the experience if the vampire enthralls them. Teeth marks will close up thanks to vampire's saliva, yet a bruise will remain. They will only become a vampire if the vampire did not enthrall them, and if they drink blood before the next full moon.

flight: Witches who have mastered air magic can fly. Only bewitched vampires can fly (if their witch supplicant is an air master).

immortality: Vampires' lives are extended by hundreds of years. They gain power and longevity by creating new blood children. They will not live forever. Witches lost immortality following the Protection, and can only renew it with vampire blood.

in-born: A vampire born of a female mortal and a male vampire. Doesn't crave blood until transformation in early twenties. Migraines clue to blood hunger. Female vampires don't give birth.

the light: Witches who do not practice demon magic and generally practice earth magic.

longtooth: Witches' derogatory term for a vampire.

phoenix: A vampire survivor of a witch's blood attack, or a vampire resurrected from ash. Rumored indestructible.

the Protection: A great spell performed by witches to end the war between vampires and witches, and to end enslavement. The Protection makes their blood poisonous to vampires, at the sacrifice of the witches' immortality.

reverie: Vampires can seduce and calm the prey by matching the pace of their victim's heartbeats with their own.

the shimmer: Vibrations vampires feel when they touch one another. The only way for one vampire to identify another vampire without seeing fangs or seeing them in the act of drinking blood.

the Sight: A rare power that enables the non-vampire viewer to see a vampire's red, ashy aura.

slayer: A mortal vampire slayer.

source: What witches call the unfortunate vampire used for their immortality ritual. Vampires refer to them as 'ash.'

supplicant: A witch enslaved by a vampire. Very rarely is the witch in love with the vampire. Usually ends in the vampire's accidental death, but often, the witch is drained of her magic and immortality.

swoon: The orgasmic result of drinking warm human blood. The vampire is momentarily out of sorts as the blood rushes through his or her system, and is vulnerable to attack at this moment.

thrall: A vampire can persuade a victim to forget the bite/attack. It can be used to enthrall an entire room, but it is difficult, and the vampire must be focused.

tribe: A vampire clan. Usually created by one or two leaders. They are bloodthirsty, powerful and have a gang mentality. Mostly found in America. Vampires can be recruited into a tribe, but tribes are usually created to increase the strength of tribe members. Their greatest enemy is the witch, yet the tribes have not yet organized to stalk and kill witches. Tribe members pursue solo vampires to join them. Tribes include: Kila (Nikolaus Drake's tribe), Veles (rumored dead vampires), Zmaj and Nava (older, unbaptized members).

vampire: To create, a mortal is bitten by a vampire, drained close to death then drinks the vampire's blood in a soul exchange. If bitten, then abandoned, the mortal must drink blood to make the change (but they will not be as powerful a vampire). Or, if they don't drink blood before the next full moon, they can be free of the vampire's curse and/or face madness. They must drink blood to survive. They are not dead.

Vampire attributes:
- increased night vision
- enhanced senses

- heals rapidly (saliva is healing agent)
- blood sustains life; soulless blood gives no sustenance
- has the strength of ten men

Vampire challenges:

- propensity to count and order things
- must be invited to enter a home, but can enter public places freely
- crosses and holy water only burn (and possibly kill) if vampire once believed and was baptized (fewer vampires over two centuries old were baptized, so the elders are quite fearsome of the holy)
- sunlight slowly burns and makes them tired; can withstand a few minutes in the shade, but must protect their eyes
- the smell of garlic is repulsive
- wild roses have no effect unless planted by a witch
- wooden stakes will kill if heart bursts
- if touched by madness during transformation, can never be completely free of it
- witch's blood is poison

* * * * *

For a sneak preview of Marie Ferrarella's
DOCTOR IN THE HOUSE,
coming to NEXT in September,
please turn the page.

He didn't look like an unholy terror.

But maybe that reputation was exaggerated, Bailey Del-Monico thought as she turned in her chair to look toward the doorway.

The man didn't seem scary at all.

Dr. Munro, or Ivan the Terrible, was tall, with an athletic build and wide shoulders. The cheekbones beneath what she estimated to be day-old stubble were prominent. His hair was light brown and just this side of unruly. Munro's hair looked as if he used his fingers for a comb and didn't care who knew it.

The eyes were brown, almost black as they were aimed at her. There was no other word for it. Aimed. As if he was debating whether or not to fire at point-blank range.

Somewhere in the back of her mind, a line from a B movie, "Be afraid—be very afraid..." whispered along the perimeter of her brain. Warning her. Almost against her will, it caused her to brace her shoulders. Bailey had to remind herself to breathe in and out like a normal person.

The chief of staff, Dr. Bennett, had tried his level best to put her at ease and had almost succeeded. But an air of tension had entered with Munro. She wondered if Dr. Bennett was bracing himself as well, bracing for some kind of disaster or explosion.

"Ah, here he is now," Harold Bennett announced needlessly. The smile on his lips was slightly forced, and the look in his gray, kindly eyes held a warning as he looked at his chief neurosurgeon. "We were just talking about you, Dr. Munro."

"Can't imagine why," Ivan replied dryly.

Harold cleared his throat, as if that would cover the less than friendly tone of voice Ivan had just displayed. "Dr. Munro, this is the young woman I was telling you about yesterday."

Now his eyes dissected her. Bailey felt as if she was undergoing a scalpel-less autopsy right then and there. "Ah yes, the Stanford Special."

He made her sound like something that was listed at the top of a third-rate diner menu. There was enough contempt in his voice to offend an entire delegation from the UN.

Summoning the bravado that her parents always claimed had been infused in her since the moment she first drew breath, Bailey put out her hand. "Hello. I'm Dr. Bailey DelMonico."

Ivan made no effort to take the hand offered to him. Instead, he slid his long, lanky form bonelessly into the chair beside her. He proceeded to move the chair ever so slightly so that there was even more space between them. Ivan faced the chief of staff, but the words he spoke were addressed to her.

"You're a doctor, DelMonico, when I say you're a doctor," he informed her coldly, sparing her only one frosty glance to punctuate the end of his statement.

Harold stifled a sigh. "Dr. Munro is going to take over your education. Dr. Munro—" he fixed Ivan with a steely gaze that had been known to send lesser doctors running for their antacids, but, as always, seemed to have no effect on the chief neurosurgeon "—I want you to award her every consideration. From now on, Dr. DelMonico is to be your shadow, your sponge and your assistant." He emphasized the last word as his eyes locked with Ivan's. "Do I make myself clear?"

For his part, Ivan seemed completely unfazed. He merely nodded, his eyes and expression unreadable. "Perfectly."

His hand was on the doorknob. Bailey sprang to her feet. Her chair made a scraping noise as she moved it back and then quickly joined the neurosurgeon before he could leave the office.

Closing the door behind him, Ivan leaned over and whispered into her ear, "Just so you know, I'm going to be your worst nightmare."

Bailey DelMonico has finally
gotten her life on track, and is
passionate about her recent career
change. Nothing will stand in the way
of her becoming a doctor...that is,
until she's paired with the sharp-tongued
Dr. Ivan Munro.

Watch the sparks fly in

Doctor in the House

by *USA TODAY* Bestselling Author

Marie Ferrarella

Available September 2007

Intrigued? Read more at
TheNextNovel.com

REQUEST YOUR FREE BOOKS!

2 FREE NOVELS PLUS 2 FREE GIFTS!

Silhouette®

nocturne™

Dramatic and Sensual Tales of Paranormal Romance.

YES! Please send me 2 FREE Silhouette® Nocturne™ novels and my 2 FREE gifts. After receiving them, if I don't wish to receive any more books, I can return the shipping statement marked "cancel." If I don't cancel, I will receive 4 brand-new novels every other month and be billed just $4.47 per book in the U.S. or $4.99 per book in Canada, plus 25¢ shipping and handling per book plus applicable taxes, if any*. That's a savings of about 15% off the cover price! I understand that accepting the 2 free books and gifts places me under no obligation to buy anything. I can always return a shipment and cancel at any time. Even if I never buy another book from Silhouette, the two free books and gifts are mine to keep forever.

238 SDN ELS4 338 SDN ELXG

Name _____ (PLEASE PRINT)

Address _____ Apt. #

City _____ State/Prov. _____ Zip/Postal Code

Signature (if under 18, a parent or guardian must sign)

Mail to the **Silhouette Reader Service™**:
IN U.S.A.: P.O. Box 1867, Buffalo, NY 14240-1867
IN CANADA: P.O. Box 609, Fort Erie, Ontario L2A 5X3

Not valid to current Silhouette Nocturne subscribers.

**Want to try two free books from another line?
Call 1-800-873-8635 or visit www.morefreebooks.com.**

* Terms and prices subject to change without notice. NY residents add applicable sales tax. Canadian residents will be charged applicable provincial taxes and GST. This offer is limited to one order per household. All orders subject to approval. Credit or debit balances in a customer's account(s) may be offset by any other outstanding balance owed by or to the customer. Please allow 4 to 6 weeks for delivery.

Your Privacy: Silhouette is committed to protecting your privacy. Our Privacy Policy is available online at www.eHarlequin.com or upon request from the Reader Service. From time to time we make our lists of customers available to reputable firms who may have a product or service of interest to you. If you would prefer we not share your name and address, please check here. ☐

SN07